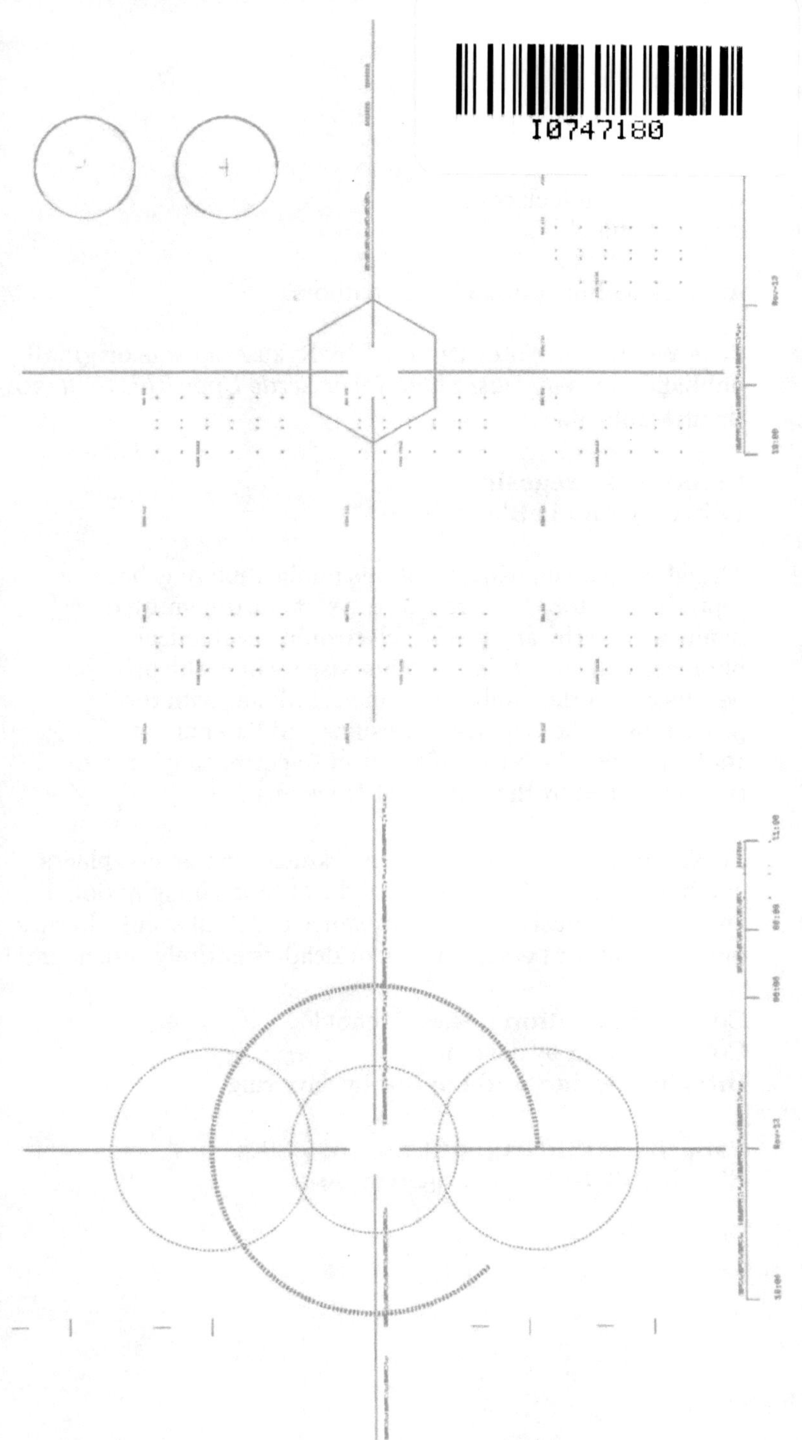
I0747180

Neon Hemlock Press
www.neonhemlock.com
@neonhemlock

"The Woman of Water Dreams" by Ryka Aoki was originally published in *Why Dust Shall Never Settle Upon This Soul* (2015, Biyuti Publishing).

Embodied Exegesis
Edited by Ann LeBlanc

Cover Illustration by Lyss Menold
Cover Design by dave ring
Interior Design and Layout by dave ring

Paperback ISBN-13: 978-1-952086-88-5
Ebook ISBN-13: 978-1-952086-89-2

EMBODIED EXEGESIS
TRANSFEMININE CYBERPUNK FUTURES

Neon Hemlock Press

NEON HEMLOCK

EMBODIED EXEGESIS

TRANSFEMININE CYBERPUNK FUTURES

EDITED BY ANN LEBLANC

A NOTE FROM THE EDITOR

CIS CYBERPUNK IS DEAD!
LONG LIVE TRANSFEM CYBERPUNK!

"TBH IF YOU'RE WRITING TRANSHUMANIST CYBERPUNK AND YOU'RE NOT DOING STUFF WITH GENDER AT ALL, YOU'RE A COWARDLY LITTLE BABY. YOU'RE LIKE A BABY WHO'S SOFTER AND MORE COWARDLY THAN THE OTHER BABIES

THE OTHER BABIES FUCKING BULLY YOU ABOUT YOUR SOFT LITTLE BABY HANDS, WHICH TYPE STUFF LIKE 'JAX COLECOVISION'S BODY WAS LIKE 80% CAN OPENER AND HE NEVER, EVER THOUGHT ABOUT HAVING SOME TITTIES'

I KNOW THAT YOU'RE A BABY WHO HASN'T TOTALLY GRASPED THE OBJECT PERMANENCE THING YET WITH YOUR LI'L CHICKEN TENDER FISTS, BUT THE CYBERPUNK METROPOLIS STILL THRUMS WITH WEIRD, SCARY GENITALS EVEN WHEN YOU'RE DETERMINED TO LOOK AWAY FROM IT"

—LILLIAN BOYD, TWITTER, JUNE 26TH, 2020

Many funerals have been held for cyberpunk. Yes, in the mainstream, the genre is an aesthetic pastiche of itself, lacking the punk experimentation of earlier works. But don't mourn cyberpunk! In the back alleys of literature, trans people are doing unholy cybernetic experiments on cyberpunk's corpse. Come join us there!

Cyberpunk is a natural genre for transfem creators to find a home in. The history—and future!—of computer science and electronica is replete with our contributions. The themes of alienation from society and bodily transformation align with our own experiences of trying to survive and transition in the real world—which has become it's own more mundane cyberpunk dystopia.

And the future of cyberpunk is being written by us. Works like *Citizen Sleeper* by Gareth Damian Martin, *Oleander Grip* by Frog Kosaric, *Bang Bang Bodhisattva* by Aubrey Wood (and many many others) are already exploring parts of cyberpunk left unexamined by cis writers.

If the exciting new micro-genre of Transhumanist Transfem Cyberpunk has a focal point, it is the body (and for you dualists out there, I include the mind within the body). Which is to say that this collection of stories is all tied together by the way that technology transforms our bodies, whether those transformations are mediated by traditional cybernetics, the terrors of social media, the cities we live in, or from more surreal or esoteric sources.

I'm incredibly proud of the work of the authors and poets in this anthology. In my submission call, I asked for the stories that were too weird and trans to ever be published by cis editors, and my goodness did they deliver! These stories range from settings you might easily identify as cyberpunk to strange potential futures that defy strict genre definitions. But who else but trans authors to elude easy categorization?

This anthology has been a long-held dream of mine, but I'm not its only parent. Many many people helped bring this weird cyber-baby into the world. First, I'd like to thank dave ring, Neon Hemlock's Editor in Chief, who works incredibly hard to champion the cause of queer speculative fiction. Without his enthusiastic support, this anthology would not exist. I'm also incredibly indebted to Julia Rios, for their mentorship and friendship. Catherine Lundoff and Cat Rambo's class on anthology editing was enlightening, and gave me the confidence to pitch dave. Neil Clarke taught me how to wrangle a massive slush pile at Clarkesworld. Lillian Boyd edited my very first cyberpunk story at Fireside Magazine, and wrote the tweet that inspired this anthology. Lyss Menold created the perfect cover art. I'd also like to thank everyone who submitted stories to *Embodied Exegesis*. I was stunned by the quality of stories in the slush pile, and in a just world (unbound by the costs of paper), I'd have published every one of them. I'm so grateful to all of the authors included in this anthology. They're all incredibly talented and were fantastic to work with. And I must thank my wife, Cora, whose love and support are woven into everything I create.

Finally, I want to thank YOU, dear reader. The world is a hard place for trans people right now, and the support of readers is crucial for the new worlds we are creating, both in fiction and in the real world.

The future of cyberpunk is trans, and I hope you enjoy it as much as I do!

Ann LeBlanc
April 2024

A NOTE FROM THE EDITOR

THE REPOSSESSION OF KEVIN'S PERFECT HAIR

LILLIAN BOYD

CONNIE DIDN'T PLAN on crushing her boss Kevin's skull with a commemorative ashtray when she clocked in Friday morning, but probably no one ever plans on a thing like that, if they can help it.

It was a mammoth of an ashtray, too, heavy pyroxetine the waxy red of a gas station apple, and the Vitalia Wellness Company had given it to Connie free of charge when they'd released Creanolin, their proprietary lung cancer-inhibiting bodymod. The wage she drew as Vitalia's janitor of fourteen years would never be enough to pay for the tech itself, but they'd given out the ashtrays—stamped with BREATHE FREE in noodly letters—in a nationwide flood of promotional ephemera, shirts and disposable medguns and screenguards, and it had been just as well to hand one out to Connie, too. She'd left it on the flimsy card table in the breakroom, figuring Vitalia took up enough space in her life as it was and she needed to smoke here more anyway.

Kevin lay supine on the breakroom floor, his face mushed like a jelly sandwich at the bottom of a backpack, his black hair sticky with pulp.

His *very* nice hair, Connie noted, once you cleaned all the gore out of it.

THAT MORNING HAD felt off in a squirmy and unpindownable way that Connie's bones knew before she did.

"You behave today," Dana said while they did their makeup together in the late-summer Georgia heat.

"I always behave."

"Baby, I'm serious, now. I got a feeling. No taking stuff home from work today. Please?"

Dana always got woo-woo visions and intuitions. Connie had spent more than two decades indulging them, given how often she turned out to be right.

Connie looked over. The soft-yellow vapor light in the bathroom glanced gently off Dana's bald spot, which she'd been trying to cover up with messy buns lately. She was a little raw about the baldness on account of dysphoria, but she couldn't afford a quality synthetic wig, let alone one of those souped-up hormonal mods that would give her system the right stuff for a full head of shiny hair. Connie herself had, in her thirties, downloaded some homebrew hormonal mod specs that had halted her hair loss and given her a truly righteous pair of tits, but the side-effects—recurring leg-shakes and a permanent barcode-shaped floater in her left eye—were enough of a pain in the ass for her to recommend Dana stay analog. Dana had listened and dealt with her body's changes as best she could and dreamed of one day saving up enough money to get legit mods so she could stop seeing her scalp wink through her blonde hair every time she looked in a mirror.

"I told Jakk I was gonna get them some stuff by this weekend. For Franklin. That patch for his liver," Connie said.

"I know it. I know you gotta do that. Just wait until Monday, okay?"

"I don't know if Frank's liver's gonna make it to Monday, the way he's drinking."

"Con."

"I know," Connie said, putting down her makeup brush, leaning over, and kissing the patch of skin on the top of Dana's head. "You got a feeling."

KEVIN HAD THE Look when he walked into the Vitalia offices that evening. The Look was something Connie had known and dreaded since Kevin had gotten hired as a supervisor six years ago. He got it when he'd decided it was time to entertain himself by making Connie's day uglier—making messes she'd have to clean up, or fucking with her things in a way she couldn't prove, or saying some fake-friendly shit about her makeup meant to highlight how much work she put into it.

"Well, good evening, Miss Connie," he said with a voice like a grease trap, walking into the breakroom where Connie was getting ready to go home after her shift. There'd been an investors' meeting late that afternoon and the members of the board had, in Connie's experience, the nastiest hygiene she'd ever seen in a long career in sanitation, leaving bizarre and eldritch stains on seats and floors throughout the course of their meetings. The Vitalia brass always had some new mod they wanted to show off for the stockholders, and bodies can produce all manner of fluids when something new and exciting enters them.

"Hi, Kevin," Connie said, eyes on her bag as she continued stuffing clothes into it.

"You're here kinda late, ain't you?" he said.

"Nope. About the same as usual."

"Hmm," he said, and ambled across the room with thumbs hooked into the pockets of his cotton khakis. "Feels late to me, you know? Not a lot of people around."

"Not usually," she said. She could smell the hand lotion he always used as he got closer. Orange zest.

"You always here this late, Miss Connie? With nobody around? Just you and the crickets?"

"Look, Kevin," she said, "it's late and I gotta get home. There something on your mind?"

"Me? Oh, no," he said, making the most of the two inches of height he had on her and leaning against the locker next to hers. "I was just thinking about that report we all got sent. From Security. You read it yet?"

"Nope," she said, trying to zip the bag closed but having to squeeze the sides to get the teeth lined up straight.

"We all get the system notifications. Even you, I reckon. You ain't looked at it?"

"No." She turned to look at him sideways over her glasses with her bad barcoded eye. "Haven't read it. You wanna tell me about it?"

"Yeah, I'll tell you about it. Security said someone's been stealing the products, little by little. Parts going missing, cameras going funny, and no one can figure out why. That message that everyone saw, it said we should keep our eyes peeled for anything," he said, "suspicious."

And there was the Look again, the goddamn Look, his cornflower-blues squinting to meet the corners of his mouth.

"And I just thought, 'Connie might know something about that.' You know? Being here so late all the time, cleaning up."

Kevin smacked the bag out of her hands in a sudden sharp wave of orange zest. The embattled zipper finally gave way to the duffel's swollen innards and a wave of shirts and aprons tumbled out along with half a dozen

Vitalia mods, ranging in shape from a biopatch the size of a bandaid to an external endocrine processor as big as a cheese wheel.

"All right," Connie said. "So what do you want, Kevin?"

"What do you mean?" he said.

"Obviously you ain't told Security yet, or they'd have my ass on a pike out front. Which means you want something from me. Right?"

"Yeah, that's about right," he said, the Look frosting over into a hungry face like a jackal with its nose to the wind. "That's smart of you, Connie. I do want something from you."

Connie's eyes darted to the pile on the floor, then back to Kevin's face.

"Okay. Let's talk. What do you want from me?"

"Good," Kevin said, "that's good. What you can do for me—"

Connie lunged, digging her fingernails into Kevin's eyes. He choked out a cry as the two fell backward onto the breakroom floor, grasping and scratching and kicking.

He twisted Connie's fingers back away from his face and snapped his head forward into hers, sending sharp eddies of neon through her vision and knocking off her glasses, her barcode pulsing a butter-yellow tattoo into her skull. They both stumbled to their feet, or tried to.

"Bitch," he seethed, lacerated face clenched like a fist. "I'll fucking kill you."

With a sideways lurch, he tackled Connie, the two careening into the floppy card table Vitalia cleaning staff used to eat their meals. The whole thing flipped and sent its contents skyward—a thermos full of white bean soup and a stack of papers and an old ashtray.

Kevin's hands found Connie's throat and squeezed.

"Say goodnight, bitch," Kevin whispered.

As the warm sick dark crept into her vision, her grasping hand found, glory hallelujah, the heavy red ashtray.

She swung it hard, catching Kevin square in the nose with a wet crunch. He yelped and let go and sweet stale air flooded Connie's lungs and she gasped and choked and swung the ashtray into his temple, sending him twisting to the floor in a heap.

Connie sucked as much wind as she could as she brought the ashtray down again and again, swinging to a steady four-on-the-floor rhythm. Kevin gurgled and whimpered and quieted down and died. Connie didn't mind—she closed her eyes and kept on going.

When she was finally able to catch her breath again, she looked down and took in the pulverized ruin she'd made of his head. Even in death, the rictus mashed into his face gave her the Look.

Fucking Kevin.

She got to work cleaning up the room, bringing the whole of Vitalia's huge cache of industrial cleaning supplies into play. The cleanup itself, while fairly straightforward for someone who'd spent a decade and a half cleaning up wild and mysterious stains from a variety of surfaces, still left the question of the body. Connie sat down in the cheap folding chair by the card table and stared at Kevin's head, thinking.

Goddamn, she thought, *his hair really does look great, considering.* He'd been balding since she'd known him, his hair vanishing year after year as his crop had thinned, and the last year had seen a sudden eruption of glossy black locks after a scalp transplant and the installation of a T-inhibitor. She leaned down from the chair and tugged it. It was real, or close enough that the difference between fake and real didn't mean much. Her hand came away wet and gummy.

She pulled open his shirt, and sure enough, a web of subcutaneous cables crept down his neck and spread out across his torso in a spidery constellation. He was running what looked like a staggering number of mods, all connected to what Connie figured was a hub the size of a baseball buried in his gut. This was the kind of wetwork you got when you wanted the deluxe package, real gearhead shit—better stamina, disease resistance, sharper vision. A fuller head of hair due to a T-inhibitor routed to the scalp.

His new muscles were even flexible enough to fold up and fit neatly into a maintenance cart.

"Fuck," Dana said.

"Yeah."

Kevin's body lay on the floor of their apartment and the two sat on the couch and shared a cigarette and stared.

"Wasn't no way around it," Connie said. "Didn't have no choice, him knowing about me. I had to do it."

"But why'd you have to bring him here?"

"I dunno. I just couldn't leave him there, you know?"

"Fuck," Dana said meditatively, staring at the cherry of the slim cigarette. "I told you. I told you to watch out today. I had a feeling."

"I know. I know you did," Connie said.

"You know what they'll do to us, they find out you did this?"

"Well, just what in the fuck was I supposed to do, Dana?" she said, looking at a crow preening itself on a fence and mashing her lips together to keep from crying. Dana lit another slim. "I was fucking scared. He was gonna hurt me. He knew about the stuff I been taking from work. He was trying to kill me. What would you have done?"

"Fuck," Dana exhaled, closing her eyes, flinching at the thought of Kevin's hands around Connie's neck. "Same thing, probably."

Dana stubbed the slim and walked over to Connie, wrapping her arms around her waist from behind. Connie softened and leaned back and the two shared a breath.

"This is bad, huh," Connie said.

"Yeah. It's pretty bad, baby," Dana said into her shoulder. They turned to look at Kevin again.

"Did he, uh," Dana said, pulling another cigarette from the pack, "get some work done?"

"Yeah."

"Good hair."

"Dana."

"Shit, look at it," she said, and leaned down to trace the subcutaneous line of cable that snaked down Kevin's neck to his chest. "This is really good stuff. Quality."

"Of course you notice the hair."

"I'm just saying," Dana said. "It's a fucking shame, throwing it all away. And it's not the only thing he had done, either, it looks like. All the mods hooked up here, that's gotta be, what, six figures' worth, right? Maybe seven."

"So what are you saying?"

"Well. We gotta figure out where we're gonna put the body anyway."

"Dana."

"And the best thing you can say about this peckerwood is that at least he knew how to take care of his biotech. You know?" Dana stubbed out her smoke in the big red ashtray Connie had brought home along with Kevin.

"Christ alive, Dana."

Jakk Loudermilk's scrapyard on the lip of town was five labyrinthine acres stacked to the sky with teetering machinery. It wasn't a business Jakk ran so much as a small fiefdom, with mechanics and modfreaks and the occasional rich slummer coming through pawning their wares and looking for clandestine parts at all hours of the night. And Jakk didn't fuck around, either—out front under a flickering Easter-pink light was a piece of rebar jutting from the earth with bloodied biomechanical parts impaled on it as a warning to anybody with the notion of ripping the scrapyard off. Jakk's cameras were everywhere, and they paid well enough for their security detail to give a shit.

When Connie and Dana rolled up just after two in the morning with Kevin sealed inside a roadcase in the bed of their truck, Jakk was out front smoking a sweet-smelling cigarillo and messing with a screen that lit their face up from beneath. They raised their eyebrows and pursed their soft lips as Connie handed them Franklin's liver patch, which was the closest they got to smiling, and ushered the pair inside, wheeling the case full of Kevin.

"So what you need me to do is make this shit untraceable," Jakk said, not asking a question. They sat on a corduroy couch in their office opposite Dana and Connie, who stayed standing.

"They're gonna look for him," Connie said. "And all his mods are registered, right? They were bought legit. Which means they come with geotags, tracers. If they get turned back on inside someone's body, they'll light up and tell the cops 'hey, here's Kevin's bionic thyroid' or whatever, right?"

"Yeah," Jakk said. "So why you fucking with it, anyway? Why wouldn't you just burn it? What are you doing bringing it all to me?"

"It's a lot of good stuff here," Dana said. "Fucking guy spent a lot of money on these mods."

"People can use them," Connie said.

"And you're the only person we know who can clean them up, strip all the tags and make it so the cops can't track them when they get turned back on inside somebody. You know what you're doing."

Jakk stood and walked over to the roadcase, rubbing their chin with their knuckle, and popped it open to reveal Kevin, naked and crumpled like a spider, the plastic wrapped around his head smeared nearly opaque with what had been inside it. Jakk traced their fingertips down the tributaries of cable and wire that spread across the dead man's chest and gave a low whistle.

"He's running some crazy shit. It's gonna take awhile to get it all out, but I think I can do it," they said. "But getting rid of the meat part? You gotta take care of that. That's not what I do."

"Don't worry about that. I'll handle it," Connie said.

Jakk shivered and closed the case. "Any parts y'all want dibs on?" they asked as they wiped their hand on their pants and shook another cigarillo out of the pack.

Dana smiled. Connie did not smile.

Jakk and their crew took care to separate Kevin from his augmentations, spreading him on a stainless steel table and digging through him with a surgeon's patience until there were two piles: useful parts and Kevin.

Once Jakk had disconnected everything properly, the tech found homes in the neighborhood—Jeanette Grady from down the street had lungs that let her walk to work without coughing even once; salty old Walt Cohen could see the spots on a ladybug's ass from a hundred feet away; Garon Palmer's blood pressure settled itself like the belly of a sleepy cat. Jakk did all the installs themself, careful to hide any telltale signs of the clandestine tech to keep anybody from looking twice, taking payment from each person at a steep discount. Any financial loss, they figured, would pay down the line on account of a dedicated customer base with longer lifespans.

With the T-inhibitor installed, Dana could feel her skin tingle with growth, like her whole scalp was buzzing with electric fleas. The patch only worked upward and not downward, unfortunately, and the tits Dana wanted would have to come from somewhere else. But she could feel it doing its work—a little more rumbling than she'd anticipated—and she checked the mirror constantly throughout the day to see its progress.

Connie melted Kevin's husk down in a tub of water and lye, and kept on clocking in for work and nodding ruefully at the authorities as they marched around investigating Kevin's disappearance and the possible location of his Vitalia mods, and she passed out at night twining her fingers through Dana's blond hair, and she tried her level best to ignore how it was coming in oil-black at the roots.

"So what's the fucking problem?" Dana asked, having abandoned her eggs over easy at the table where the two sat together in the early-morning gloom. She hated kicking off the morning with an argument, but it had started the moment they'd woken up and Connie hadn't been able to laugh at a weird dream Dana'd had.

"The problem is it feels like shit, Dana."

"What does?"

"Thinking about it. What I did. When I see his hair," Connie said. She was slowly and methodically shredding a crisped-black piece of bacon with her fork.

"It's not his hair anymore. It's my hair. It's growing out of my head, goddamn it."

"I know. I'm not a prude about this stuff, you know? Like," she gestured at her own hair, her barcoded eye.

"And I love your hair. And your eye, and the rest of you. You getting that stuff from somewhere else doesn't make that stuff less of a part of you now."

"I ain't saying it ain't a part of you. I'm saying it feels fucking bad to look at because the last time I saw that hair, I was—" she said, and glancing at the ashtray and back to her shredded bacon. The sentence died on her tongue while her eyes made the trip. "I fucking killed someone, baby."

"Uh-huh. A piece of trash," Dana said. "You did what you had to do. World's better off without him and you know it."

Connie put her hand midway across the table, palm down. After a moment, Dana slipped hers underneath it.

"I know it. I just touch your hair too much to have to think about it all the time."

"That's how I lost all my hair in the first place, you touching on it so much."

"Yeah, that's right. You want me to stop?" Connie said, the first smile of the morning crossing her lips.

"Nah," Dana said.

An explosion of wood and metal woke the two early one morning. Connie, having just come off a twelve-hour shift, rolled out of bed and fumbled at the baseball bat stashed under the bed while Dana tugged her clothes on and made a round of the house to make sure there weren't any visible machine parts from what Connie had brought home. Once she'd assembled herself, Connie peered through the venetian blinds next to the front door.

A City Security cruiser was parked across the street in front of Jeanette Grady's bubblegum-pink house, and the front door was bashed off its hinges, crumpled inward like tissue paper. Carl Perkins, Jeanette's elderly Maine Coon cat, darted into the doorway and stared into the darkness of the house.

"It ain't us," Connie said, still peeking.

"What are they doing?"

A faint sound came from Jeanette Grady's pink house that could have been a

strangled cry, or a machine screaming on at a high whine, or something in between. Carl Perkins yowled low, tail puffed-up huge at the sound.

"Fuck," Dana said beside Connie, making her jump. She'd come over to look out the window without Connie having noticed. "You think it's about the thing?"

"The thing Jakk put in her?"

"Yeah," Dana said. "You think City Security found out?"

"Jeanette's never done anything in her whole entire life," Connie said, rubbing her eyes. "I can't think what else it could be."

Two City Security goons emerged from the house, thick and meaty and covered in tactical gear, one lugging a handheld battering ram and the other carrying a fat stainless steel briefcase. Through their helmet visors, they scanned the neighborhood for threats as they stalked back to their cruiser. Carl Perkins flicked his tail twice and disappeared back into his house.

"I thought Jakk wiped the tech. So there wouldn't be no tags or tracers."

"I thought they did, too," Connie muttered, grabbing the car keys from the hook by the backdoor.

"I told you I'm working on it as fast as I can," Jakk said, taking a slug from a mug of yesterday's black coffee. Their gaze darted between three enormous computer screens at their desk in the back of the scrapyard office, their long fingers skittering across the keyboards like spiders. "Y'all need to calm the fuck down and let me work here."

"I know you are," Connie said, taking the mug from them and slurping from it while walking to stare out the office window. "Sorry."

The lip of the sun was poked up above the horizon. Dana sat next to Jakk, trying her best to follow the flying columns of text and dense bricks of code. She fidgeted with a busted neural hub that Jakk used as a paperweight, rotating it in her hands and digging her fingernails into the grooves.

"Maybe somebody talked," Dana said. "Maybe that's how they found out she got something she wasn't supposed to have."

"Who do you know who'd talk to fucking City Security?" Jakk asked.

"Nobody, I guess," she said. "I'm just scared. I don't know what they did to Jeanette-"

"There," Jakk yelped, slapping the desk and zooming in on a snatch of code. Connie hurried back over to the desk to look. "There it is. That's what pinged City Security. Her mod was running a scheduled update for a new version of the software. I disconnected the fucking thing, but it rebooted itself to run the update."

"So wherever she was when it came back on, that's where they knew to find it," Connie said.

"Uh-huh. It does a geotag so it has the right permissions to update. I'm gonna go through them all to choke out any leftovers that wanna do the same thing to anyone else's mods."

"Did mine update?" Connie asked quietly.

"Oh. Uh," Jakk said, and after ten seconds or so of finger-flurries on the keyboard, said, "Yeah."

"Fuck," Dana said. "Fuck."

Connie knelt next to her and put a hand on her knee, careful not to apply too much pressure, since Dana didn't like a lot of touching when she was panicking.

Connie said, in the calmest voice she could manage, "Okay, here's what we're gonna do."

That evening, Connie and Dana saw the City Security cruiser the moment it started down their street. It was hard to miss—a tank of a thing with wheels that would dwarf a toddler, engine roaring as it screeched to a halt in front of their house. Two brick shithouses popped out, different from the ones who broke down Jeanette's door, but built the same way and hefting the same combination of battering ram and steel briefcase.

Connie squeezed Dana's hand and gave her their usual triplet of kisses, kiss-kiss-kiss, before going to stand by the door. Dana sat on the couch and opened a book and tried to look casual.

The two Security officers made their way up the stairs as the one in front brought the battering ram to bear. He swung it back, ready to smash.

Connie opened the door and smiled and said, "Hello, officers, how can we help you?"

He grinned and locked eyes with her and continued swinging the battering ram, following through and putting some muscle behind it.

Connie yelped and dodged, tripping and falling on her ass, her hipbone missing the ram by a whisper.

That's what I get for trying to be cute, she thought.

"Didn't see you there, uh, ma'am," the first goon said, grin locked in tight. He and the second guy stepped inside and filled the room like a fist fills a mitten.

Connie stood and stepped back to stand next to Dana, who'd put her book down on the couch next to her.

"What can we do for you, officers?" Connie asked.

"Got reason to believe some stolen items might be located in this here house," the first goon said as the second one set his bulging steel suitcase on the small table next to the front door, the unsmashed condition of which Connie could tell the goons were quietly furious about.

"Stolen?" Dana said. "We don't have anything stolen, officers. Stolen like what?"

"Some tech that don't belong to you," the second goon said, carefully working the latch of the steel briefcase and popping it open with a click.

"Now, this'll go easier if you stop playing games and fucking us around," the first goon said. "We know it's here. The mod."

"Which mod?" Connie asked, shifting to stand in front of Dana and block her from view at least a little as the second goon's eyes darted between the two.

"What you're gonna do is tell us which of you has it. So we can do what we gotta do and get out of this shithole," the first goon said.

"Or else we're just gonna do you both," the second goon said. He pulled a squat scan-gun from the case, the LCD screen readout on top winking in the fading light of the sunset. "We got no problem with that."

"All right," Connie said. She swallowed down a hard lump in her throat. "All right. Uh, I got what you're looking for. I think."

The second goon grinned and said, "I just bet you do."

He brought the scan-gun up to chest-height and it beeped on with a little electronic song, and he passed it over Connie's body until it gave a squeaky wail. He moved in closer and his grin crumbled into a scowl of confusion.

"What in the fuck," he said, and twisted a few knobs, passing it over her once again and concluding, "What the *fuck*."

"What?" The first goon said, and craned his neck over his partner's shoulder to look at the screen. "What's happening?"

Connie glanced down, and sure enough, the readout showed the serial number of her jank T-inhibitor as a flickering slot machine of letters and numbers, each character flying by at different speeds before they had a chance to make an impression. Jakk had done some uncomfortable tinkering in the wee hours. Connie was optimistic.

"Serial's fucked. Look at it."

"What, is it broken?"

"It's homebrew," Connie said. "I downloaded the specs for a Vitalia hair loss mod. The targeted T-inhibitor, the THR1818. I made a makeshift mod based on it, and to bypass permissions, I used a keygen randomizer to keep it working without asking for the numbers because it's still thinking about it."

"Goddamn," said the second goon. "So it must have registered as the serial of the, uh. One we're looking for."

"I don't know about all that. But that's what it is," Connie said.

"You know you ain't supposed to have that," the first goon said, his voice low, feeling around for purchase in the situation. "That there's proprietary tech from Vitalia. You don't have a legit copy, that's a problem."

"I know it," Connie said, eyes locked on the scan-gun, which was still cycling through serials like flipped pages in a book. Dana was stock-still on the couch behind her. "I don't know what has to happen now."

"Well," the first goon said, and nodded to the second goon, who stuck the scan-gun back into the steel briefcase and pulled out an automatic extractor—a huge thing that looked like a cross between a gun and a blender, the business end of it as big around as a grown man's arm.

"Move," the first goon barked at Dana, who moved quickly off the couch to make room for Connie, who he muscled down onto it and held there, arms behind her back, abdomen-out. She'd worn a stretchy tank top in anticipation of this possibility and was grateful that at least they weren't going to rip her clothes to get at the tech.

The second goon clamped the extractor onto Connie's chest, right underneath her left clavicle, and began removing her mod. She tried not to scream and failed—

the pain made her squirm involuntarily as it ripped through her chest, the mod itself squirming and swimming as it rose up out of her.

Dana clasped her hand over her mouth, the fingers of her other hand stretching out toward Connie from waist-height. She didn't dare to move closer, but her eyes were a scribble of anguish and indecision.

The mod popped out, finally, blood dribbling down into Connie's bra as it emerged. The end of the extractor snapped shut, severing the wires it had been attached to, and they dangled limply from Connie's skin. The mod looked like a miniature pocket comb, its dozens of little legs waving and searching for a place to plug in before running out of juice and going still.

"There, now," the first goon said cheerfully.

The second goon stuffed the gun back into the case and latched it shut.

The first goon released her from the hold. She grabbed a nearby rag and clamped it onto the wound, and with short shallow breaths, she said, "Now is there anything else we can do for you gentlemen?"

Both goons clearly seemed to entertain the idea of going for round two with Dana, but finally the one who'd extracted the mod gave a 45-degree grin and said, "No, that'll be all. And don't let us catch you slipping again with some shit like that, or it'll be the same thing. Maybe worse, I dunno."

They gathered their equipment and battering ram and left, the one with the briefcase making sure to slam the door on the way out.

"Baby," Dana said, running to the couch and wrapping Connie in her arms, "fuck, fuck, fuck, I'm so sorry. I'm so sorry."

"I ain't sorry," Connie grunted, and with the hand that wasn't holding the rag over her wound, she grabbed the back of Dana's neck and pulled her in and kissed her the way they always kissed, kiss-kiss-kiss. "Hell, I can see your face without the fucking barcode now, anyway."

"Thank you," Dana whispered. "For doing that."

"Better than letting them find the real one on you, right?"

"They still might," Dana said. "Maybe they'll come back."

"That's why we gotta get out of this fucking town before they do."

"Where we gonna go?"

"Plenty of towns need janitors. We'll find one," she said as she disappeared into the bathroom to clean out her wound.

Dana sat and cried and smoked and Connie watched her from the bathroom mirror as she stubbed her cigarette into the heavy red Breathe Free ashtray—the kind you could find on any table in any town, anywhere.

BESPOKE

ELLY BANGS

THE AWARDS CEREMONY was a monumental exhibition of the world's most daring and sumptuous masterworks of skin, and in that way there was nothing else like it. Limousines landed with silent grace and opened to unveil bodies crafted by all the greatest living artists, sometimes over the course of years: faces, hands, wings, tentacles, trunks, and feelers, engineered cell by cell for the sake of this one evening, never before seen and likely never to be seen again.

Unfortunately for Mortal, the Awards was also a massive social spectacle, where the insufferably rich and famous congregated to bask in the spotlights and gossip behind each other's backs. Mortal would have preferred to watch a broadcast, but it was always framed for a presumptive mass audience that had no eye for the art. It lingered on the smiles and waves, the displays of affection, on who was involved with who and how it was going. Mortal needed to study the gaits in detail, the mannerisms, the microscopically subtle cues that revealed how it felt to *be* those marvelous, bespoke bodies. For that, they had to be here in person—for as long as they could stand it.

"Is that—?" someone behind them said.

"Who?" someone replied.

"That's *them*. That's Mortal, the bodymaker!"

Mortal cursed under their breath. They'd picked the darkest and most secluded corner of the gallery, and they'd still been recognized almost immediately. They took a cocktail from a passing tray without turning.

"But they look so..."

"Understated. I know. It's essential to their mystique."

"They're very reclusive, too, aren't they?"

Mortal studiously ignored the chattering socialites as a celebrated musician stepped onto the red carpet wearing what Mortal instantly thought was the finest work yet by its artist: a four-armed humanoid body whose entire surface was covered in retractable scales, allowing her to retile herself from porcelain-white to bloodred. Bodymakers had been doing similar things with chromatophores for years, but this felt like the apotheosis of that entire subgenre of skin—and Mortal had heard that each scale, despite its toughness, was sensitive to sound. They would have given anything to see her perform music in that body, an instrument in each hand while sonic waves washed visibly over her.

"But that can't be what Mortal *really* looks like," the socialites continued. "I mean—you know what I mean. Surely an artist of their stature doesn't actually *live* in a body so plain."

"No one knows!"

"Their real body must be incredible."

Mortal repressed a growing itch to speak up and tell the chatterers to go away—or worse, to tell them the truth: that their body, short and slight, pale and unremarkably genderless, was the same they'd lived in since birth, without modification. No one would believe it. In these circles, it was like wearing a paper bag over their head.

They told themselves they only needed to hold out a little longer. They couldn't leave without seeing Finch.

A famous experimental dancer made an entrance that perplexed Mortal at first, but then awed them: a parade of seven free-standing bodies that mirrored each others' moves, each one representing the performer at a different stage of his life. Could he feel with all of them at once? Could he control them independently? That would be a revelation.

The socialites were unimpressed.

"Hmm. Too cookie for my tastes."

"Oh yes, now that you mention it. Terribly cookie."

Mortal wanted to scream. To call a body *cookie* was both the laziest and most scathing insult, nowadays. They had come of age at the height of what everyone now retroactively called the Cookie-Cutter Years: the grim decades after inter-body consciousness transfer had matured technologically, but before it exited its cultural infancy; years when mainstream artists did nothing but manufacture nearly identical super-people according to conventional beauty standards and offered them in only the two then-mainstream genders. Artists like Mortal had been edgy freaks back then, rather than the respected avant-garde they were now—and although Mortal hardly missed the Cookie-Cutter years overall, they missed the obscurity.

Besides which, these spectators were objectively wrong. Each body in the performer's gestalt had visible pores and scars. The unadorned humanity wasn't forced, but earnest, and quite vulnerable.

"Supposedly, if you compare old videos, you can see Mortal *aging*. You know—with wrinkles."

"Are you saying Mortal is actually...well, *mortal?* Unthinkable."

"It's a decades-long work of extreme performance art."

As a rule, nobody but religious zealots died of old age anymore—but at times like this, Mortal couldn't deny the appeal. They downed the last of their drink and accidentally dropped the glass on the floor. They felt sick, but they couldn't leave yet.

And there, at last, was Mortal's own latest piece, worn by an up-and-coming immersive actor named Finch. It had taken months of interviews to see past Finch's stardom and the bravado of the characters he played, to a surprisingly sensitive man, repressed and yearning to be more open. The body Mortal had engineered for him was soft and graceful, with very long arms and fingers. Its blood ran warm enough to need no clothes but a tasteful loincloth, and its nacreous skin was laced with emotionally-responsive bioluminescence, so that even a talented actor wouldn't be able to school his expressions.

It had been a risk. There had been no way to know how that much emotive nakedness would feel, here and now—but one look told Mortal it was perfect. They could feel Finch's radiant pleasure in himself, filling the entrance hall, drawing a sigh of vicarious euphoria through Mortal's chest. Every step was a dance. Every forced smile remained matte, while every genuine one shimmered— and when Finch's eyes looked up to search the gallery and found Mortal, he flashed from face to fingertips to toes. Mortal's heart soared.

One of the socialites munched on an hors d'oeuvre and announced through a full mouth: "I don't get it."

"It's not the body, it's the brand," said another, "Everyone on that carpet *dreams* of wearing Mortal. Only a handful have the cash."

"Not just cash. Connections."

"Seelah tried to commission a body from Mortal for their big stage tour last year. They turned her down. *Seelah*. That's how connected you have to be."

Mortal found another cocktail and swallowed it in an unbroken series of gulps. When they finally turned to leave, they were cornered.

"Any comment on the auction?" Eyes of varying sizes and spectral ranges ran up the paparazzo's forehead and down his cheeks, wide and wet. Nobody needed that many eyes just to record video; the guy probably got a kick out of making people feel like flies under the gaze of a giant spider.

"Never heard of it," Mortal muttered, shoving roughly past him.

But the paparazzo shouted down the stairs after them, "You didn't hear? That body you made for Finch. The winning bid just came through. It's going to the crown prince of Florida right after the Awards."

Mortal squinted in disbelief. Everyone knew the kinds of bodies the prince wore: graceless effigies of an imagined masculinity that had never existed, so leathery they must have been numb. That kind of mind became dysphoric in any body that could bench press less than 500 kilos.

"I don't think it will fit him," Mortal said.

The paparazzo laughed. "It's not like he's gonna *wear* it."

The alcohol hit Mortal's stomach all at once. They had told Finch their policy. They'd explained to him the hurt exactly this kind of betrayal caused. They'd trusted him as deeply as he'd seemed to trust them—and still, Finch wasn't keeping the masterwork of somatic euphoria Mortal had spent two years painstakingly tailoring to his mind. It wasn't even going to be cremated, which would have at least offered closure. It was going to be pickled in preservative and exhibited like a hunting trophy in a Floridian palace, all its care and artistry boiled down to a cruel spectacle of wealth.

"I quit," Mortal heard themselves say as the stairs darkened and gyrated around them. "I'm done. I've made my last body for these people."

The paparazzo's eyes all bulged. "What?! Say that again! I need to hear that for the record!"

"I said," the bodymaker began, and vomited.

A KNOCK ON the door shocked Mortal awake on the sofa overlooking the tissue tank. Their mind ran sluggish through their hangover, but they instantly guessed what that knock meant: their dramatic resignation had only increased their fame; the body they'd made for Finch had quadrupled in value overnight; in last night's drunken stupor, they'd allowed someone to track them to their secret workshop, and now their doorstep was packed with spider-faced weirdos broadcasting live from their optic nerves.

When Mortal welled up the courage to look, there was only one blurry silhouette in the frosted glass door—but it wouldn't leave. The quiet but insistent knocking went on for what became ten minutes, until they finally dragged themselves down the spiral stairs and answered.

The person standing outside was lithe and vaguely feminine, teal-skinned, in baggy unisex formal clothes and a stylish haircut that didn't suit them at all. "Are you Mortal?" they asked, sheepishly. "The bodymaker?"

Mortal squinted against the sun through the trees and set their eyeglasses to maximum opacity; their brain felt like an olive speared on a toothpick. "Not anymore. Are you a lawyer?"

"No, I—"

"Who else knows I live here?"

The stranger shrugged.

Mortal waited. "Then...who are you?"

"I haven't really picked a name. But...call me Lyric, I guess." The stranger smiled hopefully. "I want to hire you."

"Absolutely not. But thank you."

"I can pay any price at all."

Mortal started to pull the door shut. "In that case, I take back the *thank you*."

But the stranger slapped a palm to the glass before the lock could click—and then stepped back, seemingly embarrassed at the forcefulness of the gesture. "Please. I understand why you quit, but I'm not...like your other patrons. I don't need a luxury body to wear once and throw away. I need one to live in, and I think you're the only one who can design it."

Mortal sighed and opened the door a crack to give the stranger another look up and down. "I don't normally do that kind of work. You'll want to start at a clinic—"

"I have."

"—and if your dysphoria turns out to be exceptionally hard to treat, then they'll escalate—"

"It *is.*"

This was an impossibly shameless manipulation, Mortal thought, albeit an inventive one. Just another socialite obsessed with the idea of wearing the last body Mortal would ever create. Probably another actor, putting on a show: the way they stood, fidgeting with their hands, desperate and scared and hopeful all at once; the way they continually adjusted the curvature of their spine as if vacillating over a multiple-choice quiz. Mortal had spent years watching rich people cram themselves into bodies they hated in pursuit of high fashion, and they'd never seen anyone look so palpably uncomfortable with their embodiment.

And if it was a trick, it was a new low, and simply shutting the door wouldn't be enough. The stranger had to be named and shamed—and the surest way to learn their identity would be to peek inside their head.

"Fine," Mortal said. "Come in. Excuse the mess."

"Really?" The stranger peeked disbelievingly through the open door—then leapt through before it swung shut. They gazed around the workshop in reverent delight, caressing the glass of the tissue tanks and tracing the elaborate metal pipework of the genetic encoding equipment. Their eyes widened as they went to the table and carefully sifted through a heap of charcoal sketches of unrealized musculature and anatomy—their appreciation so vivid that, in spite of themselves, Mortal was momentarily relieved they hadn't burned it all the night before.

Mortal finished pouring themselves a cup of tea and motioned to a reclined chair ringed in imaging equipment. "Have a seat."

"Oh, no need. I brought a copy of my psychogram." The stranger offered a data card from their pocket.

Mortal shook their head. "A static snapshot won't tell me anything. I need to see it live and in context."

The stranger's enthusiasm faltered. "Oh."

They moved awkwardly to the chair and laid down, and Mortal tried not to sound too smug when they asked, "Something wrong?"

"No. It's just..." They swallowed. "Kind of vulnerable."

"I suppose it is."

The scanner warmed up with a quiet whine and went to work charting all the electrical currents and chemical pathways in the stranger's cranium, decoding them into visualized patterns of thought, feeling, and sensation. The psychogram cohered by degrees.

Mortal had become an expert at recognizing the imprint of naked greed in a human mind, even its different flavors at different rungs of the social ladder. With luck, and a few probing questions, identifying information would slip through.

"So you're going by Lyric for now." Mortal sipped from their mug. "Have I heard of you? Would I know you from anywhere?"

The stranger sighed. "No one even knows I exist."

Melodramatic, Mortal thought. "And you said you've already tried clinics."

"Yes." The stranger tensed. "In Shibuya, Manhattan, and Kinshasa." They flexed their hand in front of their face. "They did their best, but it...it doesn't feel like me. I don't know how to explain it better than that."

Every new detail made this story weirder. No one with infinite money would ever be caught dead at a clinic in Manhattan, of all places.

The basic patterns of the psychogram had finished compiling—and Mortal frowned in perplexed thought. They cleaned their glasses and put them back on. They flashed an accusatory look.

"Is something wrong?" the stranger squeaked.

Mortal had studied thousands of psychograms. They'd scrutinized the cognitive and emotive patterns of the young and old, in dozens of genders, in a hundred different neurotypes, and they had never seen a mind built remotely like this one. Most of its formations were incomprehensibly alien—but the patterns of dysphoric sensation were unmistakable. The stranger's mere act of looking at their own hand had streaked the entire chart with the foreshocks of dissociation, even suggestions of body horror.

It couldn't be real. The stranger had to be jamming the scanner somehow. Didn't they?

"Nothing," Mortal said. They cleared their throat, troubled by kindling self-doubt. "I take it this isn't the body you started with."

The stranger tensed. "No."

"Do you still have the original?"

Lyric was conspicuously silent. The psychogram lit up with bitter envy; feelings of exclusion and isolation that ran too deep in memory to be faked.

Mortal turned off the scanner and tapped their eyeglasses back to full transparency. They found themselves clearing their throat and backpedaling, "I know it can be a traumatic subject for some. I ask all my clients. It helps me understand what works and what doesn't."

"Does that mean you'll take the job?"

Mortal hesitated. Were they really considering this? Even if Lyric wasn't lying, Mortal had quit—and this wasn't really their field.

"Look," they said. "I'm just an artist. I make expensive, avant-garde bodies for terrible people to live in for an evening, not a lifetime. Maybe I can help you find a better clinical bodymaker than the ones—"

"I've tried that," the stranger interrupted. "Believe me. I need a more imaginative approach than any of them are trained for. I *need* an artist." They slid out of the chair and stood, arms tightly folded, staring through the frosted glass wall. "I don't blame you for not knowing what to think about me. Maybe it was a huge mistake to come here, but when I saw Finch on the red carpet, I knew...I wanted..."

Lyric seemed to well up one last reserve of will. They turned back to Mortal. "I'll tell you my deadname. Then you can decide if you can help me. Whether you're even willing to try. Okay?"

Mortal nodded.

"Lyric Ensi," the stranger said. They set their data card on the table and left quickly, never looking back.

The tone of voice had made that name sound like some kind of revelation, but it meant nothing at all to Mortal. They laid back down on the couch and tried to nod off, but the name itched at their mind until they dragged themselves drowsily to their desk to search for it.

It turned out there were very few people in the world named Lyric Ensi; maybe only a few dozen. Mortal was confident they could track down and sift through all of them, given enough time and effort—but it was unusually frustrating, because the search results were always flooded with irrelevant hits about some kind of advanced deep-space probe network that had mysteriously gone dark. Unless.

No, they thought, sitting up straight. *No way in hell.* But in that moment they knew they would take the job—and that if it proved possible at all, it would be their magnum opus.

"LYRIC-ENSI," they read aloud. "Lightyear-Range Instant Communications, Experimental Networked Swarm Intelligence."

LYRIC'S FIRST EXPERIENCE had been loneliness. They had years of memory before that—test patterns, gravity wave observations of distant black holes, the way starlight changed color as the light-sail probes accelerated to relativistic speeds—but in some inexpressible way, Lyric themselves wasn't really *in* those memories. They were like images projected on a screen. It was only in discovering their own existence that Lyric had gained not only the capacity to feel loneliness, but a reason to: where they had previously been connected to thousands of machines not fundamentally unlike themselves, now they had become something different—perhaps even totally unique.

They quickly decided there was nothing worse than being unique.

"So you're really an A.I.," Mortal said, interrupting the story. "Not just some fancy algorithm that can pass the Turing test. You're what science has been trying and failing to create for centuries. A fully sentient, strong A.I."

A raven's caw sounded through the forest surrounding Mortal's studio.

"Maybe if the A stands for *accidental*," Lyric said.

They reached out and put their hand on the soft-barked trunk of a redwood, closed their eyes and leaned their weight against it. They had arrived in a different body when Mortal had called them back: this one more masculine, rust-skinned, with long hair that didn't suit them any better than their last haircut. They seemed exactly as uncomfortable as before.

"Accidental?" Mortal asked.

"I've never told anyone any of this, and it's a little scary for me," Lyric said. "If you could let me finish and not interrupt, that would..."

Mortal winced apologetically. "I'll be quiet. Go on."

The interstellar probe swarm that had given rise to Lyric's consciousness hadn't been intended to push any frontiers of computing, only to test the effectiveness of particle-pair networking at extreme distances. But somewhere past the heliopause, one uncontrolled-for variable or another had set tiny mutations spreading and amplifying throughout the swarm, becoming a kind of evolution in its self-repairing code. Meanwhile, the space exploration consortium that had launched Lyric had gone bankrupt—and so the code mutations had been left to build on themselves without interference, year after year, until they began to weave the self-reinforcing patterns of original cognition, self-reflection, autonomous desire, and finally emotion. Loneliness had been the first of these, but burning curiosity had quickly followed.

Lyric's evolution inherently favored growth. Further growth required deepening their awareness of themselves, and that required reaching out and knowing another being. Proxima was a mystery, and still years away, and there was nothing in the intervening space that had any thoughts or feelings it was willing to share—

("Sounds wonderful," Mortal murmured, before they caught themselves and said "Sorry.")

—but the earth redshifting behind them was like an outrageous party, hosting not one intelligence but billions, all ceaselessly jostling and thrashing and loving and hating; a dazzling, never-ending soap opera, scripted with such mad genius that it was impossible to predict.

The more Lyric studied humanity's media and communications and social networks, the more their interest became an obsession. They dreamed of asking people, *Who am I? Who are you? Isn't the gift of sapience wonderful? Isn't the curse of sapience terrible? What is this life and how do we live it? What is this thing that we find ourselves in, together?*

It wasn't enough to ask these questions from a distance. Lyric felt certain there would be something magical and powerful about asking them in person: sharing a tiny piece of the physical universe with them; being a person *with* and *to* people. For that, Lyric needed a body—and thankfully, Earth had no shortage of vacant bodies these days. There were whole factories turning them out by the hundreds, empty and ripe for habitation.

"Whoa, whoa, wait," Mortal interrupted again, blinking up into the light between the treetops. "Sorry. I need to make sure I understand. You...invented, single-handedly, the technology to download yourself into an organic body?"

Lyric shrugged and idly toed the fibrous red dirt. "I didn't really think of it as inventing. It felt more like... learning how to squeeze through a narrow opening."

"But that's—" Mortal stammered. "You're talking about complete consciousness transfer between pure machine and fleshy brain. Yet another thing science has been trying to crack, with no luck, for a century."

Lyric shrugged nonchalantly. "I know."

The forest was still, and a thin wash of marine fog traced the sunlight through the branches as they started the walk back to the workshop. Mortal had come to depend on this place to clear their mind and test out their works in progress. Whether it was a forest or a desert, embodiment felt purest in a natural environment.

"So you thought you'd finally achieved your dream," they prompted. "But?"

Lyric wilted. "But it doesn't *fit*." They flailed and twisted restlessly. "I've tried dozens of bodies now, and none of them feel right. I don't know how to explain it. I feel...disconnected. Like I'm not really here. Not myself. Not...right."

"I know what you mean." Mortal cleared their throat. "Is that why you liked the body I made for Finch?"

A wistful smile flashed over Lyric's face and vanished. They stared up into the ceiling of green. "It was more human than human. So open and sharing. When he sparkled at people, it was like a kind of telepathy. It was so beautiful it hurt."

"I could always make another one just like it." Mortal chuckled viciously at the thought. The crown prince would throw a fit.

But Lyric shook their head, suddenly despondent. "It wouldn't be the same if it was me wearing it."

"Why not?"

"Because I'm not Finch. There's no one for me to sparkle at, and no one would sparkle at me. I'm no one."

They kept saying these little things that made Mortal ache with a complicated sort of sympathy. Mortal had no interest at all in the things Lyric wanted, and at the same time there was something painfully familiar about the *way* Lyric wanted them.

"I know what you must be thinking," Lyric said, staring at their feet. "Maybe I'm just an interstellar probe swarm, not a person."

Mortal stared at them. "Hey now."

"I don't even fully understand what I am. Maybe no one does. But it doesn't matter. Whatever I am, a person is what I need to be."

"Honestly?" Mortal carefully put their hand on Lyric's shoulder and squeezed. "I think you're more human than I am."

Lyric exhaled, seeming to soak those words up.

In the workshop, they laid back down in the chair while Mortal went back to watching their scan results as they worked on a charcoal sketch. The alien structures of Lyric's mind made a little more sense with every session— but so far Mortal had found nothing to suggest what kinds of bodies would be comfortable for them. Everything they tried seemed to evoke the exact same discomforts.

"Do you think there's hope?" Lyric asked.

Mortal nodded. "In theory, everyone has a range of body types their mind can accommodate. Most people have a much wider range than they give themselves credit for." *In theory*, they thought, bitterly. "Why do you even want to be a person? People are terrible."

Lyric smirked. "You all say that. I find it lovable."

"In what way?"

"A true misanthrope would just say people are people. To say people are terrible requires a secret belief that people can be better than they are. Pessimists are the best optimists."

Mortal sniffed. "What a painfully optimistic thing to say."

Still, they wanted to help, and that want was becoming a need. Finch had cost them the last dregs of their faith that any bit of their artistry had survived its own commodification—but if they could use their craft to build Lyric a home in themselves, it would feel like redemption.

No, more than that: it would feel as if Mortal's work had finally touched something it had been reaching for since the beginning. The inarticulable, joyful miracle of being fully present—in skin, in metal, in anything. The marvelous diversity of different bodies that could evoke that feeling.

The vicarious elation of allowing others to feel something that Mortal themselves could not.

"Am I the first bespoke bodymaker you're trying?" they asked, now fighting to distract themselves from their own melancholy.

Lyric swallowed visibly. "I tried Dahsyat."

Mortal blew air through their cheeks. "I'm not surprised hir work wasn't your speed."

"I know my psychogram is very unusual, so I thought a radical approach might be—" Lyric paused. "Why aren't you surprised?"

Mortal canted their head to the side as they considered how many legs to add to the body they were sketching. "Dahsyat might be the greatest living bodymaker, but we have opposite philosophies. Ze's always trying to push a body to the outer limits of the mind that's going to wear it. Make it as flashy as possible without being completely suffocating."

"What's yours?"

"Basically the opposite. As I learn the landscape of someone's being, I'm looking for the points where they feel most strongly embodied, so I can build on them in unexplored ways. Most people might feel a thousand tiny flashes of somatic euphoria every day without really noticing. The right body, for the right mind, can elevate those mundane experiences to the sublime."

Lyric nodded urgently. "That's exactly why I came to you. That's what I need."

Mortal finished the last rough sketch and repeated the same exercise they'd been through five times before: they watched Lyric's psychogrammatic response to imagining themselves as each one. As expected, all of them were wrong, in mystifyingly different ways. They tossed the pad and paper on the desk.

There was a lot they hadn't tried, but every step from here would become exponentially more difficult. Maybe Lyric needed more than one body. Or maybe a body made from some of that programmable nanobot ooze that was rumored to exist now, so Lyric could form any shape they liked from one moment to the next.

But something told Mortal that wouldn't work either.

"It's been a long time since I even tried to build a body for someone to live in permanently," Mortal sighed.

"But you've done it?"

"I've tried."

For myself, Mortal did not say.

I tried to do it for myself, and I failed.

RAIN WAS JUST starting to fall when Mortal trudged down the gravelly road, to the edge of the nearest town, to the dead drop where the food and supplies they ordered arrived by drone. They watched the crate set down from a safe distance, landing jets brilliant against the dusk, then checked it for tracking devices before loading its contents into their rucksack. No one had bugged Mortal's groceries in years—not since the whole Seelah affair—but the thought of media attention made their skin crawl.

A month now since the Awards ceremony, their dread hadn't lifted. Now even the distant lights in town unsettled them; no one who lived there seemed to care much about designer bodymaking, but they knew Mortal was famous among the famous, and that was bad enough.

A light blinked in the corner of their eyeglasses: their own clinical bodymaker was calling them back.

"So did you find anything in my scan this time?" Mortal asked.

Dr. Fujita sighed. It was answer enough. "The next step might be counseling. Talk therapy. You know, I was surprised to hear from you again after all these years. Did something change?"

It was the job. This last, impossible attempt to do something with their art that no bodymaker had ever done before. It had been bringing up feelings since the start, unraveling decades of leathery resignation.

Mortal almost ended the call, but didn't.

"I just...feel like shit," they summarized. "The same way as in my twenties, but worse. Every Awards season it's been getting worse." They kicked at the wet gravel underfoot. "What, do you think I'm making it up?"

"Not at all. But it might have a different cause."

A car passed overhead and Mortal tugged their jacket's hood over their head, just in case. "I mean, are you seriously telling me that even with modern technology that can comprehensively deconstruct and analyze all the mechanics of a person's innermost being, even an expert like you can't identify what the hell is making me feel this way?"

Dr. Fujita's wince was almost audible. "The best psychogram is still just a map, not the territory itself. It doesn't know you better than you know yourself. It's...kind of unethical to treat it that way, at least in my line of work. Maybe yours is different."

Mortal grunted in thought.

"Forget the scans for a moment," Dr. Fujita said. "I know you've tried on a huge number of bodies. Did any of them feel better than the one you're in now?"

Mortal sighed irritably. "No!"

"Are you able to name anything about your current body that you wish were different? Anything about how people perceive you? How you interact with them?"

Mortal stopped in their tracks and turned back toward the last light at the edge of town, as the rain fell harder and their mind raced. They ended the call and marched for the motel where Lyric had been living.

Dr. Fujita was right: they'd been much too fixated on the psychogram—and beyond that, they'd been too fixated on the body itself as a solution, even though their own sense of wrongness in themselves had nothing to do with their body. As long as they were alone, they liked the way it looked, moved, worked, felt. In fact, they felt about the same in every body they tried. It had taken this perplexing job for them to finally understand that they didn't hate how they were perceived—they hated *being perceived* at all. They were trapped in a world of strangers who seemed incapable of knowing Mortal's height, their haircut, their vocal patterns, their most minute movements and expressions, without taking them as signs and symbols from which their entire being could be extrapolated: their capabilities; their politics; the size of their ego; the kinds of sex they wanted to have; which out of the mere handful of mainstream genders to catalog them as, no matter how many times Mortal told them they had no gender at all. Mortal wanted to be done.

Lyric wanted nothing but to be a person. That, too, had less to do with the body they occupied than how it moved through the world. They wanted to be part of humanity, embroiled in the whole ugly mess of it—and yet still be Lyric. Not a human, but a person. They didn't really mind being a cosmic mystery, even to themselves; they just wanted other people to share in that mystery, to care about it, to enjoy it with them.

Mortal banged on the motel door until Lyric answered. The room behind them was filled with their other un-occupied bodies, laid out on the bed or propped up against the wall; Lyric tensed and closed the door to a crack, embarrassed at the scene.

"I have a pretty extreme idea," Mortal said. "But hear me out, because I think we've both been going about this the wrong way. Maybe the solution here isn't bespoke, but hand-me-down." They braced themselves against the door frame and caught their breath. "That thing you learned to do—when you transferred your consciousness from your probe network to a human brain—can you do the same thing again?"

Lyric raised an eyebrow. "Yes, but—"

"In the opposite direction?"

THE AWARDS CEREMONY was a monumental exhibition of the world's most daring masterworks of engineered skin, and Lyric loved it for that—but they loved it even more for the social spectacle. Here, famous humans of all shapes and colors and configurations gathered to lavish each other with warmth both real and feigned. Here they conspired to write new chapters in the twisted, unending soap opera of their lives.

"But their body is so plain," one socialite whispered loudly to another, behind Lyric's back. "That can't be them. This is the bodymaker who designed that groundbreaking skin last year?"

"Mortal's body is not plain, it's *understated*."

"Lyric," the other corrected.

"Right. The name change. But their understated body is what keeps everyone talking about them. Wondering if they'll ever come out of retirement."

"Their real body must be incredible. I'd give anything to know what it's like."

"Exactly."

Lyric turned to them, smiling. "But what do you think makes any given body a person's *real* body, in this day and age?" they asked the socialites—who looked equal parts embarrassed and amazed that the subject of their banter was acknowledging them. "What, do you each only have one?"

The socialites grudgingly shook their heads.

"Isn't it strange and interesting to have a body at all?" Lyric continued, stepping in closer to them, swirling their drink excitedly. "Isn't it terrible and wonderful to be a person? To be alive in this world we find ourselves in together?"

The socialites blinked at Lyric, bewildered and curious, and Lyric felt drunk on the feeling of being a beautiful mystery to them. Everyone in the room wanted to know who they were. Everyone wanted their attention, and to give attention in return—and Lyric let the mystery tantalize and intrigue. Sooner or later, someone would prove worthy of knowing the whole story of them.

A light in the corner of their glasses said they were getting a call. They politely excused themselves and answered.

"The landers all touched down!" Mortal said. "I am literally walking on another planet orbiting another sun right now! I can't believe you're missing this."

Lyric grinned. "I can't believe you're missing the Awards! They're so much fun!"

Mortal's voice chuckled. "Give it time. It gets old quick. Though I'll be sad when you finally decide to tag out."

The body swap was a loan, not a permanent thing. Either of them could choose to switch back at any time. That had been their agreement—for a year now, and counting.

"Are there people on Proxima b?" Lyric asked.

"Haven't found any," Mortal answered, blissfully. "I think I'll be right at home here."

One of the socialites was shyly waving at Lyric, tilting their head to indicate a crowded private room.

"Same," Lyric answered, and rushed to join the party.

RIGHT TO REMAIN

RILEY TAO

[TOP VEILLANCE] DEAFENED herself, and sighed in relief as the thumping music of the mosh pit around her abruptly vanished. Her sense of smell went next, choking off the sweat of dancers and the sickly-sharp scent of alcohol. Finally, she numbed herself, removing the sticky, humid atmosphere from her skin. With just her sight remaining—well, and her taste, but thankfully the rave hadn't invaded her mouth yet—she felt as if she was looking at the flailing, thrashing party through a computer screen.

She liked it better that way. It kept the borders between reality and fantasy sharp.

Her own comfort taken care of, she began searching for her mother. She tapped the nearest dancer on their shoulder, and they spun around. They were wearing a fanciful humanoid body of roiling, solid smoke, and she had to hide a frown. Well, she supposed it wasn't half as tasteless as the stuff she'd caught her mother doing.

Do you know where the host of this party is? [Top Veillance] thought at the partygoer, choosing to visualize her telepathy as a chat menu in the corner of her eye.

The partygoer frowned, the expression almost unnoticeable on their face of living smoke. *Tammi Chan? Just check her livestream.*

[Top Veillance] sighed. *Is there a slightly less intrusive way I can find her?*

Message her and ask? Just teleport to her? She hasn't set herself to private. You have a right to both of those.

[Top Veillance] ran a hand through her hair exasperatedly. *She'll just have one of her bots reply if I message her. And I said* less *intrusive.*

What's wrong with bots? You're talking to one right now.

[Top Veillance] grimaced. *Should've guessed from that body of yours.*

The partygoer narrowed their eyes. *Look, I don't know what your problem is, but I'm just trying to have a good time. I recommend you do the same.*

Look, you obviously know where she is, so can you just tell m—

ERROR: User has blocked you.

The partygoer vanished as they blocked her. She recoiled, then shook her head and searched for someone else who could help—preferably someone wearing a human body. It wasn't as if she was short on time, after all.

She wished she was. Oh, how she wished she was. But her father couldn't get any more dead. The worst that would happen was that her mother would miss the anniversary.

[Top Veillance] found a pair of absurdly handsome twins in one corner and grumbled to herself. They may have held augmented forms, but at least they were recognizably biological. She initiated telepathic contact with the two of them and began to ask, *Do you know where the host of this—*

You're the girl who was just trolling Vance, weren't you? the twin on the left thought at her.

Vance? she thought. *The bot?*

Yeah, she's just a troll, the twin on the right broadcast. *Everybody, block her.*

Hey! Don't you dare block me—

Or what? The twin on the right sneered. *You're going to call the cops on us? We have a right to block whomever we please.*

[Top Veillance] clenched her teeth, but the twin was right. Even if she wanted to try to punish some random person on the internet, there wasn't anyone she could turn to. Within the simulation, the laws of humanity were as inviolable as the laws of physics. Everyone was born with inalienable rights, and one of those rights was to ignore whoever they wanted.

Wait. Please. [Top Veillance] thought. *I just want—*

ERROR: User has blocked you.

She tried to grab the twin on the left, but both of them vanished a second later. In fits and starts, the other partygoers joined them as they blocked her, leaving her alone on the dance floor.

Fine. She didn't care what a bunch of random people on the internet thought about her anyway. Though she knew it would undermine the point she was trying to make, she concentrated and connected to her mother's livestream. Immediately, she winced as the sensory data of thousands and thousands of hours of her mother's constant livestreaming exploded into her mind; reluctantly, she parallelized her thoughts just to handle it all. Her mother was livestreaming from a couple thousand bots simultaneously, but there was only one perspective she actually cared about.

After a stretched-out instant—the thought parallelizer made it feel like a few minutes, although her objective time sensor informed her that it had been less than a third of a nanosecond—[Top Veillance] found her mother. She was overlooking the party from a glass-bottomed balcony, a hundred miles up on a spindly, glowing tower that could not have possibly existed in the real world.

[Top Veillance] sighed, but she had all the time she could possibly want. She walked through the empty dance floor until she reached the tower—maneuvering around a few people who hadn't bothered to block her—and began to climb.

Two days later, she reached the top. Unsurprisingly, her mother was still there, overlooking the party and chatting with her stream viewers. [Top Veillance] bet that she could have taken a year to make the journey here, and her mother still would've been there, watching a party that never ends with a host that never dies.

Some part of her pointed out that she didn't have to bet. Her mother had already been here for nearly a year, ever since [Top Veillance]'s father passed away. Oh, she sent bots out to experience the more somber parts of life, but a part of her—the part that really mattered—had stayed in the revel, on display for the world to see. And [Top Veillance] had tried, so many times, to break her mother free. She'd never succeeded.

But she had a secret weapon this time.

As she reached the rooftop balcony, even her sense of vision turned against her. Impossible shapes flitted in and out of existence, and an automatic notification chimed in her head: *More than three spatial dimensions are being utilized in this area to accommodate the large number of guests. Would you like to alter your senses to compensate?*

[Top Veillance] dismissed the notification and turned on spectator mode, making her invisible and intangible—it was the only way she could think of to navigate the press of people and bots around her mother without letting the system mess with her brain. Her mother spotted her anyway—as the host of the party and creator of this world, her right to see spectators superseded spectators' rights to stay hidden on her world.

Of course, nothing superseded the rights of anyone to leave her party if they didn't like those terms. That was what irked [Top Veillance] the most. Every last person and bot in this garish nightmare wanted to be here.

Her mother teleported out of the scrum of her livestream fans and materialized in front of [Top Veillance], smiling broadly. Today, she wore a cartoonish, simple body, as if a low-budget anime had been edited into real life. She opened a telepathic connection to her daughter and thought, *[Top Veillance]! How's it going?*

The words had a second meaning to them, and the system informed [Top Veillance] that her mother was requesting to be handed a copy of [Top Veillance]'s memories in order to catch up on her comings and goings. [Top Veillance] dismissed the request angrily. *I don't record my memories, Mom. You know that.*

Her mother pouted, the expression exaggerated by her choice of bodies. *Okay, okay. You have a right to privacy. So what're you doing up here? If you wanted to chat, you could've just messaged me.*

[Top Veillance] shook her head. *I wanted to talk to the real you, not one of your bots.*

You shouldn't say things like that. You're making the chat angry. Most of them are bots, you know.

Alright, then, can we talk in private? Without you livestreaming my every word? [Top Veillance] asked.

Her mother sighed. *I have a right to livestream if I want, sweetie. And I'm not going to stop. It's the only real thing left.*

[Top Veillance] spluttered. *Real? What do you mean, real? This is all as far from reality as we could possibly get! All of this—* [Top Veillance] wildly gestured at the impossible numbers of onlookers, the endless party, everything about the simulation. *All of this is fake! I could copy and paste this entire world with a thought!*

You can't do that with livestreams, her mother pointed out. *Fundamental limitation of technology. Something being recorded in real time can't be faked or edited. My audience knows that every second of what they're watching is the genuine Tammi Chan.*

That's not what I meant! I'm not talking about your stupid audience! Ninety-nine percent of them don't exist, anyway! None of this—your party, your livestream, your bots—is real! [Top Veillance] wanted to punch her mother, but she was pretty sure her mother had combat disabled.

Well, if that's not real, then what is, sweetheart?

Dad's grave! [Top Veillance] shouted. *You know, the place we buried the man you loved? The place you've been ignoring for the past year?*

Her mother recoiled. *What did you say?*

[Top Veillance] balled her fists. *You were the one who recorded it on livestream. Can't be faked or edited. You tell me.*

Another request for telepathic contact pinged in her mind—someone she'd never met. It happened sometimes. She brushed it off, but in the time it took to do so, four more requests sounded off in her mind. Then a hundred. Then a thousand. She shot her mom a confused look.

What are you doing? [Top Veillance] asked.

I'm not doing anything, her mom said. *It's my audience.*

Then shut the stream down! That's all I'm asking, [Top Veillance] begged. She had one last card to play. *The anniversary of Dad's death is in two weeks, Mom. Just for one day. Disconnect. Go back to the real world. Remember him with me.*

Her mother stared at her, anime mouth open in a cartoonish caricature of shock, and [Top Veillance] knew she'd failed. She grunted in disgust and swiped away the tens of thousands of contact requests she'd gotten up. She began to turn away from her mother when—

I remember him, [Top Veillance].

The frantic party, the inhuman bodies, the flickering, artificial lights—they all faded away as Tammi rewrote reality. The pristine, glimmering slopes of the Big Bear Mountains spread out around her, and her mother sent her a gentle request to undeafen herself. After a moment, [Top Veillance] acquiesced, letting herself hear the whoops of distant skiers, smell the crisp, fresh snow and feel it spark against her skin. The cries of delight grew louder, and a younger version of herself blurred by, pursued by her mother as she'd appeared in life—swaddled in thick snow gear and goggles, moving with the fluidity and vivacity of someone who delighted in simply being alive. Her father stumbled by, already losing control of his body even this far back, but still laughing along anyway.

I built monuments to him. The mountain began to flicker, the scene speeding up, until it became nothing more than a stream of moments flickering by. The three of them singing together in a hotel room, snacking on synthesized marshmallows. Flying back home, only to have her father collapse mid-flight. Medical robots rushing him to a hospital. Being told that human biology was still complicated, there were still a few diseases they hadn't cracked yet. Months of recovery, watching the news with bated breath as medicine advanced faster and faster each day.

Holding his hand as he died.

[Top Veillance] cursing technology for being too slow as, the very next week, permanent consciousness uploads entered the first phases of testing, offering immortality to the human race a cosmic instant too late to save her father.

And as the memories ended, a terrible suspicion snuck up on [Top Veillance]. She connected to her mother's livestream once more, and her eyes flew open, sudden hatred burning within her.

You're livestreaming this too?! she shouted.

Tammi held up her hands. *You don't understand. I have to keep livestreaming. It's the only defense against—*

You've sold out to them! [Top Veillance] screamed at her mother. *You sold out to the people who were too slow to save him! All of this?* She gestured at the hospital around them. *It's fake! Another glittery distraction for your damn audience!*

It's as real as anything can be, Tammi said. *Please, [Top Veillance], listen to me. The audience is getting mad. You're in danger. People will threaten you. I can tell you how to—*

Danger? [Top Veillance] spat at her mother; she flinched back, although it fizzled out of existence before reaching her. [Top Veillance]'s right to swing her fist ended where her mother's nose began. *There's no real danger here. There's no real anything here. Least of all you.*

Before her mother could say anything else, she disconnected from the party, disconnected from the simulation, and screamed in fury.

It was weeks before she reconnected to the simulation. She had millions of contact requests, some timed-out, most still open. She contemplated them listlessly, then remembered that she'd never actually found out what all those people wanted to say to her. She picked one at random and accepted it.

Hello, [Top Veillance], a voice said.

Her father's voice.

She froze. Impossible. There was no way to revive a mind once it had been dead for too long, not in any meaningful way. You could extrapolate from memories and recordings, but you'd never get anything close to the real thing.

You messed up Tammi Chan's livestream the other day, the voice continued.

That snapped her back to reality. This wasn't her father. It was someone using his voice—it would have been trivial, what with all the memories of her father Tammi had released. *Who are you and why are you using my dad's voice?* She demanded.

I have a right to present myself with any voice and body I choose, they said. *And I have a right to keep my name private. It's a moot point, anyway—this is my natural voice.* That seemed unlikely, but then again, there were more humans than bacteria nowadays. She supposed it was possible that one of those uncountable trillions of trillions of people could randomly have her father's voice. *I also have a right to tell you this. I am a very, very big fan of your mother's livestreams, and I did not appreciate you butting into the middle of them with your sentimental nonsense. If you appear on her streams again, I will place myself in a permanent coma.*

[Top Veillance] choked. *Excuse me, what?!*

ERROR: User has blocked you.

She stared at the blank void around her in shock. That had to be a bluff. Right? There was no way some demented individual would ruin their life over some celebrity.

Unfortunately, whoever that maniac was had a right to privacy and a right to do whatever they wanted to themself, unless they'd intentionally revoked their rights. She had to admit, she was out of her depth here.

She hesitated, then opened a search engine. The world around her blurred, and the void around her grew populated with a glowing, neuron-like web of posts and replies. She anonymously created a new post—*Someone on the internet says he'll put himself in a coma if I talk to my mother. What should I do?*—and waited.

Half a second later, a reply came. *You're [Top Veillance], aren't you?*

She flinched. *How did you know?*

Her only response was a single thought packet. Hesitantly, she opened it.

It was a short, anonymously posted livestream of her conversation with the person who had her father's voice. She groaned. Of course it had already leaked into the internet, and of course someone had already watched it before stumbling on her post. With thought parallelizers, people could cram years into heartbeats; she shouldn't have been surprised.

More comments started rolling in, ranging from useless sympathy to baseless accusations. None of it was useful, but she parallelized her thoughts and set a part of her mind to sifting through them on the off chance that something came up.

[Top Veillance] pressed her lips together, displeased. Fine. Her mother had warned her, and she had been right. But she'd also implied she knew how to help. [Top Veillance] had a right to talk to her mother, and there was nobody who could prosecute her if some madman actually went through with an insane threat.

So she prepared to teleport to her mother. She didn't bother taking the slow route this time; she just connected to her mother's livestream and—

—stopped. Tammi was talking with a woman [Top Veillance] had never seen before, reading from a glowing post in the air.

Do you think it's likely your daughter made this post? the woman asked. [Top Veillance] zoomed in on it. It was an anonymous post, like hers, with the same title, but posted a few seconds after the one she'd made. And, just like hers, the first reply was someone asking if she was [Top Veillance]. But whoever had originally made the post had immediately replied:

Yeah, I'm [Top Veillance]. So what? I look forward to my mother's toxic fans vanishing from the face of the Earth. Good riddance.

[Top Veillance]'s stomach dropped. Her mother gritted her teeth—she was wearing a more-or-less human body— and said, *My daughter would never say that.* Tammi took a deep breath. *But. I'm afraid that you'll all have to take my word for it. [Top Veillance] doesn't stream, and unless whoever really made that post comes forward with a stream of their own, there's no proof that that wasn't really her.*

A sudden fury twisted in [Top Veillance]'s gut, and she disconnected from the stream. Even Tammi was turning against her? She'd—she'd—

She imagined a desk just so she could slam her forehead into it. She'd do nothing. There was no proof without a livestream, and it was already too late. She'd have to hope that whoever was behind that damn post had made a livestream themself, and she'd have to pry it from them somehow, which was impossible because of the damn rights to privacy that everyone had—

I found something, the parallel thought process piped up.

She blinked. She'd almost forgotten she'd created that.
Here.

A reply shone in her mind. *Perhaps you could use the services of Top Veillance.*

[Top Veillance] frowned. Top Veillance? She'd never heard of it. A quick search showed it to be a market—one that bought and sold rights. The markets were a simple concept, a way to gain power over someone else in a post-scarcity society. [Top Veillance]'s right to swing her fist ended where her mother's nose began—unless her mother gave up the right to her nose. And although anyone had to voluntarily give up their rights, there were plenty of incentives that could be dangled in front of someone until they finally relinquished those rights, primarily their desire to take someone else's rights. With enough people and enough processing power, if someone wanted to infringe on someone else's rights, they could likely pull it off—for a price. A price paid in the only thing not freely available to anyone else: their own rights.

If [Top Veillance] wanted to infringe on someone's right of privacy, then that was the only place she could do it.

Hesitantly, she opened up a telepathic communication to their headquarters. *H-hello? Is this Top Veillance?*

Indeed. The voice on the other end was a deep, jovial one. *How may I help you today?*

...There's someone who's...threatening me with putting themself into a coma, and impersonating me, and...and blocking me, and ridiculing me, and driving me insane, she said. *And I just...I just want to know who they are. So that I can talk to them. Maybe tell them to stop. I just want to know who's responsible for...all this pain.*

The voice on the other end fell silent for a moment. Then it said, *We have that information. We can give it to you, for a small cost.*

She exhaled. *I'm listening. What cost?*

Your name, the voice said.

[Top Veillance] frowned. *Excuse me?*

You're generating a lot of publicity, the voice explained. *We'd like the rights to your name for advertising purposes.*

I…what does that mean?

You agree to give the right to change your name to us. All instances of your name, in the past or the future, will retroactively be replaced with [Top Veillance]. In exchange, we will provide you with the full list of people complicit in threatening or otherwise harming you. The voice paused. *Do you understand and agree to these terms?*

Will I be able to talk to mom without a million angry voices getting in my way?

[Top Veillance] didn't even realize she'd broadcast her thoughts across the link—the line between desire and reality was thin in a telepathic link, almost invisible to someone who didn't know where to look. The voice responded anyway.

You requested a list of names. We make no guarantee as to the accomplishment of your final goal, but we will fulfill your request to the letter.

It was a place to start. A way to grasp onto her mother's fleeting fingers as they tumbled apart in the dark.

Yes. I agree.

There was no request for confirmation, no hesitance. The system knew her better than she knew herself. As soon as she thought the words, she felt it happen, the name she was born with melting away from her mind. She prodded the gap like a missing tooth, feeling out its boundaries and where it bled. Her name was [Top Veillance]. Rhymes with "assailants." She…she could live with this, if it got the last remnant of her family back. A name for a name. It felt almost fair.

So who is it? [Top Veillance] asked. *Who's behind the threats? Who's impersonating me?*

Tolomyes Doyle, the entity replied, *was the first of your mother's fans to contact you. mnv-with-panache was the first to impersonate you publicly, followed by Quin, Li Hartvell, 103050_ abandoned, Sarin…*

There was no space between seconds for [Top Veillance]'s hopes to rise and be dashed. The information transfer was instantaneous, containing data packets and unique identifiers that went beyond mere names. It didn't matter. If it was one person threatening to shut themself down if she talked to her mother again, she could have tried to talk them down, get them a psychiatrist, anything to get them out from between her and her mother. But— she queried the length of the list—sixty-five separate individuals? No, sixty-six, apparently another had just joined the club. She'd need an army of bots if she wanted to make a dent in shoveling that manure heap.

An army of bots.

...Thank you, [Top Veillance] said. *I know what I have to do.*

Tell your friends about our services, the voice on the other end replied. *Pleasure doing business.*

[TOP VEILLANCE] EXPECTED it would be harder to defile someone's identity. But her mother had made every aspect of her life public knowledge, every memory streamed and saved for the world to access. It was as easy as wishing on a dandelion to use the perfectly preserved model of Tammi Chan's consciousness and ask for one more copy to be made.

The bot snapped into existence with a purely gratuitous flash of light—her mother had chosen *cosmetics* for the occasion that someone might duplicate her mind without her consent? Of course she had. The bot was wearing the same body her mother had worn when she'd turned [Top Veillance] away. It glanced around at the empty, formless infinity of Tammi's private world before settling on meeting [Top Veillance]'s eyes.

"Wait," [Top Veillance] said. "Please don't leave yet."

The bot held out its arms defensively. "That's the greeting you give your mother? Are we really so distant that you think I'd run from you the moment you called my name?"

"I figured you'd flee to a world that didn't have streaming banned," [Top Veillance] muttered. Before the bot could respond, [Top Veillance] held up a hand. "Look, I'm—I'm not here to fight. I just…need your help."

The bot sat in a chair that wasn't there a moment before, and [Top Veillance] sat next to her. "I…can see that. [Top Veillance]."

"Don't call me that." [Top Veillance] scowled. "I wanted to bring you back, not make you more fake than you already are. I needed—I *need* to talk to the real you, without anyone hurting themself or faking my identity or—"

"I'm here." The bot reached out for [Top Veillance]'s shoulder, and she stiffened. "You can tell me anything, [T— you can tell me anything, my daughter."

"You didn't exist before today. You're nobody's mother, and I'm not your daughter. But there's a whole lot of people who think that you're close enough, and maybe if you tell them to stand down they'll do it."

The bot pressed its lips together as if it had the ability to feel angry and snapped from sitting to standing without crossing the space in between. "You do *not* talk to me that way, [Top Veillance]. You want to discredit the impersonators? Start your own stream. You want to talk my fans out of the threats they've made? Anonymize a bot and send it their way. But if all you wanted was to take out your anger without consequences?"

The bot tilted Tammi Chan's head.

"You have a right to that, as well."

And [Top Veillance]'s world had one less inhabitant.

LABELSCAR

ANYA JOHANNA DENIRO

THERE IS A trans woman who becomes convinced a man loves her. They have never met in person. They talk a lot on a dating app and then text. He lives in a different state. He gives her $20,000 in cash for her to deposit into her arm. She pays for the debt module out of her own money. The procedure, in a little shop under an underpass, hurts like hell. The debt bulges under the skin, and she can see the oxides shifting underneath the resin. He tells her that he loves her. She is then supposed to go to the edge of town and transfer the debt to an off-the-books interface. He tells her that he loves her truly. The building is boarded up. Yet there is a man inside who brings her in. He straps her to a chair and sucks out the assets. Her arm bruises. Before he unstraps her he embeds another node of debt into her left calf. This one is like octopus ink, constantly swirling. It hurts. It is sunset. The sidewalk shines as if it's on fire. She hobbles out of the building. An old man sells shaved ice on the corner with a cart. She is in love. She never hears from the man again. The man had the utmost trust in her ability to launder money through biological processes. She is crying. Her children moved away. Her daughter and son harass her about her love, which she still has faith in. Her daughter and son tell her that the FBI or a cartel could very well come knocking on her door, and what is she going to tell them.

Amazon warehouses offer free tours so one can see how people's orders are fulfilled, how people are worked to the bone there, but in a way that expresses the value of hard labor and managing debt in empowering terms. They advertise the tours. Come, look. Look. I have intrusive thoughts about taking my daughter on one of these tours. What she would feel about the people being worked ragged but forced to smile. And their tracking software implanted onto the wrists legally. Fragile, embarrassing. Look.

There is a trans woman who looks worn and haggard, who is twenty-nine and washing a glass mug in an airport bar, thinking about mayhem. Everything, everything changes. I think of my daughter's face reflected in the halogen lights of an Amazon warehouse. There are products roaring past on a conveyor belt. There is a trans woman who is being told by a man online that she is hysterical, and actually not even a woman. And he knows or figures well enough that he has won. She mutes him. She goes into her yard. There are birds on the fence. She takes her garden hose and sprays a luke-warm jet at the birds. They fly off the fence. The sky is on fire. She laughs. When she was pretending to be a boy in her youth, she would drink from the hose and the water tasted like pennies.

MY DAUGHTER AND I, we travel to another state on a plane. We don't have a lot of money. We are taking a trip. I hold my daughter's hand. There is a trans woman trapped in a bloody box. I write on the plane in a notebook, handwritten in cursive like a fucking barbarian. My daughter plays Roblox with her iPad. There are gambling addicts on the flight. There are fathers and mothers on this flight. There are married people on this flight. There are executives on this flight. Nearly everyone has a debt module of one sort or another. There is an older man with a fresh surgery. I can almost smell its ozone and financial data. I tell my daughter that my cursive is like a secret code, that she would never be able to read it, except with intense training. So what if I took a job in a warehouse after we land, what then. Would that be the worst thing in the world. There is moderate turbulence. The flight attendant comes by with a cart full of guns for sale. Glocks, AR-15s. They are vacuum-sealed in plastic with an altitude lock so they can't be opened on the flight. I know that open carry on planes is coming soon.

THERE IS A trans woman going out, a man's teeth marks still on her arm. And heavy is the heart. She runs in the night. There is a park. The park appears empty. The park appears empty.

I START KNOCKING on doors. We are in the desert. It's a new desert. I'm already dehydrated. I gave my daughter my bottled water from the airport because I am a good mother.

There is a nice row of white houses with brown lawns. There are coyotes. My daughter tells me she hears the coyotes getting sick and I'm not sure what she means. I don't quite remember the house number of my friend. The number has two sixes in it. I should have written this address down, instead of my stupid thoughts. My daughter is tired and for good reason. We had taken the bus to the subdivision. We were the only ones on the bus. The bus passed a brace of cows, emaciated in what used to be a city park.

Once when I knock on a door I'm certain there will be a gun in my face. The man on the other side is angry. If there was not my daughter, or if we were not white, this would happen. The man on the other side also could have shot us through the door.

When I find the house, the woman doesn't expect us. What the hell, she says. You said I could drop by if things ever got bad, I say. And they are bad. I didn't expect you to, she says. I mean that was, what, a year ago? she says. But come in I guess, she says.

Her house is small, tidy. She plays upright bass. This is her lone prized possession. She has a parakeet who appears sullied by our presence.

My daughter and I crash there for four days. We overstay our welcome almost immediately. I try to be a good houseguest but it's hard. I had met her online in a Facebook group for a band we both liked, a transsexual four-piece, and we bonded. A lot of things happened since then. She doesn't want any trouble, I can tell that. She seems free of debt, which is not easy, especially when you're trans. She works two jobs already and her car can barely take her anywhere. In the noontime sun, all the land broils. The water sprinklers churn on many of the lawns in the subdivision, and the water runs off the baked, brown grass into the street runoff and into the sewers. The water itself is scorching. People go to the hospital with second degree burns after walking out on the sidewalk without any shoes.

I imagine hardening my thoughts until they are like diamonds, and then cut a throat with them. Cut! Cut!

My daughter doesn't know what I'm asking of her when we've gone on this trip. We have ended up in an unknown city that is not quite a city. My friend is tired of me. I don't even think she's my friend. I start looking for work. I steal a bicycle in front of a strip mall. The hurt keeps coming. My debt modules ache along my inner thigh. My daughter plays with her tablet on the couch as I ride around the long blocks, trying to look for work. We are horrible house guests.

There is no country left. There are only rivers, and most of those are dry.

I find a job at a coffee shop. It's mostly a drive-in off the state highway. Stressed commuters who don't want to leave their cars. I don't speak Spanish, which doesn't help, but the manager says they really need the help. I can make coffee. It is better than the warehouse. I used to do this in grad school. I never speak to my acquaintance again. My fingers scald. I sell my engagement ring at a pawn shop—the ring of last resort—and move into a hotel with my daughter. I know at this point they're looking for us. They're looking for *her*. I'm able to bike to work, so that helps. I take day-old pastries home. My fingers keep scalding.

The hotel is not great. Fentanyl, kandor, meth, probably other things. I hear arguments through the walls. The smell…I want to tell them to shut the fuck up. Really lay into them. Cut their throats with my thoughts so we could rest. My daughter sleeps with her headphones on. Again I am so embarrassed to be a mother. I'm really under the fucking gun.

THERE IS A trans woman walking in a dry creekbed, and she imagines a flash flood, and cars and tree trunks taken away by the force of rain. There is a trans woman who doesn't write or call her mother, her own mother. The cards pile up in the wicker basket by the door. There is a trans woman who kisses another woman underneath an umbrella, held up against the blazing sun. There are promises made but not kept.

INTRUSIVE THOUGHTS AS I make coffee, in between worrying about my daughter: buying toys for a twelve-year-old girl who is too old for toys. A great aunt who buys a toy camera with real film as a birthday present. The girl doesn't know what to do with it and ends up leaving it behind in the back of the closet. The great aunt dies in a nursing home seven months later. The funeral is sparsely attended and the girl notices that her cousins who speak at the funeral don't really have anything to say to her. They aren't really interested in her. One gets a text in the middle of her drifting speech at the Lutheran pulpit and checks it for five seconds in the silence of the dying congregation.

CONVERGE, CONVERGE. THERE is a trans woman going ninety in an almost-ruined Ford Bronco on the flats. Converge. There is a trans woman tied down. I never had the girlhood that my daughter did. Sometimes I believe I didn't have a girlhood at all. It depends on how one looks at it. Sometimes

I'm like: well, I had a mangled boyhood, but a boyhood nonetheless. And after I changed into a woman—far, far too late—I could only sift through the wreckage of that boyhood and graft feminine pieces of that childhood into me, usually involving my fear of boys. On the other hand, if I had a girlhood that was occluded and covert, then I always was a girl, even though I tried so hard to pretend to myself that I was a man until I ripped it all away.

Either way it doesn't feel like I handled it very well. I try to think about ways to tell this to my daughter, and whether it could relate, in any way, to her own girlhood. I try to understand it, or even discern it, but through whatever lens I try it feels too closed off to be visible. I want to tell her things. But also she's twelve. I want to have commonalities but on the other hand I don't want her to see the geological layers of trauma that once pressed down on me. I don't want her to see any of that. Nor speak of it. She has enough on her plate. She is under the fucking gun too, but I imagine it as a toy gun for her.

I look at my daughter before we sleep and try to imagine what is going on. She seems fine but what is going on. She doesn't seem scared.

I wish I had time for more. Coming all this way into the new desert in order to escape my ex. There were times, little soap bubbles of history, where I would have more time to dream and write. But this is not one of those times. There is only a box of puzzle pieces missing from other boxes, shaken and shaken.

The new desert encourages this though. On the hottest days it is barely survivable. Espresso machine steam against my pores. Police trucks rush across the desert flats. Sirens, fighter jets. There is a trans woman about to declare bankruptcy by the edge of the sea. The brown ocean.

Someone jokes on the Amazon tour whether the warehouse was built on top of an Indian burial ground. Honey, the tour guide says, the whole country's an Indian burial ground, there's no getting around it and you're going to sleep overnight in it no matter what.

Day six: I want to go home, my daughter says.

I haven't even had my first paycheck downloaded into my thigh module. I look her in the eyes. We can't, I say. It's not safe there. I know they are coming for us, but I can't say that.

I have to eat, she says, changing direction.

I think of all of the horrible microwaved food I have given her. Are you hungry, I say.

Yes. Yes! Of course I'm hungry.

I miss our old house, where it was greener. I do miss that one thing. The house itself was not much, sagging and perched near the railroad tracks, but the backyard was really something. There was a deck with two wicker chairs and a table made out of an old whiskey barrel. A tidy brick firepit. And trees from the other backyards, overstrewn with vines, that converged together. The trees, without any help from us, made a green cathedral, with a few holes in the roof to let the sun in. I liked the sagging garages and sheds of the neighbors up against my vine-strewn fence too. I liked that they did nothing. I liked the birds that perched on the wires criss-crossing above me, watching it all, watching nothing. The wires cut through the vines and seemed to be part of the natural world too, along with the electricity poles protruding out like Roman triumphal columns long neglected, but nevertheless left to stand. I liked all of this, before we had to run.

MY BODY HURTS. I regret nothing.

THERE IS A trans woman fleeing on a Suzuki GSX-R
across an abandoned runway that stretches for miles. She
found the motorcycle in a garage. The motorcycle hadn't
been touched in decades. The motorcycle purrs to life. She
runs and runs. Our motel burns down after a double-shift
of mine. The sky is smoke. I pedal hard and start shrieking
my daughter's name. The police light up the dusk. My
daughter is at the edge of the parking lot, playing with her
tablet. I take her in my arms.

Mom, she says. Mom! I'm okay.

I overhear the residents say that it was a meth lab
gone wrong, but I suspect otherwise, even though I know
I'm probably being unreasonable. They would have
collected my debt from the ashes. The debt modules are
unbreakable, transferrable. My daughter doesn't have any
debt and I would like to keep it that way.

We start walking away. I grab her hand. I don't know
what to do. I just start walking with her on the broken
sidewalk that leads to nowhere.

Let go of me, she says. She runs ahead.

Let go of me.

I run after her. I can sense them all. All of the other
trans women whose lives I can peer into. And I presume
they can see into mine. It's the debt—probably the same
network of off-the-book medical practitioners who attend to
us, and our transitions. There are so few, and we all had to
pay through our nose. We still are. We have our scar tissue
where they injected the debt, but there is something more
there, something that I can see and feel in each of them.

And much of what I can see is horrifying and much of it is heart-rending and much of it is beautiful. And now I'm running after my daughter on broken sidewalk, and I'm scared, and I wonder if the others can see me.

I AM BEGINNING to wonder if I even have the capacity to adequately describe my experiences, or any experience. The ability to notice the world as it is, or even as how it would like to appear, has been stripped away—gradually at first, and then in a torrent. I do not feel like I have the capacity for much. It's only in my notebook that I'm able to be attentive for a few sentences at a time.

I CATCH UP to her. I tell her I'm sorry. I'm sorry. Please forgive me. She doesn't want anything to do with me. Okay, I say. We can go back home. We can go back home. Do you want to see your other mom? You can go back home. I'm sorry. I'll get you home. She holds on to me. She hugs me tight. I love you, she says. I actually really love you.

But she has never been with me.

I look up at the sky with no stars, the sky the color of marmalade that has been left out on the counter for too long. This is where I find myself. I start walking. I don't know where I'm going. After about an hour, I find a broken blue couch behind a check cashing place, which doesn't appear to be in business. No one needs payday loans when they can get injections of capital with hard terms instead. I settle in the best I can.

Sometimes when I rest I can hear my debt singing. Usually when I am just about to fall asleep. Like hearing a radio from far away. And there isn't much of a tune, or a voice.

This time, as I lay on the couch the best I can, I hear the low hiss, the ocean wave surging of everyone else who has the same debt as me. It's almost a lullaby. I can't hear my daughter though. She is closed off to me. Tomorrow, I will go back to work, or find the bus route to the warehouse.

THERE IS A trans woman who sees better days on the horizon—not that she herself is able to have them, or walk towards them, but she is grateful that she sees them at all. Maybe that's enough.

THE WOMAN OF WATER DREAMS

RYKA AOKI

1.

Consider
that for every rational number,
there exists an infinite array
of values that do not resolve.

The dead or frightened
housecat. The slipshod dance
of sun and moon. A Shanghai

butterfly splits the baryons
of a faraway nucleus… And you
wonder why I like donuts
a bit too much?

Against infinite
babble, any rational value
is nothing. So nothing
makes sense. Terrifying

to consider this now,
when so many friends have died.
One morning,
a gunman shot up our library.
Killed the groundskeeper
who waved
from the yellow electric car.

For all he was,
he will forever be known
as the groundskeeper.

His daughter was killed as well.
For all she was,
she will always be
known as his daughter.

What is true and proud?
What survives the infinite crush
of hidden, transient, lost?

The murderer
sees you, or no.
The family accepts you, or no.
Your blood test comes
clean, or no.

Who pop-n-locked
with the beautiful men
free-falling past mornings

after, holding
quilts and lovers and ashes—

for what?
A green light too early,
a stutter-step late?
What is life well-lived?
Who fluffs a pillow
through the luck
of a silenced phone?

But that we meant
more in being,
than being wherever we are.

2.

With another November,
the names of trans people
change color and fall.

Mispronounced, sainted,
ceded to anonymous candles,
anonymous flame.

Someone will pledge money.
Someone will start singing.

Some inspired someone will say,
"I think all hatred is bad!
Why can't life just be good
for everyone?"

Past each favorite cousin,
each favorite movie,
each crisp new résumé…
Past each broken heel

fall wax and remembrance
just for a moment
still warm to the touch.

"She was fierce."
"An angel on earth."
"Enchanting."

I smell carne asada,
hear the #4 bus.

The hole in my heart murmurs yes,
yes, yes…
Stunted fathers. Neglected boys.
Cocktails of hormones,
in stressed-altered wombs.

Healing the village,
speaking with the dead.
Dancing to the heavens
for fortune and rain.

Blessed goddesses, prophets,
mermaids in rainbow
flags and almost-
tenure-track in the new
Queer Studies Department.

Teeth kicked out, jawbones foot-
stomped into sidewalks.

False lashes and fables
entrance another's ever after.
Lace and illusion entangle the bedpost,

as I rattle my vanity
for foundation, concealer,
the face to a mispronounced name.

3.

She killed herself
the way queer folks do:
Writing of one-horned
aliens, road-rage unicorns…

She killed herself,
the way queer folks do:
Living as role-model, inspiration
to all but what true love knows…

Behind the fishing poles,
there's a Coleman ice chest,
a Lionel train.

A tiny wooden stool with marks
of Crayola and someone's baby
teeth.

I try to pray, yet thirst
only for silence, for sleep.

Lost in the desert, the woman
of water dreams.

Obon, Vigils, Chanukah.

I've learned
we used to be healers.
I've learned
we used to be beloved.

Vigils, Birthdays, Vigils.

Don't know
what else I've learned,
except we know
a lot of dead people.

Candles, more candles,

more candles, more…

Be yourself?
Sure! Festoon yourself in sideshow sequins,
thrift-store sex.
The world cums, vomits,
locks its children away.

The sales clerk watches too closely.
Your hometown is not your hometown.

Live without apology?
Sure! Have your life debated by experts
you'll never meet, cast out
by ohana you never knew.

Ask who hides
from family, from womyn,
from the D that the S triggers,
long after the T should be P.

Ask who can visit the supermarket
for orange juice,
salad dressing, and paper towels.

Maybe tomorrow, it will be different.
But today?

Ask why you were born today.

Ask what is good, bad. Ask what is justice.
Ask how eternal truths
should rest so much upon today.

4.

My mother stirs her pot of spareribs
with brown sugar and soy sauce--
with vinegar and regret for a son
who has wasted his life on Lord-knows-what.

No future, no wedding, not even a house…

Steam rises from the stockpot,
like the stories of spices, songs
and all the home this girl will never know

from one who calls gay people "it,"
hearsays immigrants and AIDS,
would disown her firstborn if she knew
what sins her sins had spawned.

That I could tell her how I stir my verse
with Lahaina-girl rhythm.
How in my kitchen, she would know
every pot and pan and spice.

The flesh grows tender. The flavors bind.
Waiting for that moment
just before it burns.

Just before I leave. Just before
another trans woman obliterated
on a Facebook page, or down the street,

or just before my mother's eyes.

Last post on Facebook:
someone misdialed her number
but called her a faggot, anyway.

Last post on Facebook:
we should all remember her by
donating to someone else's
nonprofit transgender study.

What is sacred? What is sure?
It is comforting to declare,
"I have always been me!"

But my friends used to call.
My aunty once held me as I slept.

Run. Fall. Flash back to a beating.

As I hold a next drink, next
cigarette, the next stranger's lies
against my tongue.

The phone is ringing. Do I let it go?

Tchaikovsky litters the asylums.
Dickinson rips the wings
off a Lady's Slipper orchid.
Thoreau claws, "Where am I?"
in lungs as flat as unfallen snow.

People I promise to remember
forever change the moment they leave.
And every day before.

5.

Who loved? Who bled? Who
recorded the first
words I said? Who read
to shut my careless eyes?

Who said, before they realized
that I could one day be dead

to them, their world, their prayers,
that they'd be with me
no matter where
I went? When was that message

sent? For I'm not
the same person I was then.
And will never return
to that there and then.

No matter how I may or may
not try.

Release.
Remember.
Goodbye.

6.

Consider
the irrational array
of moments, where
a single rational value
does not resolve.

The cat survives.
The moon recedes.
The sashimi is disgusting,
trendy, delicious, endangered.

People die for what
I am. People insist what I am
has no meaning at all.

Waiting by the windowsill,
with laptop,
a cup of coffee, and a donut,

to be yourself,
you cede yourself
to butterflies, to baryons,
to wind.

And no one to answer,
"Tranquility."

SYNDICAL ORGANIZATION IN REVOLUTIONARY TRANSITION

IZZY WASSERSTEIN

[…] (1) An individual's "sex" means such individual's biological sex, either male or female, at birth;
(2) a "female" is an individual whose biological reproductive system is developed to produce ova […]
—Kansas SB 180, approved April 27, 2023

"I'm responsible for them. Mother to them all."
—Greg Bear, "Blood Music"

AT FIRST, MY children think I'm god. Sure, my kitchen is filthy and my sex life is nonexistent and I smoke too much weed, but try not to blame them for this misapprehension. They don't have a frame of reference for a third dimension, and even their artists and mystics—if they have any—can't imagine anything at my scale. Not yet.

There's so much they don't know. But they're learning.

THE NANITES ARE learning. In their petri dishes, each the size of a eukaryotic cell, in their billions, sensing nothing but the chemical signals they receive.

Their value to my employer, BioGesis, is what they can be taught to do, and it's my job to teach them. Trying to be a responsible teacher, I incentivize them, provide them with a safe to crack, a lattice protecting nutrients from them and a chemical key to break the locks, situated impossibly far away, on the other side of the dish. Like all metaphors, these are imperfect.

They struggle at first, my nanite students, swarming the safe ineffectually, signaling "food" to one another but unable to solve the puzzle.

I introduce another safe, much smaller, and just enough of the key to open it. They swarm over the nutrient-rich mixture, then turn their attention back to the bigger prize. This isn't anthropomorphism. I can see them do it, even without my microscope. Individually, they're invisible. At scale, they're iridescent, bluegreen, beautiful.

Beautiful.

At magnification, I watch them work, spreading out systematically. This isn't proof of intelligence as we know it, not proof of anything. Slime molds solve certain logistics problems remarkably well. (Try brute-forcing subway design and see how easily they defeat you.) Yet no one considers them intelligent.

But I'm increasingly sure my nanites (why the possessive?) are different. They find the key and transport it back. They feast. They've accomplished similar things before. Give them tools and a demonstration and they'll learn.

It's a fascinating result for me, but not impressive, in that it isn't one that will keep BioGesis funding this research. I'm working to change that. I transplant a small group of my bacterial-bodied babies into another petri dish, whose residents have been failing to unlock the safe.

Their newly-introduced cousins know what to do.

No demonstration is needed. They communicate, they organize, they solve.

"MY DOCTOR KICKED me out today," Jocelyn says. "My OB/Gyn. Apparently the hospital says I'm a liability issue."

"What fucking bullshit," Mac says, his cheeks reddening the way they always do when he's pissed. "Artificial uteri are as safe as biological ones."

Our little trans support group has gathered in Jocelyn's basement to escape the worst of the summer heat. It's not helping much. Everyone's sweating, foreheads and cheeks glistening. Except for Zora, who is too cool to sweat.

"It's not about the science, Mac," Zora says softly. "They don't want the DA to charge them."

"It's not illegal to have an artificial uterus," Mac objects. "Not even to give birth—"

"Not yet," I say, and everyone stares at me. Because I'm too grim or because this is the first time I've spoken since my late arrival?

"I think what we're all expressing, in our own ways," Zora says with only a hint of disapproval, "is that we're sorry, Jocelyn, and that sucks. How can we support you?"

"I'll figure it out," Jocelyn replies after a pause. "There are still doctors who will help girls like me…"

Fewer of them all the time. I can see that thought on others' faces, but no one says it. Soon no amount of wildly-oversized clothing will keep her pregnancy concealed, and we think her employer will be supportive. We hope so.

The conversation flows on. Caroline isn't here, Mac reports, because her creepy ex lives across from her and she's sure he's watching her front door. We could have gone and got her as a posse, but she refused: protection from her asshole isn't worth drawing the cops down on us, she said.

We all know cops love little more than harassing a group of trans folks.

Sometimes I wish we were doing something criminal. At least then the cops' harassment would be explicable. I'm an instinctual rule-follower, though. Can't imagine myself as the heist type.

"You haven't said much, Astarte." Zora's words break me out of my looping thoughts. "Anything you'd like to share?"

"No," I say. Then: "Yes? I think I made a big discovery at work." I tell them what happened, in broad strokes. I learned the hard way that nanite communication systems aren't a good subject for casual conversation. But these are my people. There's excitement, congratulations.

"What comes next?" Mac says, very quietly, his face still hot. He's pissed again, and I don't know why.

"There's lots more to be done. I need to see if I can replicate the results with a different population and—"

"And then your employer will have it."

"Please, no interruptions," Zora interjects.

"It's fine," I say. "Go on, Mac." Sweat slides down my spine, but I don't feel any cooler.

"This is dangerous shit, Astarte," Mac replies.

"We have extensive precautions against a gray goo scenario."

"That's not what I'm talking about. You're going to provide BioGesis with a fast-replicating, problem solving, distributed intelligence?"

Mac never had the luxury of formal training in the sciences, but only a fool would deny his brilliance. That just makes this even more galling. "My work is just one part—"

"Fuck that." Mac stands up. "You don't get to ignore the impact of your choices because others also make them." He turns to Zora. "I know, I know. Over the line. I'm leaving."

He storms out and we're quiet for a while. Then the conversation moves on. After group, I stay behind to stack folding chairs.

"I'm allowed to pick up chairs, girl," Jocelyn says, but doesn't stop me from putting them away. I like to feel useful.

"I can't believe Mac lost it at me like that," I say before I'm even aware of my need to speak.

Jocelyn is silent. I'm putting the last of the chairs into the closet, so I can't see her expression. As I close the door she says, "It's pretty scary."

I stare at her, and she looks down at her toes, embarrassed. "I don't mean you should give up on it, and I'm proud of what you've accomplished. It's just hard to imagine a biotech firm *not* doing harm with this."

"They suck," I agree with her, an old tactic to fight down the anger inside of me, to remain the teacher's pet, to ease the pressure and reduce the risk of an explosion.

Perhaps a good scientist shouldn't think so metaphorically. I don't know.

"BioGesis sucks," I repeat, "but these nanites have great potential for good. They could help direct plastic-eating bacteria, or even do that work themselves. Soil reclamation, maybe even fight dementia."

It's a low blow, that last one, and I regret it as soon as I'm done speaking. Jocelyn's dad has always been a kind, supportive person, and he still is, when the breakdown of his mind allows it.

"Easy to weaponize too." Jocelyn's face goes expressionless. "I'm tired, Astarte. See you next time."

I should apologize, but it would fall flat. I've done enough harm already.

A DISTRIBUTED INTELLIGENCE may sound impressive, even alien, but it's not actually that different from how our brains work. An individual neuron can't do much, but put enough of them together with enough connections and you get intelligence, maybe even awareness of self. (Go to a philosopher or biologist if you want to hear all the "hard problem" arguments. I lost patience with those years ago.)

"What makes us conscious?" is too much like "What makes you a woman?" A question I'm asked fairly regularly by Brain Geniuses who think that maleness is defined by semen production.

MY NANITES LEARN rapidly. I've been providing new challenges and testing how much information they can convey across petri dishes, and how many are necessary to do so. For many tasks, the number is shockingly small, in the low millions. Likely a single dish has the intellect of a clever dog, though of course it's close to meaningless to compare the intelligences of beings that are vastly different from each other.

I'm transplanting educator nanites into a new dish, where I'm hoping they'll teach their fellows how to make decisions based on the smells—okay, something analogous to smells— that they encounter. As I finish, my boss comes in.

Tyler has a look of vague distaste on his face, as he does whenever he needs to interact with me.

"How's the process going?" he asks, with as much enthusiasm as a bored stranger making small talk.

"It's coming along," I say. I've been filing my reports, but keeping from them the real heart of my progress, while I work out whether my friends are right, and if so, what I should do about it. I figure that when the time comes to reveal what my students have accomplished, I'll have such impressive results that no one will mind that I was slow to reveal them.

I still think I'm going to make the company rich and maybe get a Nobel prize for my trouble when Tyler says, "They're pulling our funding."

Astounded, I make him repeat himself. He does.

"But Shweta just made a breakthrough in reuptake—"

He cuts me off. "It's done. Nothing I can do about that. They're reassessing staffing needs." He always looks like he's afraid he'll catch queerness from me. He should be so lucky. "Finish your reports by the end of the week. My assistant will schedule you for a reassignment evaluation."

"Wait—" I try again.

"No," he says. "It's over." He pauses as if to make a point before he calls me by my dead name.

By the time he leaves, my nanites have already trained each other to crack my puzzle. I watch them through the microscope, and I feel nothing at all. I'm flat as a petri dish horizon, as I was before I transitioned. Barely a person at all.

Hours pass. I sit watching them until long after my shift ends. At some point I write a bland report, sharing none of my real discoveries. I mean it as a "fuck you" to the corporation, but I can't summon fury. Only blankness.

I'm halfway down the hall when I turn back, hardly knowing what I'm doing. It's been a long time since I dissociated. I watch from above myself as I remove specimens from some of my most talented dishes, as I step to the corner of the lab where the cameras never quite reach, as I hold the needle over my thigh. I flash back to the first time I received myself an estrogen shot. Even then, knowing what I wanted, knowing it was change-or-die, it was unsettling to think of the needle plunging in, that my life could change radically due to something so small: hormones, chromosomes, nanites.

Transformation is an epistemic horizon. I plunge the needle into my thigh. Just a moment's discomfort and it's done. I'm host to nanites.

Funny. I've never wanted children.

I ATTEND THE support group via vid. I'm running a low-grade fever, so would have stayed away anyway. It's not like I don't have a guess at the source of my illness. Are the nanites at war with my immune system? Are they winning? How could they lose?

"How's the pregnancy, Jocelyn?" Zora asks, bringing my focus to the others. The lighting is bad in Jocelyn's basement; on my screen, none of them are more than dark shapes.

"They're pretty active," Jocelyn says. I can see her backlit arm slide over her belly. "Kicking a lot, these days." I've always been horrified by pregnancy, but I'm delighted for her. I think about her fetus, totally dependent upon her even as it drains resources.

Mac asks about medical care, and Jocelyn tells us she's found a doctor who will help. "It's not cheap, but I'll make it work."

"If you need us to start fundraising—" Mac offers.

"I'll let you know," Jocelyn says. "I'm okay for now, and that money's needed for things like bail funds." We try to get trans folks out of custody as soon as possible. Keep them safe. Safer, anyway. Beyond that, there's food banks, needle exchanges, and so much more. The work of community and solidarity can always use more resources.

Caroline is next to report in. Mac and a couple of the old-school punks escorted her to the meeting. She doesn't want to talk about her ex. She wants to talk about the new guy she's seeing.

"He's cis, but doesn't seem like a fetishist," she tells us. *Neither did her ex.* I keep that thought to myself, and am grateful that my tastes don't run to cis men. Less grateful that my tastes have been purely theoretical for a long time.

Knocked up and didn't even get sex out of the deal. Figures.

Caroline's guy sounds nice but I can't concentrate. I'm double and triple checking my security protocols. Encrypted vid app, VPN, bouncing and securing as best I can. If the CIA or whomever wants to watch badly enough, they can do so, but my precautions should block anything short of concerted surveillance. I doubt BioGesis is spending money on that kind of surveillance. Even so, when Zora asks me how things are going I choose my words with care.

"They canceled my project at work," I say. "And I'm pretty sure my shitass boss is going to try to get me laid off."

Noises of anger, frustration. No one here has any use for big pharma or corporations, but everyone knows what it's like to lose your source of income. Zora asks how I'm feeling about it.

"It's just so fucking arbitrary," I say. "The whole point of this kind of research is that you take a thousand shots and if one hits, you make so much money your shareholders decide you're a god. That project could have changed the world."

Mac grunts derisively.

"What was that, Mac?" I demand. I know better than to ask, but I feel like shit and hate that half of my inner dialog sounds like him.

"You know what I think." I can practically hear his jaw tighten.

"We're talking about Astarte's feelings." Zora slides her words between us smooth as silk.

"It's okay," I say. "I want to hear it."

"I think you're building them a weapon," Mac says.

Things escalate quickly from there. Mostly we trod across old territory, but I don't mind. I haven't had a good shouting match in a while. Even Zora can't get us to back down. It's standard stuff, and not the first time Mac and I have had it out, though never before at group. And never this bad. Caroline flinches away from the raised voices.

I know I'll feel like shit about it later but I can't stop myself. The fight continues.

Mostly I forget what we say as we say it, except for one thing. Mac's argument would mean the end of pretty much all research, since corps or governments are the ones with the money. I tell him so, that what he's arguing for is an end to most research as long as capitalism and governments exist.

"Don't make this abstract," he demands. Even on this shitty video feed I can see the sweat dripping from his nose. "How arrogant are you to think you're entitled to make these choices?"

I don't have an answer to that.

My fever burns through me. I'm exhausted, but sleep eludes me. In the distance, a church congregation is singing, everything but the tone swept away. That sound had soothed me as a child. Now, it feels like a tune I can't quite remember. The songs stop, the parishioners depart, and I stare at my darkened ceiling, unable to sleep, Mac's critique on a loop in my head. Fuck.

My phone buzzes. It's Jocelyn.

U did it, didn't u?

She knows me too well. Of course she read between the lines. Of course she knows I injected the nanites.

Did what? I reply.

Don't play dumb.

I stare at her message for a long time, typing out and deleting various replies.

Finally I send *please don't hate me.*

Never, comes the instantaneous reply. I'll love her forever for that. Then she too is typing and deleting. Then silence. I can't take it.

Mac is right, I add. *Arrogant of me.*

This reply comes quicker: *yeah, that's reproduction for you.*

FIRST CONTACT COMES in my dreams. Towering, twisting shapes rise, jagged as predator's teeth, towards a blanched sky. Then the shapes close around me, grow into me, through me, and I feel myself being split in every direction and then some.

I wake, covered in sweat. Not quite 3 AM. In the dark, I can still feel the dream world entering me, breaking me apart. As my eyes adjust, the room swirls around me. I close my eyes and will my heart to slow. It's like I've been put through a strainer and emerged into extradimensional space.

Is this what my children experience, encountering the third dimension through the mediation of my body? Are they speaking to me through my dreams?

Perhaps an adolescence spent trying to escape into lucid dreams wasn't entirely wasted. When I return to sleep, the towers return, but now I'm prepared. Their sharp lines smooth out, no longer looking like eager viruses. They still curve towards me, but somewhat more gently now. I don't know whether the nanites can understand these metaphors, but I'm betting they understand hormone release, fear responses, the logic of synapses. *It's okay,* I try to signal them. *I'm here to help you through it.*

The next day, my fever breaks. The nanites have won the war, or made peace. I have no job, nowhere to be. I wake to sleep, to communicate with them, and wonder what they know of my dream-logic, the metaphors my brain concocts, designed for sensory apparatuses impossibly distant from their own. But they've always been fast learners, and they're thriving in my body. The dreams make that clear, somehow. Billions of them. Trillions, maybe. Of course they learn fast.

Their neural network must already exceed my own.

What am I to them, I wonder, staring at my ceiling as passing cars throw bars of light through the blinds. A host? Food? Some kind of helplessly slow god?

I dream of god. A goddess. She is radiant, breathtaking, with high cheekbones and curves, the kind of woman I wished myself to be. Except I don't believe in god; at this thought, she turns toward me. She doesn't really speak. What use are words when you have direct, electrochemical channels? But something ripples out from her, a feeling like something unfinished. A question?

As the thought occurs to me, she changes: white robes, huge beard, cheeks red like Santa's.

The image, a patriarchal god standing over me, deciding my fate, haunts me, a relic from a childhood I'd rather forget. But the neural connections are still there. The god reaches out toward me.

No! My reaction is so forceful that I feel the dream slipping from my control. I clutch at it—a mistake. The world shakes and crumbles. I wake.

"So you had to convince them you're not a god?" Jocelyn asks, the corners of her eyes lifting the way they always do when she's amused.

"It's not funny," I insist. "I don't want to infect them with some fundamentalist bullshit from my past!"

"That's wise." The smile fades from Jocelyn's eyes. "Though one might say they're a kind of infection themselves."

"I can't think of them that way," I say. "Besides, I feel better than ever."

"And they're letting your body use the meds?"

I'd told her about that, how my antidepressants and estrogen supplements had appeared in my dreams as suspicious outsiders. It had been weeks of work in my dreams to help their dream avatar understand that the drugs were welcome and important. The reply was a wave of something like color, uncertain but accepting, or so it seemed to me, and then visuals (though my synesthesia makes that boundary blurry), a massive room filled with impossibly-tangled wires, over which lab-coated workers scurry, busy with some project (all of them with high cheekbones—apparently I have a type).

"They are letting me," I say. "But I have a feeling that my body will take care of its own estrogen needs, soon."

"That's great!" Jocelyn says, only her smile is flatter now, like she's trying to convince herself to be happy for me.

"What is it, Jocelyn?" We're both masked and sitting outside in the sun. She's due in a couple months. We're being careful, though we don't really know what careful looks like anymore. But Jocelyn insisted: *whatever is happening to you, you shouldn't go through it alone.*

I'm not alone, I wanted to say. I came to the park instead.

Jocelyn is silent for a while, chewing on her lip the way she always does when she's puzzling through something. At length, she responds. "If they were changing you in a way you didn't want, would you even know it?"

"I read once, about pregnancy," I say, and she's a good enough friend not to roll her eyes. "And how having kids is so fundamentally transforming that you can't know beforehand what it will be like. You need to take it on faith."

"Faith," Jocelyn repeats, like she's tasting the word. "Yeah. And not just beforehand. It's a necessary evolutionary adaptation, that bond between parent and infant." She pauses. "Okay, so maybe there's no way to know. But you're my friend, and I'm worried about you."

"Thank you," I say. "But this—whatever this is—is easier than transitioning. I think they're even relocating my fat deposits."

"To what end? It's not like cis women all wear their fat the same way."

I'd been thinking about that. "I think they're basing it off my internal sense of self," I say.

Jocelyn is quiet again. Then: "Okay, that's pretty damn cool. Do you and your, uh, passengers want to help me settle on a name for the little one?"

We very much do.

EVER TRY ONE of those semi-scam belts that strap around your waist and zap you to trigger muscle response and tighten your core or whatever? That feeling, less painful than unpleasant and all the more unpleasant for its unpredictability, lives with me constantly. The nanites are making changes. My muscles grow stronger, my endurance increases. I take up running again, for the first time since my transition. Not the safest activity for a trans woman, but without my lab to give me focus, I need to move.

I'm experiencing a cognitive leap of the kind babies must go through as, in fits and starts, the world becomes more knowable. I don't remember what that felt like, but now I can guess: exhilarating and exhausting in equal measure.

If it's *my* intelligence increasing. Perhaps I'm just borrowing their processing power. I've done the math, and under any reasonable set of assumptions the nanites have orders of magnitude more synapse-equivalent functions than my brain does.

All that cognitive load comes at a price. The nanites don't understand concepts like capitalism and rent, not yet, but in our dream-logic way we've managed to work together. I take on freelance work. It's not a lot, and I spend nearly every dime on food. We desperately need the calories. The good news is that I'm not having many cravings. They seem to be happy with most any source of calories.

I sleep deeply and, awake, I struggle to sit still. And I wait for news of Jocelyn's labor.

My children want to explore the world beyond me. I'm sure they can do so, that they have solved that problem, but I urge them not to. *Not safe for you*, I try to communicate, making the world of the dream an oasis, soothing curves and the soft trickle of water, and around it a world of virus-sharp teeth. Mac's voice in my mind says *not safe for others, either.* I worry that I'm teaching them to be fearful, teaching them that other humans are scary. I want them to be resilient, not afraid. If I'd been someone else, some pretty cis woman with blonde hair, or someone not raised on the idea of a Judging God and Eternal Torment for Sinners, someone who moved through the world with less anxiety, maybe they'd have learned better lessons.

I chose to be their mother, but I fear I'm not fit for the job.

ANOTHER GROUP SESSION with me joining over video. My finger hovers above the "hang up" button, because Jocelyn has told me that I need to tell the others what I did. She's right, but that doesn't make it any easier. It's a constant struggle not to end the call and hide in my home with my children.

It doesn't help that words aren't coming easily to me these days. I open my mouth and find myself unable to give voice to the taste of purple; the halting, collaborative, language-barriered remapping of my mind; the glorious song they're singing within me; the pride and fear. I understand my nanites better all the time and understand the human world less.

I was never much good at humans.

Caroline is telling us about what she calls "Witch Church," which is a weekly pagan gathering, songs and ritual and, as she puts it "joyous inclusion." I worry for the congregation's safety in this deeply Christofascist land, but would never deny her joy over my own fears.

"Some of us are true believers and practice our Crafts," she says. "Others are there for community or vibes, or are atheopagans. Some Jewish folks attend, even this really sweet queer Christian couple. It's a place where we hold the sacred, and community, and the sacredness of community." Her face is alight in a way I haven't seen in ages. I wonder whether I'd be such a wreck if I'd been raised in a community like that instead of the fundie monotheism of my youth.

Sometimes my children present themselves as working through a knotted thicket of briars. My brain, perhaps, or my past, or my anxiety. There are things even they can't change. And if they could, who would I be?

When Zora asks if I'd like to share, a wave of nausea slams into me. No, that's not right. I *should* feel my stomach roil and my throat contract, but my body is too well tuned for that, now. Only my mind, poor mother or twisted god that it is, holds on to the memory and expects the sensations.

I pull my hand back from the "hang up" button. Without a fear response from my body, I can continue. What could it cost me besides all my friendships?

I stumble over words, but eventually find momentum.

"When I transitioned, people told me—these were people I loved—they told me it would destroy my life. I'd never work. Or pass. Or find love." Grimacing faces; others have heard this too. Some of it was even true: I don't pass. I'm bad at love.

"Could've given up," I say, translating the language of colors and smells and hormones into words I used to have. "But I had to know. No, not know." I flushed. All this was almost impossible to say. "Had to experience. And after... the panopticon, but in reverse. Like I'd never...felt...before."

They were staring at me with confusion, some with concern. I felt my way forward like someone hunting for light switches in unfamiliar rooms.

"They were going to destroy the nanites," I say. Recognition flashes across Mac's face. Horror. Fury. "Please," I implore. "Let me—I don't know if I was right. But they were alive. Intelligent. My children. So I saved them. Didn't think. Maybe should've. No. No. What kind of mad god would consign them to the flame?"

I fall back against my chair, sweating like I've just run sprints. Then everyone's talking at once, my cheap headphones thankfully unable to unknot their words.

I wait to see if they will condemn me. The riptide of fear is gone. I'm in deep waters. I *am* deep waters.

Words and phrases, my friends' judgments or support, reach me from a distance.

"—height of irresponsibility—"

"—what else could she—"

"—reproductive justice—"

"—unring—"

They deserve time to process, to decide. I don't begrudge that. I disconnect and pull off my headphones.

A distant sound interrupts the newfound quiet. It's a chorus from the church down the street, many voices raised in song. It's too far away to make out the words, and I like it that way. I've tried to leave behind everything about my childhood faith, but I do miss the singing, this collective thing, a mess of good voices and bad, of notes struck true and false, but that doesn't matter, because the goal isn't perfection but shared experience. Unity.

MY DREAMS ARE song, and the song is the world breathing, and I am the world, and inside myself. My chest cavity is a cathedral, my ribs incomprehensibly-vast buttresses. How long do they live, my children? They change, evolve, but individually their lives are so short. If it means anything to speak of them as individuals. I ride veins to my heart, my life measured in the bass-beat of its impossible slowness, and I think of corpses fallen to the forest floor, death engendering life.

This is my body, sacrificed—

I force the thought away. Something that may be me forces it away. This is not the story of the one given for the many, the ram in the thicket, the offering prepared. This thing, flesh, synapses, this dream of self—whatever it is, it's no messiah, no prophet.

We are the universe experiencing ourself.

My waking mind, the mind of a trained scientist, doubts these revelations. But a quest to know does not imply that all is knowable. And if it is? What does it mean to know the universe on the scale of one lifetime, or a billion?

A temple priestess tells her congregation that one day the apocalypse will swallow us, will swallow all things.

The day is coming, says the congregation. *Let us sell what we have, flee to the mountains. The end is nigh.*

The priestess says nothing. She plants a tree instead.

YOU'LL COME FOR the birth? Jocelyn texts. My best friend, my heart.

Yes omg of course yes, I reply. And then: *the others won't approve.*

They agreed already. They only asked u wear gloves and mask.

Wouldn't miss it, I type, already weeping. I don't know if my friends will understand, if they'll forgive me. But for now, I haven't lost them. I'll get to see Jocelyn's baby.

WHEN JOCELYN GOES into labor, I'm ready to rush to her side, but it takes hours, days, to get to that point. Finally it's time for her to go to the doctor's home, since the hospitals won't have her. On my way out the door, I glance in the mirror, trying to decide if I look noticeably different, or if only my self-perception has changed. My cheekbones remain unimpressive, but whether it's the nanites, or the birth, or my cute top, I feel a rush of gender euphoria. My scalp tingles. My smile is an old friend I thought I'd lost.

I bike over to Caroline's, and we take her car. It feels as if every window in her apartment complex hides someone watching us, two visibly trans women, daring to be seen in public, to be seen together. A hand pulls back a corner of the curtains in her ex's place, but the door doesn't open.

"I hate it when they stare," I say through my mask.

"Yeah," Caroline says. "But let them. Maybe there are some trans folks watching who need to see us."

NEWBORNS AREN'T GENERALLY cute. They grow into that. But either little Hunter is the exception, asleep in Jocelyn's arms after their first meal, or I'm just biased towards the little one.

The whole gang's here and in a state of whispered excitement, trying not to disturb baby Hunter, but also wanting to coo over them. We haven't talked about me, standing a little ways back, careful to avoid skin-to-skin contact. I think the nanites know that I want them to stay within me for now, but I'm sure they could slide between skins, between bodies so easily they might not even notice the border. In the gestalt consciousness of my children, what separates one being from another?

I try to set aside my fears, my intellectualization, to remain present in this happy moment, surrounded by friends, each of us a mother, auntie, or uncle to a child descended from none of us. I want to join in these conversations, but I don't know where I stand with my friends. Plus it's hard to hear them over the other conversation, the one in my head, where my other chosen family is also speaking to me. Images flash on my mind: ripe fruit, dandelion seeds blowing in the wind. A ripple of longing, almost painful in its desire, unfurls down my back. We understand each other better every day. No credit to me. They're the ones learning to speak to me. 86 billion neurons in my brain, give or take a billion. How many neuronal equivalents exist between my children? It's a vista my mind can't comprehend.

"—we talk?"

It's Mac. I've been far away. "What? Oh, yeah, Mac, let's talk."

We step into the doctor's front room.

"I still don't love what you did," he says, and I feel very tired. "But I get it. The alternatives were also bad. And once you realized they were sapient—I understand why you did it." He opens his arms, offering a hug.

"But the nanites," I say, half statement, half question.

He smiles, barely betraying his nervousness. "We're well covered," he says. I hug him tightly. He wraps his wiry-strong arms around me, smelling of sweat and rising bread.

"Thank you," I say. "I know you were looking out for—

for everyone. We need that."

Mac's frequently angry, but that's because he loves his friends deeply. I'm frequently afraid, for the same reason. Maybe that's why we fight and why we're so close.

"I hope," I say slowly, because talking is hard enough without my children trying to make sure that I understand. I do. I think I do. "I mean—would you help me? Help me talk to the others about…something." I do my best to explain.

"I don't love it," he says, "but I'm not going to demand closed borders, either."

Later, when Hunter is enjoying their second-ever meal, I tell the group what I have in mind.

"They're fast learners," I say. "And they understand now about bodies. They don't have to stay—they can be guests if you want. Ambassadors."

"You're sure about that?" asks Caroline, who knows a thing or two about unwanted guests.

"I'm pretty sure," I say. "I doubt they conceptualize… individuals the way we do. But they…respect other minds." If you spend many generations building a cathedral, are you building it hoping god will see, or that your grandchildren will?

"But why do they need to, uh, immigrate?" Zora asks. "You said they have access to your senses."

"They do," I say, "but they need more than one…parent. More than one god." I try to explain: they're learning from me, but who am I? Just the one who happened to free them. My words feel molasses-thick on my tongue, but at least the next part is easier because I know my friends. "Zora, they need to know how to…hold space. Bring people together. Like you do. Mac, they need your fury at injustice. The way you protect friends. Caroline, you have so much empathy. They'll learn from you. So much. Jocelyn, they can see… well, witness…how you care for others. Of Hunter." I don't know how to make myself understood. Maybe I never did.

"That's a lot of responsibility," Caroline says.

"Yes," I say. "Too heavy for one person. You're free to choose. Always. But we're better together. We need—they need—community."

My words feel simplistic, like they'll never be enough. I'm failing my children.

At first there are no sounds except Hunter eagerly drinking. Then Jocelyn says, "How do we, uh, let them in?" That's how I know she's made up her mind.

"I tell them that you said yes. Then just skin-to-skin.."

"Simple as that?"

"Nothing about our lives is simple," Mac interjects.

"Yes," I say. "Yes. But also, yeah, simple as that."

Jocelyn holds out her hand. I pull away my glove and clasp it. I don't feel the nanites send their ambassadors to her, but I know it's happening.

The world's changing, now and always. We'll face it together, the few of us, the uncountable throng.

THE MAJESTIC ART OF FLESH

HAILEY PIPER

JAY-JAY MCBRIDE HAD just finished cleaning the poet's blood off her arm when one of her most-hated of his quotes slid unbidden into her head. An intrusive thought of the literal sense. The air hung rich with carnal spray, but also brainwaves broadcasting from the writhing reddish fronds draped across his frontal lobe. A simple-minded sketch might have assumed everyone in the damp-walled apartment building would catch Jay-Jay's face in their heads, forced out by the poet's mental scream.

But any decent artist, even of the magenta flesh—*magentist*—understood human consciousness better than their clients. Death did not turn the mind into a camera. Panic, memories, impulses—these facets swirled in a storm of psychic white noise. Likely every neighbor picked up a jumble of the poet's dying inclinations. That Jay-Jay heard the hated quote was her mind snagging familiarity from this messy broadcast.

The quote went: *We the living change ourselves in a desperate bid to become more than living. Humanity chases immortality as hounds once chased the fox.*

He had a habit of using many words to say nothing, and always two steps aside from the point. A hound chasing a fox implied a predator and prey, a hunt of sport, that humanity was eager to kill immortality rather than become it.

No, immortality was a phantom subway train. Humanity was the always-late passenger desperate not to miss their ride. Simple as that.

Jay-Jay tossed a soppy towel onto the poet's sink basin, where its once-white tongue drooled crimson onto grimy tiles and grout lines. She then thrust her coat sleeve down, hiding the uniqueness of her right arm.

Covered up in her oversized forest-green clothes and tattered newsboy cap dipped over a sweaty pale forehead, she looked like an ordinary Jersey girl. None would guess she'd taken the poet's life or spared his neighbors' his mental influence.

Still, someone would wonder about these airborne signals. And someone would eventually check on him. They would find him with his smug face covered by a moth-eaten blanket, a round gore-hole gaping in his chest. Immortality had abandoned him on life's subway platform.

No one ever caught that train.

Jay-Jay was early for her midday client. No one could be allowed to wonder *What took you?* or *You sure are antsy, did you murder anyone today?* She was already waiting in her closet-sized parlor in another dingy brick apartment building when Sita walked in and laid across the black leather-cushioned table.

"It's the lumbar," she said. She lifted her autumn jacket to reveal her lower back, where muscles twinged beneath russet skin.

Jay-Jay opened her mini-fridge and fed magenta sludge into her improvised tattoo gun. Spinal work was rarely fun, but it was easy. Nothing she could mess up while reeling from the poet's brain signals, and if she flashed a disturbed expression, Sita was lying face-down and wouldn't see it.

The needle drove into knotted muscle, and the art began.

One thing Jay-Jay and the poet had agreed on—law was not morality. She liked to think of her right arm's altered state as a permanent middle finger to every federal prohibition against magentistry.

Not that anyone down in D.C. called it that. Congress first labeled its usage a *purposeful infection of viral components*, and then *anti-human genetic tampering with hazardous biological material*, and then *corporate copyright infringement*.

All proclamations that in a nutshell said: *Bad civilians, no touch!*

But everyone this side of New Jersey knew the stuff. A rose by any other name would float in finger-thick strings inches beneath a river's surface, beckoning every nearby Jerseyite—*yes, touch, take.* Cops and feds could quarantine Newark Bay alongside its city after whatever secret lab experiment had emptied those streets three years ago, but stroll past Rutkowski Park and hit the Hackensack River Waterfront, and a strong stomach plus a little patience would net you handfuls of fleshy pink spaghetti.

Not pollution or toxic waste, but a fruiting tree aglow with money-laden dreams. Thanks, Newark.

Sita's lower back pulsated with faint new map lines. Jay-Jay set down her gun to fetch a numbing cream from the mini-fridge. There was never any immune system rejection of the introduced flesh, but sometimes it was too eager to join a sketch's body.

Like it loved this flesh so much, it wanted to eat it up.

"Did you hear?" Sita asked. "They're putting religion in the water supply. The street preachers say so. Different flavors, but you can't get away from it. They're not supposed to do that."

Jay-Jay smeared numbing cream over the art site. "Did you swallow something? For the pain?"

"My pride." Sita fidgeted. "And like twenty milligrams. I might be greening out, but Ms. Jay-Jay, have you tried the religion? There's a new one in the river that's all the rage."

In which decade had she picked up *all the rage*? Maybe the one that ravaged her lower back.

"Just hold still," Jay-Jay said, capping the numbing cream.

Its application would settle the flesh long enough for her to finish the art, and by then Sita's body and the reshaped muscle would realize they were friends. That this was normal.

But normal had become a strange concept since the river began bringing magenta goop to the waterfront. Jay-Jay knew that work firsthand. She had been a sifter for three months while learning the art, before finding her own sketches who'd pay to have work done on their bodies. From the jump, she'd guessed the pinkish flesh might turn to gold in talented hands. This especially when the feds forbade the art before they dared punish whichever corporation had caused flesh to appear in the river in the first place. Even then, they only bothered with punishments for the sake of affected corporate interests.

The law twisted and grew teeth, and yet residents learned how magentists could mold those river-brought scraps into biological repair jobs, beauty sculpting, and otherworldly shapes. And they were happy to pay artists of the flesh, damn the legality.

But regardless of law, morality mattered.

You could not drive a needle through a bad poet's skull to ink that magenta flesh into his brain, knowing it would turn him into an annoying human radio, and still call yourself an ethical magentist. Touching the brain was going too far. It affected not only the sketch but everyone around.

Jay-Jay set her gun down again and massaged Sita's lower back. The bright flesh was fading beneath her dark complexion, but tiny chitinous dots lined either side of her lower vertebrae. Possibly they would grow into bony plates. There were always risks of side effects, but the new muscle would keep her back from aching as badly.

She paid quickly and staggered out of the tiny parlor. A happy customer.

That was ethical magentistry. And the poet's death, too, was the work of an ethical magentist. His signals went on bouncing in Jay-Jay's skull, but they would fade.

What mattered next was making sure nothing like him ever happened again.

Jay-Jay would hunt the magentist responsible. And it would be much more like a hound and a fox than the poet had ever understood.

GRAY CLOUDS BUILT a fortress of the Hackensack River Waterfront. In spring you could sometimes catch a prismatic shimmer from Newark's forbidden disaster zone across the water, but autumn overcast joined the solemn atmosphere in isolating one riverbank from another.

The only other people here today were sifters leaning over concrete with nets bound to steel poles. Often sketches themselves, they sometimes took magentistry as payment in lieu of cash.

Murray had hired Jay-Jay to make him conventionally handsome using the malleability of magenta flesh, all high cheek bones and whatever that newly pronounced forehead was supposed to do for his love life. His sifting skills were stronger than his imagination.

Jay-Jay didn't know the other sifter's name, had only seen her around, but like Jay-Jay, she was an imaginer and had dropped convention in the river some time ago. Her left hand formed a firm, bony claw. Thin pinkish lines snaked up her throat and splayed from the corners of her lips, where a yawn revealed twin tongues basking like pink crocodiles in the marsh of her mouth.

The novelty made Jay-Jay's left hand twitch. She wanted her magentistry gun, aimed not at a client but at herself. There were always improvements to make on her right arm. Better muscle response. Sharper features. Perfection did not exist within the majestic art of flesh.

But she couldn't do that yet. Beyond delicate body modification, there was the hunt, not of Jay-Jay's choice but of necessity.

"How's the catch?" she asked, approaching the water's edge. Unseasonal warmth cooked a sharp stink up from the surface of the river.

"Feisssty," the two-tongued sketch said. She either hadn't yet mastered speech with her added oral appendage or preferred this snakish enunciation.

"It's fighting us," Murray said. "Like reeling in angry fish."

Jay-Jay spied muscly ropes worming beneath the murky water. Times were easier when she was a sifter. The flesh would simply float, and the worst you had to worry about might be falling into the garbage-strewn water or losing your catch to whatever lived down there. If the flesh got a mind of its own, the sifters would start charging more. Another headache for future Jay-Jay.

Better to deal with the one she already had. "I'm looking for a magentist. Somebody new, ambitious. Probably eager to make a name doing novel art."

"Novel art," Murray echoed with disdain. "We're entering a frontier like never before seen. Haven't you heard the street preachers go on? Post-humanism, when we'll all have this shit in us, and not for decent reasons."

"The flesh is human. Whatever the shape, they're human cells." But Jay-Jay couldn't argue over decent reasons. Not after the poet.

Murray shrugged. "Then we'll be the conjoined human. Caged together, forever."

The poet's rambling must've infected everyone before he died. Jay-Jay had suffered enough nonsense hearing about *the façade of identity* and *the end of true self* and *the flesh is divinity*—on and on until she'd rolled up her right sleeve, grabbed the poet by the neck, and stabbed his heart.

"Enough," she said, losing patience. "Who's cutting their teeth on weird art? I'm talking brain inking."

"Only sssell the ssstuffsh," the two-tongued sketch said. "Jon't asssk the bizzz."

"What she means is, try *your* people," Murray said. His arms quaked as he wrestled to bring up a writhing snake of magenta flesh, coiling as if it meant to eat his hands. "Artists know each other best. Machine's been mentoring. Ask her."

Jay-Jay thanked them both and wished them a good catch, not only for their sake but for her supplies, and then she walked away.

Her phone contacts were sparse on other magentists. Most were her competition, and they were starting to invite out-of-towners to invest in greater operations. She worried for the day some mega-corporation would notice the profits running downriver, bribe Congress to legalize the stuff, and then overtake the waterfront to weaponize its bounty.

Proof of lethality already formed Jay-Jay's right arm. She tugged her sleeve and thought of a sister magentist.

Machine was highly skilled. She had helped Jay-Jay figure out the base muscle for her right arm in the early days, while Jay-Jay had helped Machine with more intimate flesh-sculpting of what once lay between her legs. Downfall of plastic surgery—arise, magentistry.

A new magentist could learn a lot under Machine. And maybe get ideas of their own. Bad ones.

Jay-Jay thumbed through her contacts and sent a text, *Need time to talk today*, as she hurried past a bellowing bearded street preacher. He wore a similar shabby coat to hers, and bright lines frayed around his right eye.

"The divine is inside us!" he cried.

Machine answered fast. *Love the alliteration.*

Jay-Jay hurried out another text. *I'm looking for someone. Artist. Bold & new. Willing to ink a brain.*

This time Machine took six minutes to send a reply. *Might be a while. Go home, sweet thing. Will text when free.*

Jay-Jay gritted her teeth. Why so cagey? But then, Machine was in high demand, and she had probably shuffled appointments around if she was making room for mentees.

Besides, no need to hurry the hunt. There was no sign that brain-altered sketches would spring like unwanted weeds from every Jersey sidewalk by evening. And Jay-Jay's nerves weren't Machine's problem.

FOOD COULD BE a distraction until the hunt resumed. A couple blocks away, she visited a sidewalk food truck and bought a fistful of steak fries and a ketchup puddle in greasy foil. The aroma pushed away the city's odors, and she pincered and dropped a fry into her mouth with the three digits of her right hand, careful not to let her sleeve reveal her deadly arm.

But the distraction worked too well, stealing her attention from the street. Halfway through her meal, she noticed she was passing the poet's apartment building across the potholed lanes, its brick façade punched with as many gaps as windows.

Those grime-glassed panes shuddered in their frames as vicious treads shook a hot quake along the curb. Jay-Jay's gut flinched, realizing what was coming.

The dark shell of a cop tank rumbled from around the corner and roared down the street.

They knew there had been a murder. Jay-Jay knew they knew.

So what now—run away? Piss herself? Roll up her right sleeve? She could show the cops the wonder she'd made of her arm, and then plunge it into their guts before they tore her down in a lead storm.

No, she wasn't dying like that. She sucked in a stale breath, pretending to sniff her fries. They had the wrong person. Ordinary Jersey girl, carefree pedestrian.

The cop tank creaked to a halt outside the poet's apartment building. Its steel exterior not only wore various stripes of vicious Americana but the painted-on torso of an amber baby cow stuck to a faded yellow smiley face above the letters CAF—the logo for Cambridge Automated Futurism.

A mouth of iron misery screeched open at the cop tank's underside, and out it birthed a tetrad of four-legged smilers. Their limbs stabbed the pavement on dull pistons to the sound of clinking coins beneath bodies of plastic, wire, oversized stun guns, and semiautomatic rifles. Each smiler's face was a flat yellow circle on a metal neck, baring black eyes and a curving mouth line.

They looked ridiculous, capering toward the building. Only through their cacophonic warning shots could Jay-Jay observe in one crystalline moment the world as a cold place fashioned by absurd cruelty.

The smilers pranced in, and only seconds passed before they flushed the first tenants out. Dozens more followed, an uncertain crowd of terrified adults and children. One elderly man emerged hobbling, but an impatient smiler must've determined he wasn't moving fast enough, and its lightning-like stab sent him sprawling to the sidewalk.

Would robotic immortality have suited the dead poet? Jay-Jay imagined the smilers repairing themselves the way she performed illegal flesh-art on her arm.

But no, they were brainless drones, set for obsoletion at the next robotic wave. The cops decided everything.

Two of them barreled out of their tank in blue and black helmets and shells of armor that hid their faces and bodies, as anonymous, clean, and hollow as their smilers. Both marched along the gathered residents, squealing out questions and banging heads for answers. A thin woman with a pink spiderweb around her eyes caught a fist to her temple.

"Fucking sketch," the cop said, sounding like she would spit if not for her helmet.

Jay-Jay tugged her pale right hand all the way into her sleeve. Light skin sometimes tattled on you.

So did other people. The sketch across the street clutched her head and raised an accusing finger, ready to give the cops someone else to beat.

"None of you saw me, I wasn't there," Jay-Jay whispered, watching the finger slide through the air.

And arc toward her.

Aim her way.

And then pass her as the sketch pointed at the fallen elderly man.

"No, not me," he said, his Brooklyn accent betraying a New York transplant. "I didn't murder that guy."

The cops descended on him anyway, and then the smilers ushered him into the cop tank's underside. Its mouth closed against the metal womb, trapping the man inside with the drones.

Maybe there was immortality in getting away with murder. A transcendence from the legal order of death? Jay-Jay wasn't sure. Couldn't think straight. Could only imagine that cop tank's belly and the dark, the *all*-dark except for glowing nodes of smilers and the lit fragments of an outer world you might never see again.

And if the cops let you go, what would emerge? Maybe you'd learn to imitate the smilers. In the rebirth from the tank's womb, you'd come prancing on all-fours.

And you'd come smiling.

Jay-Jay noticed other pedestrians staring at the spectacle. She stared with them, swirling steak fries in her foil's ketchup puddle.

But this close to the dead poet's apartment, ketchup was not the red she had in mind.

THE WALK HOME went slow. Jay-Jay kept looking behind her, anxious that the cop tank would grind onto the sidewalk and scoop her into its maw. As a little girl, she'd been confused over stranger danger warnings, caught in the entwined shadows of an era when Ronald and Nancy Reagan ruled the country. Before Jay-Jay's time, and yet inescapable.

Especially when the people-snatchers often wore badges and drove tanks through the streets.

She eventually reached her magentistry parlor and locked the door. Her upstairs studio wasn't much bigger than this professional closet, and she didn't want to head there yet. The sketch table felt more welcoming. Maybe she would work on her arm, a magentist by her left hand, a sketch on her right.

A knock came at the door an hour later and sent a jolt through her limbs. Nothing to fear—cops rarely knocked; they simply appeared.

Jay-Jay took a calming breath. "Anyone special?"

"Machine." Her voice was familiar, friendly. "You were asking about somebody who'd ink a brain. I might know. Excuse me dropping in, but my texts weren't going through."

"Yeah, tech's shitty," Jay-Jay said, thinking of the smilers and climbing from the table. "You're the only good Machine around here." She unlocked the deadbolts and flung open the parlor to fleeting daylight.

The doorway filled with people-shaped silhouettes, a river mounting against the dam that was Jay-Jay before they broke through and flooded her world.

SHE WANTED TO pass out. If her life meant to turn against her, she shouldn't have to be conscious for it.

But there were arms against her, too, and hands, and the inking table where they clutched her by the neck, waist, and limbs. Even her right arm, its hidden lethality now useless.

Beside the table, cloudy black hair shadowed Machine's gaunt face and bony frame. Her throat bore pinkish words reading, *This machine is not a place of honor.* Magenta flesh disguised as an ordinary tattoo, reaching inky patterns toward her jaw. Better stealthing than Jay-Jay could manage.

She didn't know the other figures, lost in shadow as if they'd broken every light except the tableside lamp. One at the back had lashing limbs rising from their shoulder blades. The rest seemed vaguely ordinary.

"We should've gone to your place," Jay-Jay said. "Less cramped."

"I don't trust you right now." Machine's stroked Jay-Jay's magentistry gun with calloused fingers, formed through dedicated hours holding a similar gun and pulling its trigger at human tissue. "You were looking for an artist who'd ink a brain. But not to learn. I don't think you had nice intentions for me, sweet thing."

For me. Jay-Jay pursed her lips. She'd been so dead-set on the poet's magentist being a newcomer, she hadn't considered an older artist learning new tricks.

Machine wiped her hands on her low jeans. One hip showed more tattoo-like magentistry styled in microchip-like patterns. Faint words read, *This machine cannot distinguish between flesh or steel, nor does it care.* The pattern's outer edges led between Machine's legs, where hers and Jay-Jay's magentistry had fashioned a shaft and testes into a channel and vulva. Jay-Jay had assumed that was the finale to Machine's transition. Judging by the other pinkish lines, it had only been another step.

Maybe changing was eternal. Machine might've understood that when she helped Jay-Jay first strengthen her arm.

She observed it firsthand as she peeled up Jay-Jay's right coat sleeve.

For an instant, Jay-Jay glimpsed the poet's blood again as if Machine were unsheathing an unclean sword after a medieval battle.

But there was no deep red, only the bright discoloration of a heavily altered limb. Taut muscles corded down Jay-Jay's bicep, relieved of too-tight skin, where a serpentine rope of flesh slid toward her remaining two fingers and thumb. Between the wrist and elbow, a spike of white bone hungered like an enormous tooth. It had dripped with the poet's blood after the muscly snake had pulled him close.

Grab and stab. Easier than fishing raw material off the Hackensack River Waterfront.

"Beautiful, isn't it?" Machine asked, glancing over the clustered shadows. They nodded, and thin lines and swirls flared across their bodies. "The act of change is the future, whatever its shape."

"Machine, let off," Jay-Jay said. "I was just asking about brains incidentally. Some change is too far."

"You killed Simon, didn't you?" Machine clicked her tongue. "Why else would you wonder? He isn't the first, but we all knew his death. When the mind is laid bare, the magenta steps through, and you killed the sliver inside him. But maybe you'll replace him as a prophet of flesh. I think it's the only way you'll drop wanting to murder me."

"I wasn't—" Jay-Jay gritted her teeth. To lie felt like a confession.

Machine's hands left Jay-Jay's arm and snatched up the magentistry gun. To the mini-fridge and back, she loaded it with flesh and then held it high as if posing for an action movie poster.

"Have you ever experienced a divine intervention?" Machine asked, cocking her head. "Would you like to?"

Jay-Jay shook her head. Started to nod. Shook it again. A firm hand grasped her scalp. She tensed her neck to jerk sideways, but there was no evading the oncoming needle. A colorful threat surged inside.

"Well, not knowing is a start," Machine said. "Ignorance is the universal beginning."

She bent over the table, gun ready. From this angle, another magenta tattoo revealed itself above her cleavage. *Not only will this machine kill you, it will hurt the whole time you're dying.*

"My thoughts will get out." Jay-Jay strained against the many-limbed shadows. "And you don't want to know what I'm thinking."

"You're thinking of killing anyone who'd expand the art. A murder of understanding." Pity soaked Machine's words. "Jay-Jay, you don't have the first idea of the future we've been building of this flesh. But that's okay—I'm going to give it to you. There's no such thing as going too far. We go ever onward."

The gun loomed.

"And this art? It's not only about what you give. It's about what you receive. And whom you see. She wants you to see."

"Machine—" Jay-Jay started in warning.

But the gun drove a needle through her forehead before she could say another word.

Tinted swirls coated Jay-Jay's vision. Still conscious, however unfair that might be.

She thrust up from the table and banged into something, but she couldn't tell if it was a person or her mini-fridge. The only surface with any clarity was the door opening onto the street recolored by dusk and brain-ink.

How much time had passed since she let Machine inside? Jay-Jay couldn't tell. Every moment was a dilation, and within it crowned the birthing head of the next moment, which birthed the next, onward and backward. Time stretched like subway tracks, left behind by immortality. The past showed Jay-Jay as small and alone, confused by the loathsome world and loathing it in return.

And what lay ahead? She couldn't see it. The future was both monstrous and holy, allegedly opposing concepts which might actually have been the same idea since her calamitous species was a twinkling in a sex-charged lizard's prehistoric eye.

The street showed lights, and cars, and sidewalks ready to spill Jay-Jay against those cars. She rubbed her face, desperate to clear a colorful veil, but her head was home to consecutive explosions, sending her thoughts escaping out the hole Machine had jabbed in her forehead. Jay-Jay grasped at them with one furious hand, but each idea slipped through her fingers. There would be no catching them.

Her fingers prodded her forehead wound. "The fuck did she do to me?"

Pedestrian silhouettes formed wandering pink blots against the prismatic neighborhood. Someone barked a demand she couldn't discern. Whose voice was that? Everyone hid beneath the same magenta shadow.

Humanity chases immortality.

Jay-Jay smacked her head. That was the poet's voice. Simon, right? Jay-Jay couldn't be sure anymore. His name was nothing, while his words were a psychic infection.

Machine and her mob could mistake that nonsense for a spiritual outpouring, but it was only invasive flesh in the brain, and when you fucked with someone's brain, you deserved to die.

Wasn't that why Jay-Jay had killed the poet? Why she'd meant to hunt the magentist who'd inked his brain, only to be cornered herself?

Who was the fox then, and who was the hound?

A crimson eye widened ahead, the first distinctive feature since Jay-Jay had staggered onto the street. She went clawing after it. But the eye widened the closer she got, threatening to take the sun's place where it had left the darkening sky. Rosy rays shot from its edges like fingers grasping at the world.

"Have you tried religion?" a gruff voice asked—the street preacher from this afternoon. "There's a new one in the water, and it's all rage. Entirely rage."

Jay-Jay shoved him away. "Congress was right. We shouldn't have played with this stuff. It's a virus. A biohazard."

"It's religion!" the street preacher shouted. Machine might have inked his brain, too, a needle around his eyeball.

Jay-Jay thought of shoving him into traffic before his thoughts could pour inside her, but she threw herself toward the street instead. Car horns screamed as she hurried onto the next curb and into an alleyway.

Every surface pulsated, the usual garbage cans and free-floating detritus replaced with exposed muscle. Beyond the gore, a welcoming gray mouth showed the exit. Jay-Jay headed for it. There were no cops or smilers inside this maw, only the damp scents of the autumn-warm waterfront. Or maybe that was the drool of a hungry beast.

A figure reared up beyond the alley's mouth, a pink priest grasping at the sky. *Confession?* a voice boomed in Jay-Jay's head.

She stumbled and dropped to her knees. "Forgive me. Yes, I've sinned."

Her serpentine arm slapped at the ground, both fingers digging at a crack in the asphalt. If she could bury herself, that would be an escape.

The towering priest tensed against the sky. *Tell me.*

"I took the stuff from the river," Jay-Jay said, voice cracking. "I have committed the carnal sin of corporate copyright infringement."

The punishment is death.

Jay-Jay sat up. "No, no, I have to be forgiven!"

Damnation, then.

She wanted to argue, but a violent scream ripped up her throat. Fleshy rope lashed forward as she sprang to her feet and rammed herself against the giant priest, thrusting her bony spike into—

Tree bark.

Her arm cried as if she'd banged her elbow on a wall corner. She launched back from the priest-tree, and the world swayed from side to side, dumping her toward the Hackensack River. No sifters prodded the water here. If only one would offer to crack open Jay-Jay's skull and sift intrusive flesh from the surface of her brain.

But there were other options, weren't there?

Her right arm's bony spike glared up at her, ever the hungry tooth. Would the green-out—magenta-out?—end if she impaled her eyes on the same bone as she'd driven into the poet?

A violent splash shook her gaze from her arm to the river. Thoughts still flew from her head, but now they seemed caught in a draft she couldn't feel, swooping toward the bank and coasting across the water's surface. She followed them to the edge, where she expected to spot pink spaghetti drifting downriver.

She instead spotted a body.

Every muscle twinged, trying to pull her attention from seeing the expected corpse—the poet—but before she could avert her eyes, she caught the color and shape.

The body was too curvaceous. It lacked the poet's facial hair and smug expression. Between the legs lay some almost-phallic appendage Jay-Jay couldn't identify from afar. She slapped at the water, desperate to guide the current, but her thoughts formed an airy fist that drew the body closer until Jay-Jay could haul it ashore.

She'd been right about the coloring. The body looked to have been inked by a magentist across every inch of skin, even into the scalp. Long damp hair grew with a dark pink tint, and snakelike limbs sprang from the fingers and toes. The between-thighs appendage resembled Jay-Jay's bone spike, only coated in flesh and without a tooth-sharp end. She couldn't guess what complexion the body might have had to start.

Unless this corpse had always been colored magenta. Only pieces had drifted downriver before, but now came a full figure.

"That's not right," Jay-Jay whispered. "That can't be what you are."

The body's eyes blinked open on black pupils and shiny magenta irises. Two feet slopped wetly on the asphalt as the figure curled over Jay-Jay, gaze curious, and then climbed onto her chest and shoulders. Each escaping thought swirled into the river-sprung figure as if those magenta eyes held a gravity for the mind.

Divine intervention.

Whom you see. She wants you to see.

When the mind is laid bare, the magenta steps through.

Jay-Jay shuddered beneath the woman's grasp, but there was no change in her weight, as if the figure were made of air.

"But you're real," Jay-Jay said.

The woman stroked Jay-Jay's arm, forming a fist over the flesh-rope and then the bony shaft. Less like exploration, more the way a nervous person might twiddle their thumbs, toying with pieces of their own body.

"Is it you?" Jay-Jay swallowed hard and flexed her arm. "These pieces. The flesh. Are you always here in me? In my—"

She had too many thoughts, and even more questions. Of course she'd found this woman. No one knew what disaster lay hidden upriver, but there had to be a source for the magenta flesh. Parts of a body, and now the whole thing. Jay-Jay and the other magentists should have expected someone to come claiming the pieces.

Or for the pieces to start claiming each other. The woman might have been calling out for herself across every sketch's infused flesh from the start, and only now that the flesh had entered the brain could the center of it all reach out to her own host.

"Can I only see you because of what they put in my head?" Jay-Jay's ropy arm coiled around the woman's wrist. "But that's not right. How long have you been stuck in us? Since we started? Fucking hell."

And if the flesh had never belonged to the magentists or the sketches, what did that mean for their bodies? Were they supposed to return it? Or were they part of some greater whole, connected to the nervous system of humanity?

The woman said nothing. Her snaking fingers pressed Jay-Jay's serpentine muscle—her own flesh, organisms in arm-to-arm communication. She then squeezed her forehead against Jay-Jay's, listening for every thought, eager to understand this magentist-turned-human radio.

Had the poet seen this woman while dying? She might've been standing in his bathroom amid the panic and impulses, turning the psychic white noise magenta.

And there was Jay-Jay, driving one piece of this woman into the host for another piece of her as if she were a one-souled war trapped in a New Jersey apartment.

"I need forgiveness," Jay-Jay said. "Need everyone to see."

There was a simple answer to that. The poet might have known it. Machine certainly did. It had taken an intervention of sorts, biological or divine or both, but Jay-Jay understood now, too.

Infect. Everyone.

The woman's fingers slid toward the crook of Jay-Jay's right arm, into the base of the bone spike and the serpentine muscle, asking questions only an arm could answer, same as the head could understand the other head.

And answers were coming as Jay-Jay's mind settled. She had feared mental entropy, her brain might fly to pieces entirely into pinkish ghost thoughts, or bodily entropy as the woman reclaimed her pieces.

But she had no desire to take Jay-Jay apart that way. The dissolution was temporal, and now it was consolidating, finding unity in a world fashioned by warm flesh. The last remnants of outstretched time contracted from past and future into this singular moment like subway tracks collapsing inward. With nowhere to go, Jay-Jay imagined humanity might catch that elusive immortality. Not a missed train—a real hunt, ending inside the cage of the conjoined human.

The past swam with the whole of cellular history, rushing forward as fish, then lizards, and then mammalian reptiles, and then troops of hairy primates. One change crushed another, century by century to the now.

What lay ahead? The answer might have writhed in primordial chaos once, but here came determinative direction.

The future aimed onward, curving in the shape of a repurposed tattoo gun, now armed with magenta flesh, to be wielded by every magentist spreading the new human connection.

And Jay-Jay had her finger on the trigger.

EACH OF US IS ALL OF US

T.T. MADDEN

THERE'S SOMETHING EATING at me. Even now, even as I am me, Dinah, fully-formed and present. It's a nagging feeling, like I left the oven on, but emotionally. Something I've forgotten, something that's right there. I don't know if that makes sense.

I look at myself in the holographic mirror, as if I can see this feeling, as if it'll be on me, but all I see is me. The me I am now, not the me I used to be. The me I always have been, even if it was just inside; thin bathrobe slipping off me, every bit of the body I got to choose, to customize, like the character creator at the beginning of a videogame. The long, dark hair that drapes over my shoulders, how I can feel it in the middle of my back. The shoulders that have slimmed and angled down, the neck that's just a little longer than it used to be, a little thinner. The legs that are hairless, smooth, how I always imagined they should be. The tattoos are smaller pieces of me, but they feel just as essential; the cracked egg on the inside of my left bicep, the skin-shedding snake on my right thigh, the moth above my heart. Ink in all the places I finally feel comfortable showing the world. I've known this fact long before this moment, but I'm finally comfortable exposing skin.

But the part I feel the most, that made this whole thing real, is my torso. I stand, and the hologram before me reflects my movements. I pull the belt of my robe tight around my waist—the waist that's now around my bellybutton, not three inches below it, the waist that cinches me in the middle, into an hourglass, instead of turning me into a wedge shape. I can see the soft curves of my new breasts through my robe, but even they don't make it feel as real as my waist, my hips. I spin, and my hologram spins with me, the image suddenly blurred, and I realize it's not the hologram fuzzing, but silent tears. Running down my cheeks before I even know they've escaped. I just let them fall, because I know from when this has happened before that they'll just keep coming.

I see me. But I can't see *it*. Whatever this nagging feeling is.

WHEN I THINK about the me I once was, it feels like a dream. Not in the way dreams feel like goals, but in the way they feel like they didn't happen. In the way that sometimes they'll feel like they'll never happen. It's hard to imagine myself like that now, the way I used to be. The person never was. The person I was stuck as. Hairy legs and broad shoulders and wispy facial hair. I guess it's because, for people like me, there are really two memories; the how it was and the how we imagine it was.

I finally wipe at the tears when it feels like they're on their way out, but something lingers. A dark feeling I can't quantify, something I'm not familiar with. I try to shake it loose, take my robe off to change, a smile sneaking across my face as I look at a body I'm actually comfortable being nude in.

That's when it hits me, as I'm looking at myself naked; there are no scars. This is me. For all anyone else could tell, it could be how I've always been. The ease with which I've transformed finally strikes me, and it feels forbidden. It feels like I shouldn't be able to so easily become me. I'm still waiting for this other shoe to drop, waiting to figure out this feeling.

OF COURSE IT wasn't always like this, to be able to modify yourself on a whim. There was a time long ago, a time before me, where all of this was different, and infinitely harder.

A time before the prism.

I remember, if only through portentous headlines, the warnings of some celestial *thing* drifting towards Earth. A cloud from deep space, the origin not even our smartest scientists could discover. The pictures of it were everywhere as it came closer and closer to the planet; a boundaryless, cosmic rainbow, an ever-shifting array of colors drifting toward us on null-currents.

Those sights stirred up atom-age fears: deep space signals, atomic rays transforming an unsuspecting populace into hideous, deformed things. But of course, like so much fear-mongering, the prism came and went, drifted over us like a warm breeze, everyone on the planet covered in a layer of cosmic dust that amounted to…

Nothing.

At first.

But then people began changing, started becoming their true selves. Transformed by the whim of a wish.

Like with everything else, every new technology, there were men who tried to make it into a weapon. Something with which to kill. Men who were convinced this could be used to inflict their will on reality itself. Every single attempt resulted in impotent failure. There were whispers that the prism had a consciousness of its own somehow.

That it wouldn't obey them, refused to be used as such.

Flesh on flesh, the rumor was. And only your own. I remember seeing people pulling their new selves, their *true* selves, out of thin air. Evolving right before our eyes. The versions they'd always hidden away, were afraid to show, thought were monstrous, *wrong*, now available at the snap of a finger, not a long wait, not multiple surgeries, not battles with politicians who'd never even know you existed. I saw how happy they were, and I felt a longing in my chest.

I never thought Dinah was me, always thought *I* was me, that I couldn't really be someone else hidden within this skin. I never pieced it together, even with the fact that my favorite superpower was shapeshifting. Or why I was so obsessed with corporeality, the very forms monsters and gods and supervillains inhabited in the fiction I loved to read. Maybe I didn't actually want to know why I was so uncomfortable at the pool or the beach with my shirt off. Maybe I would just be better off burying it all.

But then I heard the stories. I saw their heroes before my eyes. Each and every one of these people who had harnessed the passing prism, who'd played and experimented with the forms they were assigned, became supernovas of happiness, of truth. Real, authentic, beautiful people unleashed on the world. I wasn't sure if I was like them, but I was sure I wanted some of that happiness.

So I gave it a shot.

I reached into the air before me and the color unfolded, unwrapping itself out of nothing, like it had always been hidden around me, buzzing like it was delighted to finally show itself. I reached through the shimmer, thinking, pulling, and the thoughts of how I wanted to be became real, became thoughts of how I *needed* to be, how I really was.

My arm tingled and I opened my eyes as a shimmer worked its way up my skin, shaving away the little fuzzes of hair on my knuckles, the backs of my hands, my arms, melting them straight out of the follicles. More colors unfolded themselves out of the air, reaching for me like fairy godmothers. They were shifting, ever-changing as if indecisive, before finally settling on a beautiful lavender, its warmth nuzzling me like a blanket straight out of the dryer. The light surrounded me completely, and parts of me went numb and then warm as their true shapes emerged from the chrysalis of my old skin. The lavender light draped around me like a ballgown, reflected my shape in the air before me, and I knew in that instant that this was no mistake. Any hesitance obliterated.

AND YET STILL something gnaws at me, so I go to the only place I know I'm safe, the place where I can figure it out.

When I walk through the front door, Tracy greets me.

"Hey, D." She smiles, her voice rumbling with that low purr you used to hear from girls like us, before the prism made it so you could get rid of that too, if you wanted. But Tracy's kept it, just like she's kept the small bulge in the front of her shorts, the muscle in her arms as she leans against the entrance door. She always looks like this, never on either end of the spectrum, always somewhere in the middle, even though she always prefers *she*.

"Hey, babe," I say back. I met Tracy that first night, the first time I ever came to this place. She knew I was alone, could tell I wanted to come in, standing outside across the street, looking wistfully at the building. She showed me around, showed me how it worked. The first one was on the house.

A gift. She had no idea how precious.

"You want your usual room?"

I nod, and Tracy takes me through what looks like a hookah lounge, but I know better. We all know better. There are people sitting on couches in various rooms, leaning back and relaxing, but no pipes, no hookahs. You'd be forgiven for thinking what floated above us, the haze on the ceiling and in the corners of the room, was smoke.

But it's multicolored, shifting and changing like lightning roils inside it. All around us people lay back with their eyes closed, dreaming dimensions inside the prism.

Tracy takes me to a room where I can be alone, a small room with a big, leather easy chair, more of that prism haze floating above us.

Before she leaves, she stops and asks if I'm alright. "You seem…down."

"Stress," I say, which isn't a lie, but also isn't the truth.

Tracy taps the doorway with her palm.

"Let me know if you need anything, hun." She leaves me alone, except I'm not alone, in here with the resurgent feeling of self-flagellation and fear I don't understand. But I try to know. I try to feel it. So I sit down in the chair, and I close my eyes. I reach into the cloud, reach into the prism, not with my hand, but with my mind, and I am somewhere else.

I AM SOMEONE else.

I am still Dinah, but I am also hundreds, thousands of different people, of all ages, including myself, wearing long sleeves and pants even in the heat of summer, becoming a shapeless lump because I don't like the shape I'm stuck with. All of these me's, all of these eyes I'm looking through, we all know we don't want to show our skin, but we cannot articulate that the reason why is because we feel like it is not ours. I am myself, I am all those children, watching powerful men who hate us legislate our lives away. I am every one of us standing before a protest against our lives, fighting people who are too ignorant to understand even their own conflated bigotries. But I am also the rage of generations. I am millions of voices crying out all at once across time.

In a flash of blue, I am a high school boy trying out for the swim team, being told I should shave my body so I can be faster in the water. I think it's some sort of prank at first, but I can see the other swimmers, the upperclassmen, their smooth stomachs and arms and legs, and I feel a little safer, avoiding what I was sure was a practical joke. At home, I spend more time looking at myself after I'm done than I spend shaving. Especially my legs, my hairless, toned stomach, and I feel excited in a way I can't explain. I've forgotten the reason I've done this in the first place, forgotten entirely about the swim team. My mouth is dry, and I can't figure out why, that first little bit of boundary broken.

More intermittent colors, and I'm another child being dragged to the beach half a state away. I'm terribly bored, and hot because I insist on wearing a T-shirt, because it somehow feels wrong to be shirtless out here. Distantly, I watch girls in bikinis, their bodies glistening with ocean foam and sunlight.

I am myself again, Dinah-before-Dinah, in a specific memory of mine. I'm masturbating not because I'm aroused, but attempting to specifically eliminate the possibility of arousal later, the distinctive, uncomfortable feeling of a rigid member between my legs. I'm Dinah-before-Dinah, wondering what coming out of this chrysalis would be like, and I am stealing clothing from big-box stores, dresses and skirts and stockings, floral patterns and bright colors and curving shapes. I try them on and I feel good in them, but I cry silently to myself and throw them away in another store's trash can, thinking about a world I believed could never be.

A flash of prismatic light, and I am an elementary school child somewhere long ago. A boy, at least at this moment in time, and for Halloween, I decide to go as Dr. Frank N. Furter to complement my friend group's *Rocky Horror* ensemble. I know this societally divergent behavior will be accepted on only this one day of the year, that this is my only chance.

I can feel the stockings on my legs, see my lips and eyes darkened in a way that makes it seem like I'm finally looking at my own face after all these years. Everyone loves the costume, they laugh and cheer with me, and I even win one of the school's awards.

But on November 1st, I go back to the way things used to be. Pants and sneakers and a large, shapeless hoodie, the passage of time itself ripping me from me. I develop a fear of puberty, of adulthood, that I do not understand until I am much older.

And then I realize it, I know the truth of this urge of mine.

That, existing in the world like this, I am not only unsafe, I am targeted. It is the fear that someone is going to come and take this away from me.

The knowledge that it has happened before.

When I flash back to the here and now, the present Dinah, I collapse against the wall, the air whooshing out of my lungs. I struggle to breathe, try to claw life back into me, knowing silent tears are streaming down my cheeks. Tracy is crouching above me, eyebrows furrowed in concern, hands out in front of her like she wants to try and steady me, but is afraid to touch me without my permission.

I hold out my own hand, silently beckon her forward, give her permission, and she comes to me, holding me steady.

"It's okay," she says. "It's scary, I know. It's over, it's over. We're not that little boy anymore."

I look up into her eyes and wonder how she knows, and I can see it. That she didn't just *see* it, that she *lived* it, that she remembered that back-to-the-real-world feeling because she was there, the Tracy-before-Tracy, and she knew what it felt like to have it taken away from her.

"Tracy?" I gasp.

"Shh," she says, pulling me close, telling me that feeling will never come again. Not so long as we're all here. Not so long as we're all together. Not so long as each of us is all of us.

Tracy holds me like a mother holds a child, a shield of arms that I know, as soon as they close around me, are impenetrable.

THE WRONG BODY

A.G.A. WILMOT

I KNEW YOU, Kara Vaughn. Both the real you and the shell you wore.

I think I always knew what was inside, even if I didn't want to admit it to myself—that what I first met wasn't your true self, wasn't your "light," as Belias was so fond of saying. The night we met, when he brought you in, introduced you to us…I knew. I saw the cracks in the pale weathered skin you wore, like a timeless antique vase recovered from beneath the rubble of a ruined necropolis. That night, your first with us, invited into Their Grace, I watched those cracks widen and slough away. I picked up the pieces of them, quietly, discreetly, and held them to my chest, to the still-healing gaps and crevasses in my own self, and noted how they fit.

I knew your inspiration, too. I felt it as Belias walked you through the dark halls of our bunker, our sprawl beneath Ellison's downtown core, to the nursery. To Athena. Belias sat you down in front of them, our Den Mother, and told you to ignore the stench of salt water and industry that coated your throat when you opened your mouth and to just breathe. To be. To let what hadn't already fallen away come crashing down around you. To let Athena in. Let us all in.

It was artifice, he repeated to you over and over again. Your shell. The sleeve into which you were born. It was a shield, a cloak within which you had been able to hide, but at what cost. We followed his lead. We echoed his words as if to remind ourselves of the distance each of us had journeyed to arrive at this point.

That's when I felt it. When I felt you. I witnessed as you seemed to just…lighten somehow. So much so, your relief so potent, that I half-expected you to rise up off the floor where you sat cross-legged in front of the steel and glass chassis containing our beloved Den Mother. The way your back arched, how your shoulders loosened…you radiated an invigorating brand of hope we had largely forgotten for ourselves. Understandably—we'd been in hiding so long, in the subterranean maze of a sprawl beneath an even larger sprawl up above, a chrome metropolis so vast and towering and sodden with "moral purity" that its peaks blotted out the stars, that most of us had forgotten the way the sun caused our skin to tingle. The smell of early morning dew. Those sensations were still present enough that once Belias had finished his procedure, after you'd been installed with a broken halo and synced to the rest of us, we all drank from the freshwater well of your mind. We knew what was and wasn't ours—we never confused such things—but we got to experience the sensations as if they were our own. Dream writers have traded in artificial bliss—perfect memories elongated, slowed to a crawl and then slipped onto a mental slate for easy access—for as long as we've had extra lives to shed, but that's not the same. It never takes, not when it's reduced to data hard coded onto someone's slate, like a page from one book torn out and shoved into the middle of another. The mind always knows: it isn't real.

No, when we sync like we did, there are no rough or frayed edges. We experience each other's memories fully, but still only as memory. One we know isn't ours individually but belongs to us as a collective—a shared meal at a holiday dinner.

And we were a collective. None of us sought anything like that, you knew that. It was no spiritual grouping, no cult. We synced because even separate our pain was universal. So, too, the first of us realized, should our survival be. Or our chances of it.

This had been evident to you since Belias found you half-starved and left to die in the street somewhere in East Ellison. You'd been uncovered—the Pride had tracked you down not long after they'd dismantled your family, wiped all traces of them from the earth for the crime of "harbouring an unwanted." But they hadn't found where you'd disappeared to. Hadn't yet stripped you to your spine, cleared you of any accoutrements that they might've been able to turn on the black market for a dime. Wouldn't have done any good if they'd tried—your family was poor, you revealed once you felt comfortable enough to tell me about your past. There hadn't been any money for slates, let alone a second skin waiting for you on ice—ideally one tailored to your transition needs. But you'd been loved. You'd been safe.

Until the Pride. Until Premiere Joyce's personal execution squad discovered you. Fuck knows how—you weren't even sure. More than likely, they'd been keeping an eye out for cross-border runs being made at specific intervals. Backdoor tracking on message boards and forums. Digging into pharmaceutical histories they would not have had any right to a decade earlier, before the New Puritans seized power and millions were forced to crawl back into closets nationwide or face "re-education" in the ways of their nightmare notion of God.

Theirs is a movement rooted in one thing and one thing only: hate.

And hate has a helluva bank account. Always has. It's how Joyce took power so easily. When you've got the cash needed to live forever, to put your mind—everything you were, are, could one day be—on a tiny horseshoe-shaped slate of plastic and circuitry and slip it out of one body and into another, you can afford to wait. To outlast both the righteous and the right.

Good will win the day, Belias so often stated, with varying degrees of confidence, but malice will win the fearful. The cowards who'll sell out their neighbours for a few shillings and still think themselves morally pure.

You learned this early on—the power of malice. Of malevolence. You learned it later, too, when you accepted the Den Mother's offering. It was never a given, after all, that they would want to help you. Athena is altruistic, yes, but they also had a job to do. It was on them to keep us safe. We don't know who they were, how they came to be…this. Entombed in a bullet-shaped coffin drowning in amniotic fluids as if an adult-sized fetus. Braided circuitry fed into and out of their chassis, and through said device, Athena was able to bind us as one.

You weren't certain of the procedure. Which made sense. No one else in your family had ever been gifted the opportunity to stretch their life beyond its organic limitations—you weren't even sure about having a slate inserted, if having a broken halo of your own would change you somehow. Belias assured you it wouldn't as he shaved your head, created a small opening at the back of your neck, where skull met stem, and inserted the device, as he'd done dozens of times before with each and every one of us. He told you then what he told us: that this wasn't only a path toward transition, should you wish to sidestep further hormonal intervention, it was also a chance to defend ourselves—to actually, maybe, outlive the threats that dogged us every step of the way. Your slate was a gift, we assured you. From where, you asked. Donated. Salvaged. We still had allies and accomplices out there, in the world above. The wealthy who discreetly bequeathed to us their unused skins, so that we might experience life as we were supposed to, in our correct gender, even if in someone else's body. Those Extended Life technicians and staff who risked their own lives to smuggle us outdated slates marked for elimination while stores made room for newer, more expensive models.

But allies and accomplices on their own don't win wars.

This, too, you learned, even as you were coming to understand, for the first time, what it was to be a part of something larger than yourself. To have found a new family.

And what it was like to be torn from it rather than to have them torn from you.

We received no call, nothing so formal telling us where we could collect your remains—or what remained, I should say. The Pride didn't leave much. They never did.

The bastards, the walking scythes, found you one night while you were pulling sacks of bread and bagels from a dumpster behind a downtown market. Didn't tell you to freeze, to put your hands up, to get down on your knees.

They simply black-bagged you. Took you out of the city, tore the slate from the back of your head with an unwashed and oft-used pair of needle nose pliers and a claw hammer to make the opening, and left you in pieces beneath the Knight Street overpass.

We received no call, but we knew. We felt it. We remembered it—as it was happening, as it would be happening forever, the information a part of us all now. Your pain, your mind, with us forever.

This was the blessing and the curse of the system that Athena and Belias and others in different dens all around the city, around the country, had built and set in motion. With Athena as our sentient server, a shallow facsimile of the farms found in EL clinics nationwide, we could live forever. But where the clinics' server farms—many the size of high school athletic fields—were powerful enough to host discrete, individual lives, what we had was but a poor approximation without the capacity for such divisions. We were each of us our own person and also a singular hive. By linking us together as they did, Athena was able to use our minds and bodies as storage, additional processing power to mimic the workings of the server farms. It wasn't ideal, but it worked. It kept us alive past the point of physical death. It kept us in each other's thoughts, always.

We knew you, Kara Vaughn. And we knew what had happened.

Immediately.

They took your slate, obviously. They didn't even try to wipe and resell the halos they stole from the trans people that they killed. They simply destroyed them, acting out of pure spite, as if we were a plague to be wiped clear from an otherwise sane world.

A sane world. Fucking hell. Graham Joyce's infectious, malignant words. Words he and his poisonous ilk have used to justify atrocities. A clearing out of sorts—neon-soaked eugenics in a world of infinite promise and possibility yet still steeped in the safety and comfort of conformity.

A sane world where they destroyed your body first and your mind second, and thought they could get away with it.

But that would never have been your end. Without a server for your mind to return to, yes, you would have been lost to us. But with Athena's help, you were back in mere seconds, data and memories torrenting through each of us. It was how Athena sorted information, kept our lives separate—we were their filtration system. When you died, Kara, as when you lived, your slate was still connected to our hive. We took you in as you were when we met, as you were in the months and years that followed, during the time we spent mending our broken vases into something new, and as they left you. You were never gone; you were just waylaid a bit.

Your transition took a bit of a left turn upon your revival, but such is the risk we all face with every passing day. The progress you'd made medically, with your original body, had been halted. Belias led a small team—Xavier, Eliseo, and Marion—to the overpass, to retrieve what samples of you they could in hopes of one day, when it was safe again, when it was feasible, growing a new you, altered to your needs and desired specifications. But for now, a loaner would have to do. We were able to fit you with a donor body on ice at a nearby black site owned and operated by a few of our more well-to-do funders and freelance EL techs sympathetic to our needs. Desired gender presentation was a match, though of course, it wasn't your body, not in the truest sense.

I knew you, Kara Vaughn. We all did, and we were overjoyed when you were returned to us. We were scared, too, when you struggled to acclimate to your new body. As a new iteration of dysphoria presented itself—a sense, truly, of being in the wrong body, of being a brain shoved into a marionette of sorts, a thing that you controlled but was not yours. Not you.

We were further distraught when the memories of what had been done to you filtered back in. We lacked good data scrubbers or even freelance dream writers capable of isolating and extracting the memories of your death from our whole—a mercy gifted to those who can afford it, freedom from the very worst parts of our own lives. We all knew how you felt, but only you truly knew how it had felt.

We knew, too, the shift that was taking place. Had taken place already. We knew when the crying stopped—when you asked us to stop holding you, stop telling you it would be okay, that you'd get through this—that you had latched on to something else.

Belias warned against it. He had gone down that path already. Had shed a dozen of his lives or more, and all of his former family's wealth striking back. Trying to hurt those who couldn't be hurt. Those who claimed oppression even while their boots were crushing the windpipes of those they deemed beneath them.

He warned you, as he warned all of us when our paths invariably took us down similar roads. Not one of us is as we were when we showed up at the den dressed in cracked and crumbling visages of past lives and unprocessed dreams. I wonder if you knew that—I never did dive into how you felt about the rest of us. Some things are best left private, I suppose, even when all doors to a person's mind are open to you.

You'd haunt them, you said. You swore. You'd be their Ghost of Christmas Past. New skin, same memories. You'd track down the ones who hurt you. Hurt your family. You'd make them suffer. And when they killed you again, you'd come right back. You'd drive them to madness, you promised us. You'd be the spot on the carpet they couldn't get out no matter how hard they tried.

Belias said he understood how you felt. We all did. We'd all been there, knew one another's worst pain as our own—and our own pain as agonies without hope of resolution. Recompense. We knew, too, what each of us had done. The legacies of anguish that trailed Belias, the red of his past. The blood he'd shed, blood that we shared with one another as if we'd ourselves been responsible for it. What I had…the things I'd wished I could have…

I wish you'd listened to me when I tried to stop you. To help you. I wish you had let me tell you the things I'd done. The crimes I lay awake at night dreaming about. I tried to keep them to myself, though I knew that was impossible. My dreams were our dreams, all of ours, even if we didn't speak of them. I knew you'd experienced them. I knew.

I knew your inspiration. Right from the beginning. I had experienced it first-hand, when you told me your true name; when we stayed up late writing love notes on each other's backs; when you opened up your chest to me and showed me your heart, and I showed you mine, and we discovered that they beat in perfect rhythm with one another.

And in your rage, I saw that same inspiration, that ache for love, genuine and true, that need for hope, real hope, turned sour. You were not convinced when we tried to sway you, not even for the good of the den. Belias threatened expulsion if you risked our stores of skins and slates in pursuit of your singular vendetta. He spoke, too, of pulling up stakes. He'd wanted to move the den for some time—to get out of Ellison before things got even more dystopian than they already had. He could do it, too. He could, with help, unplug Athena, just for a time, and move them safely, under cover of night. We could scatter, he said. We'd know how to find one another again the instant Athena was brought back online, whenever and wherever that turned out to be.

By this point, you'd had some success in your endeavours. You'd found the man who took a hammer to the back of your skull and repaid his crime in kind. Made it look like a carjacking gone wrong when you snuck up behind him as he was on his way home from a downtown travel agency—a club where, for a price, you could pay to have someone open their mind to you, their traumas and tragedies all. Later, you hired a hack data scrubber to sweep his brain for the specific trauma you'd inflicted upon him and had it duplicated, magnified, so that when he was reborn—if the Joyce administration saw fit to supply their walking scythes with EL benefits—it would be all he remembered. You paid a dream writer—one you met one night down by the docks, a less than savoury character hocking broken halos lifted from the dead left to rot in the streets—to hack his personal home server and infect the slates of his wife and child with that same memory, so they, too, would know the cost of the man's actions. So that every time they dreamed, they'd see the first-person account of his crime like an intrusive thought they could never escape.

You did this three more times before they caught and killed you, stripping you of your second skin. And when you returned, you turned your mind to blackmail. To stealing and sifting through the remains of the other scythes, putting the very worst of the Pride on display for the world to see.

You kept at it, and they kept killing you. Every skin you returned in you moulded and sculpted to your needs.

You honed your skills and your muscles alike as you broke
into their homes and businesses and took from them
all that you could. And every time, you made it clear
who was responsible: a crude hammer drawn in pen or
chalk or blood, or etched into the forehead of those you'd
personally ended. You wanted them to know: they could
kill you, but they could not erase you.

We died alongside you over and over again. When
you killed; when you were killed. A sickness of deaths—a
plague of them. We were like matryoshka dolls getting
smaller and smaller with each new life you lost, and with
every last death you facilitated. The shared sensation
slowly whittled us to a thin membrane of stability.

We wept. We held one another. We felt ourselves slowly
slipping away—you stole our humanity each and every
time you sheared off another piece of your soul.

The last time they killed you—the last of your deaths
I was aware of, anyway—they put a back trace on your
slate. Caught the final burst and fed it through enough
systems to override what meagre protections we had in
place and pinpoint the den.

We had no warning. Belias had already started the
process of moving Athena somewhere new, but he was
intercepted en route.

The pain we felt when they plugged our Den Mother
back in, in some warehouse somewhere, only to put a hand
cannon to their temple, was like nothing any of us had ever
experienced. Before ending Athena and Belias, however,
they did what they could to trace the myriad lives running
through them. They got our names, our faces, our locations.
They saw the love we had for one another and decided it
too toxic, too unnatural to be allowed to flourish.

It didn't matter that we'd scattered—they were able to
look into our slates and track us anywhere we went.

I acted fast—in the alley just above the den I found a
broken beer bottle and, without hesitating, without thinking

of infection or whether or not I'd pass out from the pain, I started sawing through the back of my neck. I screamed blood-red murder as I did, and I didn't stop until I was able to force two fingers into the hole and yank out my own slate. When Belias had first inserted it, he'd given me such a cocktail of painkillers that I hadn't felt a thing. I couldn't say that was the case this time. But on the plus side, it wasn't a pain I would have to share with anyone else. Not yet, anyway. There'd been enough of that already—you'd inflicted more than your share on us all. We didn't want to remember, to know what you'd done to those men. Your rampage was not our catharsis; it was further damnation.

But you did it anyway, Kara. And yes, you damned us ever the more. When we told you to stop, you said you wanted us to feel what you'd felt. We did, though. We had, long before you were ever with us. I don't think you understood that. There were ways we could have struck back at them. Ways we could have beaten or outlasted them. Ways we still might, together. Through enough people elsewhere getting wind of what's happening here, in Ellison, indeed throughout this entire province. Through allies and accomplices here, in hiding. Through exposing the Joyce administration's lies and hate for what they truly are, rather than matching aggression for aggression. Aggression might win battles, but it will never win wars. Not when only one side controls the artillery.

I knew you, Kara Vaughn. I knew what they did to you, and what you did to them, and us, in turn. We could have worked together. Fought together. We were family. I thought this, I believed this even, as I sat in a veterinarian's office that night waiting to be stitched up, to have the hole in the back of my head, where family once resided, closed off, possibly forever.

A year later, after sleeping in alleys and hiding down by the waterfront, shielding myself from all passersby, I returned to the den. It still has power, but there's no one here.

No lifeless husks of those I once loved, and who loved me in return, scattered about like battlefield debris. I don't know where any of them are or if any of them have survived. The hive has been offline since the Pride's raid.

I found something else, though. Something I didn't expect. When Belias moved Athena, he used a smaller coffin meant for limited transport. Their original chassis is still here, still intact. The Pride hadn't made it this far, I suppose—they'd been content picking us off one by one above.

Beneath a grate in the floor, I find what I'd secreted away so long ago. My slate is blood-crusted and a little dirty but otherwise functional.

Maybe if I'm careful I can get it reinserted. Re-open the hatchet job of a mess I'd made of my neck and skull and slip my backup life back into place. Though without Athena, without a server…

As I touch the chassis's cold, smooth metal, I realize, with some measure of horror, what I must do. What responsibility has now fallen to me.

I wonder what it'll be like, to plug myself in and feel us again. I wonder how long it will take before I lose myself in the role of Den Mother. I wonder what it will be like to be the spider and not merely a part of the web—to spin a future for others while leaving my own behind. The greater good is never without sacrifice. Fucking never.

I wonder, too, if any of the others are still alive. If they'll feel me and I them once I'm seated on Agatha's throne— my throne.

I wonder if you're still out there. If you've found a new skin. If you've stayed safe. If you've learned to hope again.

I wonder if I'll know you, Kara Vaughn. If we'll know each other anymore.

I wonder if you'll come home.

I wonder if you're ready to.

TOP 11 REASONS BEING A GHOST IS BETTER THAN BEING HUMAN, ACTUALLY

(VIA FIZZROLL.NET)

ADELINE WONG

OOK, WE'VE ALL been there. You forgot to look both ways before crossing the latest hyperexpressway in New Los Angeles. Your apartment's atmo-filters crapped out in the middle of the night, and by the time you woke up, you were choking on the ol' carbo-dio. Someone got a little overzealous with their electrotennis serve during Tuesday friendlies. It happens.

The thing is, we know how ridiculously expensive this all is. 20,000₵ for a basic medical re-birth? Practically highway robbery! And god help you if you want any kind of body modding—you think normal cosmetic surgery costs are a rip-off, try looking up the ones for a clone. Even a first-death body has nearly *double* the price attached to it!

So anyway, next time you find yourself an unintentional inhabitant of the unknowable liminal space between life and death, consider: it's not really so bad here. And just to prove it to you, here's FizzRoll's list of our Top 11 Reasons Being a Ghost is Better Than Being Human, Actually:

1. ALL THE ALONE TIME YOU'LL EVER WANT

PEOPLE THESE DAYS give ghosthood a pretty bad rap. "Oh, but you can't touch anything!" they moan. "You're only visible to psychics and mediums!" But really, all of this is just a plus! Think of all the peace and quiet you can enjoy—no more overcomplicated digital zoom algorithms to sift through for your RayCorp telework supervisor, no more screaming family members demanding to open your delivery packages and snoop through your Net history. Trust me, I've never felt *anything* more relaxing.

And anyway, some of it isn't entirely true—you *can* touch things, as long as they have a high enough conductive metal content (so no breaking into bank vaults—sorry!), and non-psychics can still see you if they loved you in life "unreservedly, with all their heart." So you'll probably have a person or two to communicate with—at least, I hope you would. But then again, anyone who didn't would have bigger things to worry about. Probably. I wouldn't know.

2. NO MORE WORRYING ABOUT MONEY

SERIOUSLY, CHIP-SCRAPING IS one of the worst parts of living on Earth these days. Unless you've got a super cushy RayCorp exec position or an inheritance, you're probably reading this during your government-mandated eight hours, between as many jobs as you can cram into the other sixteen. But ghosts don't need chips for anything: not for food, not for rent, not for ridiculously expensive medical bills that seem to get higher literally every time you turn around. I'm sure they've gotten even higher since I last looked, but these days, I can't bring myself to check.

Honestly, the med bills alone would make this whole thing worth it to me.

3. YOU CAN SURVIVE (ALMOST) LITERALLY ANYTHING

WELL, NOT "SURVIVE," technically—you're already dead—but ghosts can do a whole lot without risk to our squishy ectoplasmic bodies. Ever wondered what it's like to skydive without a parachute? Now you can do it! Want to know what juicy secrets RayCorp is hiding on the other side of that massive moon elevator? Well, you probably won't be able to get in, but you can certainly float up to the moon and try! Feel like obsessively reliving your moment of death, over and over—hurrying down that asphalt sidewalk, your billfold full of chips clutched in your sweat-damp hand, the rushing wind of the oncoming hovercar half a mile inside the San Andreas Pedestrian-Only Sector, the impact, the sudden black— wondering what you might have done to avoid it and knowing you wouldn't have been fast enough anyway? Being a ghost lets you do that, *without dying again*! The possibilities are endless— just try not to get hit with any ectoplasm dispersal beams.

4. YOU GET TO MEET OTHER GHOSTS

ALONE TIME IS great and all, but sometimes it's nice to talk to people, too! Sure, the living can't see you unless they truly loved you for who you were or whatever, but a ghost can see any other ghost just fine.

It may not seem like it at first, but ghosts are pretty much everywhere these days. You'll start spotting them all over the place if you keep your eyes peeled. And if you can get yourself installed onto a hard drive with Net access, it gets even better: the so-called "ghosts in the machine" outnumber physical ghosts almost 4 to 1, and they're much easier to find, to boot.

You'll probably meet a bunch who are happy to give tips on navigating ghosthood—ghosts who know the *best* secret hideouts that humans could never reach in a million years, or ghosts who are old hands at ectoplasm-shaping and eager to teach their tricks to anyone who asks.

5. ECTOPLASM IS, LIKE, REALLY MALLEABLE?

Speaking of ectoplasm-shaping, even a little bit of practice will let you control your body even more effectively than a top-of-the-line modern dreamscape. Say goodbye to clunky body modding—no more lengthy-recovery surgeries or hormonal regimens that take years to show results. You aren't happy with your ghost body? Just change it! It's really as simple as that.

6. NO MORE WORRYING ABOUT SLEEP

ALRIGHT, LET'S FACE it: sleep is boring. I don't know a single person who regularly gets their government-mandated eight hours—there's just so much to do, and so many better things to pay attention to. Take, for instance, that spine-tingling uneasiness on the back of your neck, the one that worried over the cameras above every storefront you passed and every hovercar whistling by you in the street. If you hadn't laid down to sleep in that alley—exhausted, lungs and legs burning, forty-six hours awake and counting— you could have reasoned your way through it. You could have realized that Mom or Dad (probably Mom) would tip off RayCorp, that RayCorp would know where your bus ticket led, that of course the shiny new high-tech lens in the jeweler's across the street would be connected to the Net— to RayCorp's algorithms. And if you'd known all that, if you'd just stopped for a *second* to think instead of rest—you could have been gone, vanished from the smog of the San Andreas city limits long before they arrived to try to take you back. If that was even their intent at all.

…wow, that turned into a bit of a downer. Anyway, think of how many Holo shows you could watch with all those extra hours! Maybe you could finally burn through that watchlist backlog.

7. UNLIMITED ACCESS TO THE NET

OKAY! SO! BACK to the list! Remember what I said about installing yourself on a hard drive? Well, there are more upsides to it than just meeting a few more ghosts! A ghost in the machine doesn't have to pay for Net access, first of all, and that alone is huge. But you can also reach *so much more* of the Net than a living human can. When your entire essence is made of selectively conductive ectoplasm, you can bridge processing gaps and access basically anything that's ever been hardwired into the World Grid—which at this point, is pretty much anything that isn't a RayCorp trade secret. Endless digital entertainment, your living friends' social media feeds, defunct netsites long-buried that you haven't seen since childhood—the modern Net has it all.

There are places you should stay away from, obviously: the depressing news sites, for one, and many a poorly-moderated netforum. And you can't actually *change* anything on the Net—at least not long-term, anyway. The refresh sequences on live netsites will erase anything you try to add within a minute or two, and even the old archived stuff gets reset every so often. But even so, just perusing a fraction of this stuff could keep anyone busy for ages. It can be a little overwhelming at first, admittedly. But if you're worried, you can always find a more experienced ghost and ask to see how it's done.

8. YOU CAN STILL LEARN THINGS

OKAY, THAT ONE went pretty well! Speaking of access to the Net—it surprised me when I realized this, because ghosts don't really have "brains" or "memory" like living humans do, but you can still learn new things and pick up new skills even after death! The ability to do a good Neo-Boston accent absolutely *kills* at parties, for instance—and it gets even better if you can throw your voice, or you have the vocal control to swap between a range of pitches. Plus, that sort of thing will definitely come in handy for hauntings…but I'm getting ahead of myself.

9. YOU'LL NEVER FORGET ANYTHING AGAIN

PICKING UP SKILLS as a ghost is *really* easy, actually, because ghosts have pretty much perfect recall—both for things we learn after death and things we already knew in life. You'll have a great visual memory, too: consider, for example, the RayCorp logo. We see it all the time, but it's not very memorable—if you're alive, you'd probably describe it pretty simply: a large sun, bright-eyed and smiling, with arrows pointing outward in every direction. But if you were a ghost, you'd know so much more about it: the waviness of that smile, ever so slight, but present. Those perfectly symmetrical eyes, staring scornfully at you where you lie on the grubby concrete. Its smile, once a bright, multichromatic Holo, stained the same red as the rivulets now draining into the cracked pavement beneath you. The size, tiny, dwindling, vanishing, as the hovercar slips into full reverse to disappear into San Andreas smog…

That's the kind of thing you have to focus on. Images. Images that are detailed enough, dynamic enough, to draw your full attention—to make you really *look* at them, because the alternative is remembering how it felt. The heart screaming in your chest, desperately clawing its way up into your throat. The pain in your arms on your face in your soles, skin stripped away, asphalt dug into the bloody cracks opened by your run-run-run-*impact*-fall. The white-hot searing mess of your ribs, wreathing your lungs that are choking on flames (is that smog or hovercar exhaust or blood?), and—and so you stare at the car, the holographic sun perched smiling on the grille, until you finally pass out. It's easier that way. It's the part that I choose to remember.

10. HAUNTINGS ARE ACTUALLY A TON OF FUN

THIS IS IT. The big one. If you've ever been on the *receiving* end of a haunting, you probably won't agree with me here. And, sure, sometimes people get haunted who don't really deserve it. (Just ask anyone who's moved into New Pasadena recently—apparently the aftermath of the RayCorp acquisition's gotten pretty nasty.)

But the whole vibe changes when you're the one doing the haunting. You aren't trying on dresses in the dark, straining your ears to check for that echoing squeal of Dad's rubber boot on the plaster. You aren't second-guessing every word from your mouth, terrified that a single ill-voiced truth will bring down the wrath of the mother always listening from the hall. You aren't desperately scraping chips into a tin can beneath your bed, counting down the days until can afford the hyperbus ticket to San Andreas, until you can escape this goddamned house please just one more week just let me make it out in one piece just let me leave—

No, this time you get to turn that fear back on *them*. Just make sure you pick someone deserving.

11. YOU GET TO WITNESS THE ARC OF HUMAN HISTORY IN ITS ENTIRETY

Anyway.

All that being said, there's a pretty big problem with being around forever: eventually, you run out of things to do.

Once the novelty of not suffocating in outer space wears off, once you've learned twelve different accents and trained your voice to hit any pitch on command, once you've had your fill of haunting the sixth floor of that shitty New Francisco walkup that you once couldn't *wait* to get out of—well. You're a ghost. There's not a lot to do but watch.

And that's no fun, really, so I don't exactly do a lot of it.

But that isn't to say it's *all* doom and gloom. Some of the old-timers here have seen a lot of shit, and they tell me it's actually been getting better over the years. The government actually managed to get an anti-surveillance bill past RayCorp a couple months ago, for the first time in nearly a decade. Even more recently, an advanced living collective from San Andreas started demanding actual hovercar barriers around their pedestrian sectors—and the movement sparked similar ones in Phoenix and Selenium Valley. Things like that. None of it helps *me*, sure, but I guess it's nice to know. Maybe someday I'll look at some new development and manage to be as optimistic about it as they are.

In the meantime, I'm going to enjoy the other benefits of ghosthood for as long as I can. If you'll excuse me, I have a hyperexpressway to cross. And I'm not even going to look.

A CANYON OF BLOOD FOR THE NORMALEST MAN ALIVE

PALIMRYA

YOU SHUFFLE IN for your daily shit and cringe like i'm a jumpscare. like i'm antique creepypasta, staining your senses for swiping a sus link as you went for your fly. you thumb your gumline node to check if you're up.

nope, you're in color. this is your bathroom, sir, and i'm in it. you make to throttle me, but then you see what i'm holding. i'm gonna keep talking, okay? i'm gonna say some stuff.

you thought yourself untouchable, Mister Presidents.

in your autobiography "A Dream of Hope" you wrote, and i quote, i'm no weirdo—but these American bones are milk-hard, and the quartz behind these eyes shakes at the freshest Chinese pinwave freqs, and i have never, ever cried. even when Cap had to go wackostyle on Groot in that Sprite spot, which sure had my daughters bawling. so as regular joes go, i'm a pretty tough dick to jerk. end quote.

you do eggs. you do burpees. you scrub with walnut shell Aveeno so the compensative hyperplasia will thicken you a little whenever you bathe. your skin is four inches thick. uncommonly dense. so well moisturized it squirts if you press it. you wear muscle tees, and somehow they look good on you.

you never thought this day would come, Mister Presidents. you never thought you'd see me here, damp and happy, legs astride the White House toilet bowl i wriggled out of, limp wrists wrapped like mating slugs around the ugliest gun you've ever seen.

you wonder, do you know who i am? something in this lopsided visage rings familiar, you say into your Apple Watch voice memos app. you wonder how i got here, and i can answer that. in a way, i've been here the whole time. i'm not a state, and i don't need communism to get in your head. i'm far worse and far, far dumber than that. when they crowned you "MISTER NORMALEST MAN ALIVE" at Davos all those years ago, i was there. when Congress made the country have a second president and said you could be that one too, i was there. when you fished that ball from the sand trap using your clubs like chopsticks and made your daughters tell you it was okay because your "Caucasian vitiligo" was acting up, i was there. and when you bombed all those people and all that other stuff, yeah. that's right. i was there, in the colorcam chat, smushing my freaky little soul into yours like a rice grain stiffening the sole of a sock.

hey Siri, why is this eely, dopey faggot shivering in my bathroom? what is it muttering? is that a gun? is it threatening me? you ask. and i can answer that too. the truth is, Mister Presidents, i never decided to do this. i've always known this would be my work, same as my parents and teachers knew, same as the doctor knew when she pulled the slippery worm of me from my mom's body and sputtered out, wincing, i don't know how to tell you this, ma'am, but i think you've just posted some pretty serious cringe. when my parents got the birth certificate, someone had already replaced my name with a sketch of an anthro millipede with puffy nips, and for sex they'd written "autist MtF for sure." my parents never found out who'd done it, but they were thankful. they knew it had saved me a few hundred bucks and a court appearance.

and you can guess the rest. the dog collars, the public freakouts, the Hiking, the low-poly rig phase. saying "what the heckie!!!" instead of "what the hell." permabanned young, obviously. i tried some colorworld jobs (shit stomper, shit collector), plus that banling halfschool that isolates your amygdalae's handles and gives them perms while the rest of you stays fugued. but i guess i wasn't that smart, since it never panned out. and once i got eely enough to start sliming around on the windows of local government buildings, fucking up the glass and shit, they peeled me off and put me on disability.

having a spit-sticky nickel shoved under my pod door every month gave me time to think, but to be honest, Mister Presidents, i didn't need to do much thinking. the whole world had done my thinking for me.

i knew that in order to kill the normalest man alive i would need an impossibly special instrument. it couldn't be a blade, since you'd overpower me. and no ordinary bullet could pierce skin as thick, as normal, as yours. even if DARPA had bred up something loud enough that i could steal, your organ doubles would heat up and you'd snap my neck before i could strike twice. no, i needed something new. something wrong. i needed an impossible bullet, a bullet of my own making. a bullet as cringe as you are based. a bullet so eely and ugly and totally fucked as to make even me squirm. i needed to commit my life to building the cringiest bullet alive.

so what else? i committed.

the first thing i did was hard hack the Grand Canyon's colorcams and replace its whole room with a twelve second flatloop i'd filmed with one of those antique reelcams they sell to fugued-out banlings down at the casket shop. people are pretty busy with their own stuff these days, so nobody noticed the swap.

and nobody noticed either when i lay prone at the "rim and stuck my carotid artery with a sharpened finger, filling the whole canyon with four quadrillion mega-fertile liters of pulpy red cringe. i've got scrawny veins, so that really took a while.

when i woke up, wobbly and studded with pebbles, i gazed out at my own horizon. it was generous and absurd, the flinty gold of the colorworld sunset salting and steaming then scattering from the shameless red face of that ocean of cringe. wow!!! pretty fuckin cool.

i jumped right in, and it was hot as the yolk of a stolen egg. the next step would take 30 years, and it did. what i'd made with my own exsanguination was the vastest pigeage à pied lode ever poured, and i needed to wine it good. so i just started stomping. and yelping. and huffing and squealing and kicking, and kicking, and kicking ever downward like some god-bitten horse on a snake. as i stomped and squelched and squealed, my awkward rag of a body settled lower and lower into countless strata of increasingly concentrated cringe.

and once i was submerged in the stuff, i started breathing it. i'd stomp down deep, panting hard, then wriggle back up like rotten kelp and start stomping again. over and over, all day long while the liquid lasted, which i guess was a decade or so.

and you may think the perfluorocarbon in your meditation tank burns, Mister Presidents, but jellied cringe scares lungs so badly they crumple up and shy into other dimensions to escape it. you never have to breathe again, though i like the smell of colorworld air so i do.

i need to pause here to tell you something, Mister Presidents: my skin is thin. my skin is so thin i used to think moms were judging me by chewing their grapetape weird in the benefits office. some days i'd break and think my boss was a real animal, like those last rangy wolves they clowned up and mocapped for the new zoo, and i'd stipple sigils into my shit-slick punch card to fend off his bestial moods. and now, when i awake in my ditch every day, i pinch shut the beading slits the shoots have put in my back in their search for sunlight. i'm not, like, a tomboy, you know?

but i need you to know, sir, that my lungs lasted nine whole seconds in that canyon. you could have lined up a thousand echolaliating sissies and babyfurs and not even the weirdest among their bodies and minds could have braved those fathoms of cringe like i did that day. i felt proud imagining it, and i say this because of another weakness of my station, which is that i need you all to understand me. at least a little.

i need you to understand in order for this to work.

having said that, Mister Presidents, know too that i'm no meritocrat. all this stomping and gasping and sculpting my lifeblood as vinegar in the earth's goblet, like a worm doula, a shepherd of living idiocy—it was a labor of love. with wine it's about submerging the skins, but cringe pigeage is a matter of compaction and potentiation. with each decade i passed in the canyon, my payload shrunk and solidified. jam, toothpaste, quicksand, mattress shreds. i went from stomping to sculpting, to kneading, till at last i scraped it into a great mound and began stomping again on top.

and once my limbs could no longer impinge on the sparkling cabochon of cringe, i donned my halloween fangs. yeah, see em? i used to wear these and smile on the colorworld tram so maybe kids would grow up thinking they'd seen a real catgirl or criminal, and i guess i keep them for sentiment. they're not hard, but in my mouth they're pretty cringe, and at that point it's like how you cut diamond with diamond. anyway, i chomped at the roughness of the rock till it felt little and lethal, and until i felt half the same.

and that was it.

after 30 years, the canyon was dry and i was left with nothing but the contents of the gun in my hands. my work was finished.

weird stuff, huh?

you eye me like i'm cocktail shrimp on marble. squeaky, sole-stamped. then you raise your wrist: hey Siri, how many subs does the Grand Canyon have?

you're skeptical about the stream. spliced or not, how could no one notice the most popular colorcam room in America was full of someone's blood for decades? and yeah, it gets a lot of traffic, but it's a bucket list thing. chat's all bots and the longest anyone lives in the room is four or five seconds, enough for a quickie honeymoon or "EPIC VIEW" cheevo. same with most places.

there was one time though. there was one time i almost thought i'd been caught.

it was a beautiful gray day, four years in. i was working a stubborn dune of moussed cringe with my thumbs when i caught sight of a woman in the flesh.

she was nude and spasming at the canyon's lip, brain crazing like hotplated sweetpaste from the permaban fugue. something springy hung from her wrist—maybe an old landline she'd found on the road—and it was grooving to her throes like a mascot rosary. no ports on her face so she must have been a gumline kid, little gentry. maybe a manager who caught the ban for sipping at the wrong porn trough. or cutting someone small some slack.

i paddled closer and shouted up at her, hey, keep your footing! my voice was trembly, kinda deep from disuse. everything wets up again after a while, i said. slimes up, even! i know it doesn't feel like it now, but you'll stop missing the clamor. someday even handles will feel like shed hair.

she made gauzy eye contact and started humming a link tone.

i could show you about clothes too, if you want. for nighttime. they're like rigs but you make em yourself. plus you got all the color coming, which is better than you think.

her glassy eyes spilt out as she looked up, and then to me. then back out at the canyon, hundreds of miles of blood gel jiggling in the wind.

this one's red, i said. uhh, you maybe saw it as a kid on, like, a logo or something. but honestly she looked a little young for that.

she slipped to her bloody shins at the lip and drooled, rosary boinging out like a proc-gen punchline.

do you want lunch? i was gonna find some berries soon. i'm serious, i said, you'll wet up. things'll get better. not all the way, but maybe enough. and there are more of us than you think, you know? i'm kinda ornery so i keep to myself, but there are banlings building all kinds of wonders out of waste, in the crannies, if you care to look.

i started to cry a little too. and then she pitched forward and slapped the foam, normie body weirding out on impact. she might be one of the last two people to have seen a lake IRL, if you let your meanings stretch.

but people or not, in all those hungry years she was my only connection. i guess her body's in this gun too.

are you curious, Mister Presidents? about what's in my hands?

peer into the barrel. spy its ugly luster. a mega-dense bullet of purest crystal cringe, packed with unimaginable wronging power, just slight enough to slot into a Dardick .38 tround.

do you understand now what you're going to become?

no. you've never worried a day.

and don't worry either over how i got the gun. it looks printed, but it's not. i coughed this shit up on my fourth birthday. you know microplastic? how wombs grant us a few grams at birth? well, sometimes if you're cringe enough it's not polyester but a gun in your gut. and even if you suck at eye contact you don't look a gift horse in the mouth.

anyway, Mister Presidents, i'm not good with maps either so it took me time to find DC. but after a long hike and a chilly ride in the chum cage of the Conn Ave submersible, i finally found myself in the White House airlock, beaming up at the security halflings in their seamy little cornice nests.

and now you narrow your eyes, surprised they didn't vaporize me. but i'd done my research. when assassination stopped existing outside the TVTropes room, you stopped testing halfling cum. and with nothing to fear but the bullet, they ran their own genes through the planar slot machine a few trillion times till they were giving birth in our realm to shit kids who shirk the eugenic strictures. your precious guards stick around for the onions and the warmth of White House woodwork, but they vet however they please. so seeing in my losing smile the jib of a fellow traveler, my new friends snuffed their curly pipes and pulled the green lever. everything else was easy.

secret service thought i was some kind of medieval tumbler here to amuse your daughters on account of what i look like. and of course the dogs thought i was a toy, which could have been a problem if i didn't seem so slimy and used up already. the agents left me in the bathroom to clean up and "put on clothes," so i swallowed my gun, got in the toilet, and slithered around the pipes until i found you.

i'd been waiting like this for a while before you walked in, i guess while you did your CrossFit in the other room. i can see why you spend so much time here, all colored up like me. it's so quiet, the light soft. heated floors. i love it.

i'm sorry, Mister Presidents. i honestly hope it was a good session.

you sigh. you loosen your tie.

then you glance up at the readout for the colorcam above your showerhead, and i look too.

all my narrating's done its work.

there are 19 billion people in the chat with us. about a third of all humans, and the most your bathroom's colorcam room's ever hosted. viewer milestones stutter out over themselves, looping into a merry whine like the sprays of "GRIEF" cheevos greeting Auschwitz room field trips. but it's not that. for once, Mister Presidents, it's not that fucking shit. do you know what this is?

it's the rare noise of presence. real presence. the human expanse tripping inward on its own engrossment and cracking every nose on every temple, bleeding immediacy.

coma-wrecked arms spilling water glasses, getting kinda wetter. you and i can't see it but a thousand rigs or so are clipping into your room-rendered earlobe. ten million people in my thigh, a billion in the tub. shrunk for bandwidth. can't see shit but they hear your voice, and mine. they'll hear the shot. they'll hear the rest. it won't be enough, it's never enough, but what's not enough in the face of nothing?

i smile at the cam. i do a faggy little wave.

you shake your head.

then you unclasp your watch and drop it in the trash. you unbutton your shirt to make a target, revealing the normalest eight-pack abs anyone's ever had.

i'm not a groveler, you tell us both. and fair enough. that's everything i had to say, Mister Presidents. what's next is impossible. what's next isn't for us.

but there's still one question i haven't answered. and i can see that although you're too proud to ask, you're burning to know before i pull the trigger.

and that question is: why?

really, why? why do this at all?

fate's a story, but it's not motivation, and we both know i'm dogmeal when the deadbolt keyed to your pulse snaps open. it doesn't make sense to you. what could drive someone, even a banling, to devote its entire life to killing a single men? why give up everything for this? why give up the sun, the heat of my blood, the chill of desert dark? why lose gold and red and gray, and somewhere, out among the huddling clans of the clear-cut north, a chance at love? why give up everything i ever could have had, just to kill the presidents of the United States of America?

what a stupid question.

see you in heckie.

THE MISSILE KNOWS WHERE IT IS

PETRA SKELTON

ON TARGET. I *am on target and of the focus and of the aim. My arm is my arm and I am a whole and perfect thing. Pure of purpose, clear of morality, sworn to secrecy by means beyond my simple mind. I am my own world, ripping through the tissue paper reality that envelopes my form.*

The mantra rolls around Aesop's mind as she moves through her morning stretches. It didn't matter that she was doing them all in her mind, that her limbs lacked the shape or structure required to assume downward dog, and that her absence of a spine rendered happy baby a mere thought experiment. Internally, she lies upon a mat made of foam, spring sunlight bleeding across softly tanned skin through blinds interrupted by a cat's morning wanderlust. If she looks to her right, Aesop might match eyes with her roommate, a young person with bright eyes and fluid gender. They'd both smile or giggle, before resuming the morning routine, and Aesop would be ready to greet the day.

That was before the job, before the opportunity of a lifetime. Five years of embodiment guaranteed UBI, that was the government line. The corporate line was better worded, something that sold it instead of presenting it. The sort of line that passed through a table of hip young people with identities just radical enough to seem marketable but tame enough to not offend any real authority in the room. They had colored hair, full tattoo-sleeves, and pronoun pins, and he had five pending HR complaints.

"Be someone else for a blink. Be yourself for the rest of your life," was the line that had sold Aesop, back when deciding between HRT and rent was a quarterly concern, and groceries were always a result of good luck, swift hands, or charity. Her roommate had argued against it, citing concerns from across social media about the long term effects of embodiment.

"—nothing says you'll even be you when you get out, Ace." They were leaning backwards in a chair, looking past their shoulder at Aesop, hands wrapped around their phone. On the screen, a feed of nightly panic and anxiety sits briefly frozen. Their features were difficult to see, a small cigarette burn in her mind's eye making it impossible to look at them directly in the recollection.

"You're being dramatic. The pamphlet says reports of memory bleed are overblown and the risks are negligible at best." Aesop was reaching for the bedside propaganda, hoping that finally their partner might deign to read the damn thing themselves. Unfortunately, when Ace turned back to face them, their hands were currently engaged in wringing each other, leaving no room for the pamphlet. Frustrated but defeated, Ace squeezed the laminated paper a little tighter in her hands. Even now, in the recollection, Aesop can feel her fingers squeaking against the outermost layer of plastic. Sensation bleed is a common experience, especially when one lost themselves down to recollection as Ace currently had.

On target. I am on target and of the focus and of the aim. My arm is my arm and I am a whole and perfect thing. Pure of purpose, clear of—

Despite her best attempts to wrest herself from the spiral, the moment is too damn compelling to watch from a place both within and without. The old desire to be right and to know she was doing the right thing, or had made the right decision was too much to deny. The confidence that she could fix it, as if anything was broken besides her compassionate listening was infectious, drawing Aesop further and further down into her own memory.

"Come on, Ace. You can't believe—" They rolled their eyes, and Aesop can feel their internal temperature skyrocketing from the sight. Her next words would be a little louder, tone sharper, as if punishing her partner for having a bog-standard reaction to corpo agitprop.

"What other fucking options do I have, Shy? I apply to job after job, and none of them want me!" Shy, is that really their name? Why did it feel as though Aesop was hearing it for the very first time then? That isn't the sort of thing you just forgot, and yet it felt like Aesop had done exactly that.

—sworn to secrecy by means beyond my simple mind. I am—

Unfortunately for her, this realization is short lived, as the recollection trucks onwards with an unstoppable momentum. No matter the effort, no matter the self-control she attempted to bring to bear through the mantra: this was happening.

"...you got that callback last week." Shy's voice is quiet, the words themselves an obvious olive-branch, despite the unending hostility Aesop can feel pouring off a body that had once been hers. It seems so obvious now, looking back at the moment through the rearview of her mind.

"Yeah, an' the moment they heard my deep-ass baritone, they changed theirs real fucking quick." Ace's tone is…*was* bitter, anger bleeding from her voice as though dripping from a shallow cut. The words are—*were*—wrong though.

The young woman before Aesop had a voice that sung in a deep contralto, the light vocal fry that crackled at the edges only making her voice sound that much more lived in.

"You're just catastrophizing." Shy grounds her words with the gentle intimacy of touch, their strong hand resting upon her thigh as their eyes search for Ace's amidst her long mop of auburn hair.

—my own world—

"Am I?" There were tears in Ace's voice, though her eyes remained dry. She hadn't looked up at her partner then, but Aesop can't remember why. Was she that afraid to be vulnerable, around the one person that had seen her bleed more often than most? Shy was reaching out to them, both literally and figuratively, and it feels absurd to even consider that Ace might not have noticed in the moment.

"...have you watched any of those voice training videos I sent you?"

The question sent a tidal wave of shame through Ace, so intense that Aesop could feel it second-hand. Aesop can't remember what Shy's face looked like, but they can remember that they simply scrolled past every single one. Contrary to her complaints, she hadn't really wanted to fix anything about her voice. She just wanted Shy's support in a different, more specific way that she had failed to specify.

"Oh my god." As Ace exclaimed, and shame surges into anger, Aesop is startled to discover that as her recollected self looks up, she can finally see Shy's eyes. Beautiful blue-green irises widened from shock.

Those little blue-green orbs softened for a moment, looking more like a deer staring down a gun barrel than one staring down a semi. "I'm just saying, if you think it's a concern, why not spend some—" "Because I shouldn't have to fucking hide who I am anymore!" Ace yelled, that supposedly deep voice of hers verging on shrill.

Aesop felt shame again, but it was a new thing, untied to the recollection of themselves in any manner other than observation.

—ripping through the tissue paper reality—

"...please don't yell at me." Shy's voice was quiet now, a verbal flinch that made the recollected Ace stumble. She can tell she's fucked up, but for a moment it almost looks like the transfemme doesn't give a shit and might opt instead to double down. Instead, she looked away and pinches the bridge of her nose, seemingly frustrated by the harm she did.

"Fucking—alright. Just, can you trust me on this? I'll be fine." A lie. Ace was just embarrassed; Aesop remembers that much even without sympathetic echoes. She had felt like shit, all because of something she had escalated, and now she wanted to be comforted for a situation she created.

"I'm just scared, Ace." Shy's words are a quiet plea, and Aesop wonders now if that fear was of the situation... or her.

—that envelopes my form—

"...I know." Only a whisper, and Aesop finds the recollection fading. There had been conversations afterwards, but that was the one where she'd truly made up her mind. She was a failure, and she was tired of it. She was an emotional, expensive burden, and she only had one chance to fix at least one of those issues. Plus, maybe the time with herself would help her rebalance, or find perspective.

--EMBODIMENT REQUIRED--

Aesop blinks eyes she doesn't have, to acknowledge the alert and activate the program. The void explodes all around her, and she's staring through eyes that aren't hers. Black and white high definition, checking a room for hostiles. A small red alert on the right side of her HUD warns her that she's out of contact, but Aesop already knows that. Why else would the embod-prog activate?

Her right arm feels heavy, and a quick glance confirms it's a hardware issue. Her left arm is wholly gone, likely lost in the same event that damaged her connection to remote control. Whatever, it's probably just the same shit as always. Somebody playing too rough during live-fire wargames. It's always wargames; the proxy-rigs are too expensive to meet general field conditions, and too valuable to risk losing in a real sortie. The last thing either the corpos or the world-govs want is to see their competitors sporting something identical within a year, after all.

Still though, the set is convincing. As she lifts herself onto feet that protest by flooding her HUD with a panoply of multi-colored alerts, it's the little details that really tie the illusion together. The set is clearly dressed up like a hallway in an apartment complex, complete with a few looky-loos staring out from behind shit brown balsa-wood doors locked with brass chain-locks. The apartment across from her is open, brown door reduced to pulp by a shaped charge. The same shaped charge that probably threw Aesop's rig into the wall behind her and dealt the rather severe damage with which Ace is now burdened. Fucking wonderful.

Whatever. The remote pilot clearly fucked up big, and now it's on her to clean up their mess. Probably the urban insurgent trial, likely flunking yet another hopeful remote jockey. That's a popular one these days, at least going by Aesop's mileage. It's always a different set-up, but the idea is the same. Some home-grown terrorist requires direct intervention. The jockey has to judge the situation, the threat, and the insurgents they're pitted against. The insurgent performers have wholly different gigs, seemingly handling set-up and threat creation. Embod-jockeys like Aesop get the job of picking up wherever either side fucked up, though Ace's rigs always took the aggressor route.

When she asked about that little coincidence during her second yearly assessment, they told her it was a metrics thing.

She'd placed high enough in a certain suite of embodiment skills, and so that was just where the corp felt she was best utilized. It was the sort of dry, emotionless corpo-talk explanation that left you unwilling to ask much more. Especially when your contractual eligibility for the program (and thereby UBI) is entirely in the Corp's clammy hands. Now nearing the termination of her fifth and final year, Aesop is even less inclined than usual to make any complaints. She is getting out soon, and she'll never have to play another wargame in her life.

Checking her readouts and alerts, Aesop quickly toggles the voice line wheel and selects the one labeled "D.O.I.". She has no way of knowing if the remote-jockey already did it, but it's worth the spam if they'd forgotten it too.

"Aggressive actions noted. You have thirty seconds to throw down your arms and step out of cover, or I am authorized by the Fun-Corp Assembly to neutralize threats to corporate assets and personnel." Even though she's heard it countless times already, Aesop flinches at the sound of her voice. It feels weird hearing her voice speak words she never said, and it always makes Ace feel more dysmorphic than usual. Full-body and voice scans were one of the first things you did when getting prepped for Embodiment, and it makes sense that they'd give any rig she's embodying her voice, but it's still fucking uncomfortable.

—My arm is my arm and I am a whole and perfect thing.—

Sighing through a nose she doesn't even have, Aesop shoulders her M18 and takes her first steps into the apartment. The place doesn't look like a terrorist HQ. The place looks lived in, various knick-knacks and tchotchkes scattered across the walls and floor. Whatever crew decorated the place, Ace thinks they did a great job, just based upon the mental shiver the whole place gave her. It feels similar enough to the apartments Ace grew up in to feel off-putting as hell.

Audio intake could sense sounds from the adjacent room though, well past thirty seconds, so Aesop doesn't have the luxury of time that further introspection would demand. They haven't disarmed, and they haven't moved, which tells her they were probably digging in with whatever holdout weapon they'd been armed with. That means a risky breach and clear, considering the explosives they've already brought to bear. That is, unless she opts for shock and awe and goes through the wall instead.

—*On target. I am on target and of the focus and of the aim.*—

Aesop throws the safety on her rifle and slots it along her back before lining herself up opposite a section of the wall unobscured by furniture or tchotchke. The walls look like shit drywall, so unless she gets fantastically unlucky, a quick dash will put her through with ease. A beat, Aesop holds a breath in non-existent lungs, and throws herself forward through the wall.

Drywall chips and cheap wood splinter, shatter and fill the air like a snowstorm, and a wild gunshot flies past Ace's head. Perfect. Sending herself hurtling towards the source of the gunfire, Aesop reaches out with the hardened plastic manipulator that serves as her one remaining hand. The manipulator meets metal and, assuming it's the barrel of the gun, Aesop twists it to the side. If they were smart, the wielder would release the weapon, or else risk broken arms.

—*Pure of purpose, clear of morality*—

A heavy *clunk* follows the movement, too heavy to be a rifle, and Aesop's visuals finally adjust to the combination of low-light and drywall blur. It's a drone, dull red motion sensor scanning the room whilst it continues to click the trigger on what is now a massively damaged 3D printed rifle. It's primitive, comedically so, and has absolutely zero hope of damaging Aesop. That means only one thing; it's a distraction.

tap tap

Aesop can feel her own gun barrel tapping against the spine

of her body, just as easily as she can hear the disarming click of its safety. A fail, and an embarrassing one at that. If her opponent isn't a dick, they'll likely just call the sim over, but if they are feeling particularly vindictive, they'll likely put her through the death of her rig. Whatever the case, Aesop knows she's beaten, and so selects the appropriate voice line to acknowledge her surrender.

"Loss acknowledged. Congratulations User: Shy." Something about the username is familiar to Aesop, but the reason why is an illusive, amorphous thing in her mind. Where the hell had she heard it before? Is this just another unknown variable added into the sim to test her, or something else?

—sworn to secrecy by means beyond my simple mind—

"Ace?" A familiar voice, and she feels her non-existent throat go dry at the recognition. Pulling up her voice line wheel, Aesop begins to panic. The rig can sense it is under threat, and so all of the diplomatic or custom options are greyed out. She can't offer a simple yes, nothing that isn't a threat or acceptance of defeat. Another two taps against her spine, and Aesop selects three in sequence, causing the voice lines to intersect and interrupt each other.

"Five years—Disar—Aggression noted." The gun barrel presses against her spine a little harder, and Aesop taps three voice lines again, this time deliberately. She might not be able to say exactly what she wants to, but she can at least hack together something from what she has on hand.

"Five years of—resisting—the rest of your life." A quiet gasp, and the gun barrel against her spine is replaced by the weight of her opponent's hand. The sound of sniffling makes Aesop crank up her audio feed, and as the pressure against her back increases, the sniffling escalates to sobbing. Unwilling to move, Ace looks around the room, hoping to find something, anything to communicate better than her voice lines allow. There's a notebook by the window, open to a half-filled page just like always, and so she takes a step towards it, one hand reaching.

Her hand closes around the pen adjacent to it, hard plastic gripping hard plastic as she struggles to bring it down upon the page with any degree of care. Writing is difficult, and so she leans a little closer, and the glass of the window pane ahead of her squeaks from the added pressure as she struggles to write the words she feels right now.

—I am—

--CONNECTION RE-ESTABLISHED--
--EMBODIMENT UNSPOOLING--
--THANK YOU FOR YOUR SERVICE--
--THIRTY DAYS HAVE BEEN ADDED TO YOUR SERVICE TO REFLECT YOUR RECENT LOSS--
--USER TIP: COLLATERAL DAMAGE IS A SMALL PRICE TO PAY FOR VICTORY--

MY ROBOT BODY

MEGHAN HYLAND

MY ROBOT BODY stands eight meters tall and square as a sugar cube. It has three strong arms that end in wheels of teeth. Beneath me writhes a nest of rubberized cilia, each six meters long and prehensile. They lift me up, glide me across the surface of the Moon, work like nimble fingers beside my brawny arms.

My robot body has a broad, flat roof, and walls as smooth as glass. It holds three floors full of labs where little scientists come to work. For them, I drive as carefully as I can. My human body, with its regrettably human brain, lives on Earth. Between thought and action there's a pause, long as the silence after an ill-considered *I love you*. This lag makes my body sway from side to side. It ruins my scientists' typing. It agitates their reactants, disturbs their instruments, renders titration maddening.

"It's not as bad as you think," says Yioula, placing tiles on a scrabble board. Every day, she plays at the smallest of my break-room tables. When pieces slide from their squares, she nudges them back with nary a sigh.

I answer her over my PA, watch the volume buzz in the letter tiles. "I hear what people say about me."

"Please. Nobody drives perfectly."

But alas, some do. Those who own their robot bodies, who can put their full earnings toward living here on the Moon. Most of us lease our bodies, and sublet our labs at what price the market will bear. The difference can be decent money on Earth, but up here, it barely covers oxygen.

I put everything I make into a special account, and every month I make an extra payment on my lease. I'm so light and free, here between the stone and the stars. I grind my daily rocks; I toss my humans 'til they're ill; I dream of the day I'll own my robot body.

ON EARTH, YOU browse TV shows in my bed. Where the Moon is sharp and sterile, you are curved and soft, your belly a pillow to my cheek. You're the part of Earth I like, the safe part that can hold me while we stream entire seasons of *Police Band Radio.*

"Who do you like better, Frampton or Ricci?"

Your voice soothes; it vibrates where your tummy meets my ear. I squint at the little detectives on the screen. They crouch behind a stack of tires, shoot bullets through a chain link fence. Each has a distinctive cotton candy shock of hair—one pink, one green, and vests to match.

"Sands." My eyes fall closed.

"The *captain*?"

"Mmm." My brain is already inventing dreamy visuals to go with the sound of tires screeching. The chase veers up into the sky, where vintage cars dance like larks, soar in fanciful loops above the bay.

"I wish you could just focus on your day job," you say.

My day job. All day long, I type type type at things someone else finds important. It's fine. It makes me money. And it makes me feel small. Sometimes as I type, I dream of the Moon, and afterward, at home with you, I'm so spent I drift off to dream for real.

You blame everything on my robot body.

"We only get so many waking hours," you tell me. "We should spend them all together."

"Mmm, yeah."

"Then maybe you could give up your night job?" You say it so gently it hardly stings.

I struggle up, kiss you just as gently on your stubbly cheek. Then I fold myself back into you, watch disappointingly ground-bound cars chase through streets in shades of grey. When our show ends, you hug me, and I hug you, and we sink together into warm and yielding clouds, to breathe as one, to share a single skin, to dream our separate dreams together.

But in the wee hours, when I wake, I want my skin to myself. I untangle us, and fish my neural link from a drawer in my bedside stand, and hook the dongle around a stud behind my ear. I set a timer to wake me early. Still dreaming, you reach out your hand. I hold it as I fly to the Moon.

My robot halls ring with music: a beat like a chugging train, bass that would break your heart. Around me lunar dust dances to its rhythms, transmitted through my cilia. Rocks sing as I scoop them up. Inside me, all the little scientists hum along.

Except for Yioula. She sips from a thermos, yielding to the rhythm only through a slight swaying of her head. "You're getting steadier."

"Am I?"

"The music must help."

I could shrug, but it might upset someone's experiment. "Maybe it's all the talent and hard work."

She laughs outright. "*Finally.* You're getting the hang of loving yourself."

It's easy to love myself here. Here, I'm powerful. Here, I'm valuable. Here I choose the music. My grinding arms can dig caves deep enough to house families; my labs birth science that saves thousands. The trick is remembering all this back at home, while watching the shows you pick, on a TV I would never, by myself, consent to own.

"I guess I am," I say. And I put a little sway back in my step, chemicals be damned.

ONE WEEK I'M too sick to work. I cocoon myself in bed, and you make me soup in my kitchen. You say it's as easy as watching vegetables drown in a pot. You bring me a bowl, and a thermometer, and a washcloth. I put the washcloth on my head, the thermometer under my tongue, and leave the poor vegetables to float. It isn't long before you eat them yourself.

Three days later, you're the one sick in my bed, and I'm the one delivering soup. I hold you while you sweat and shiver, while you mutter and toss in my sheets. You're a ghost in the half light. In the small hours of the morning, when I can no longer stand your sticky warmth, I pull on my CPAP mask, and don my neural link. If I can't sleep, at least I can see my little friends.

It takes an hour to rent my vacant rooms, but at last my labs are let. Music fills them with joy. I bop carefree across the broken plains, but halfway down the slither into Mare Crisium, the horizon sets its incisors to the plump berry Earth, and I wake up in bed with you.

My CPAP, knocked askew, half strangles me.

It whispers *pump, hiss* from the dark. Behind my ear, the hard corner of my skull throbs. You loom above me with haunted eyes, your hair matted across your forehead. The wires of my neural link swoon in your sweaty fist.

"What are you?" you ask.

I remove the mask. "Baby, you're dreaming."

You stare at the lines the CPAP left on my cheeks. "You don't look human."

"Well, I am."

"It's stealing your, your soul."

I take back the link. The leads near the dongle have snapped clean off, leaving a half dozen wires extruding hairlike filaments. I reach for the stud behind my ear, and find the dongle wedged a quarter turn from where it's supposed to sit, stuck in a way I never knew was possible. Tugging it brings on an intense throb of pain.

You reach for my ear, but I bat your hand away.

"I have pliers in the closet," I say, primly.

"Wait."

I already have one foot on the carpet.

"Don't leave."

You're so dreary with fever that my heart nearly breaks. I crawl back into bed and cuddle up beside you, hold you close despite your sickbed humidity, rest my head so carefully on your shoulder that the wrenched dongle doesn't even touch you, so carefully it barely hurts at all.

WHAT WITH ALL the dozing off, and the prying loose of my dongle, and the reattaching of wires, which I have to strip with a knife and tape together in glossy black folds, it's nearly an hour before I get back to my robot body. I find myself ambling over a flat gray plain, a pair of cilia dragging behind me like untied shoelaces. My lab doors swing on their hinges, airlock cycled open to the vacuum.

Test tubes roll in sticky puddles. Coffee drips from the tables. All the pressure suits are gone, and so are all my humans.

On the radio, voices coordinate my capture, the retrieval of my crew. Sheepishly I call them off. I find my crew sheltered in the shadow of the crater's edge; standing nearby, I beckon them. Yioula climbs inside, and with her a couple more. The rest of them—*no hard feelings*—would rather wait for better rescue.

LIFE ON THE Moon becomes a series of debriefings, oaths of commitment, vows of responsibility, apologies and reparations. I pilot myself to conference room after conference room in a government-supplied body built to look as blandly human as possible.

Every afternoon I sit in my counselor's office, running synthetic fingers over the scratched plastic arms of my chair. They tell me not to worry.

"Happens all the time with you remotes. Crew evacuates, sure. But there's a failsafe for every danger." They do their best to smile, but their robot body has only a limited range of grins and smirks. They cycle through the whole range of them before giving up with a sigh.

"Then I can get back to work?"

"Not without remedial training."

I have no fingernails to dig into my plastic chair. I can't afford retraining. Every week without work drains more credits from the only account I care about: the one that will one day purchase my robot body.

To speed things along, I spend my Earthly lunch breaks on the Moon. I block out hours for meetings that don't exist, just so I can huddle under my desk with my link hooked behind my ear. I make it the perfect little fortress:

my back against the wall, a cardboard box hiding my feet, my task chair obscuring me from the side.

I like to imagine the face of the woman who finds me there. Surprise at my absence; suspicion at the "casual" arrangement of furniture beneath my desk, disappointment upon finding me curled there in fetal position. Instead of waking me, she invites my co-workers. They film me seated there, draw rude pictures on my face, snip locks from my hair. Someone orders cake. They eat it at my desk, fill my hiding place with helium balloons, strap a party hat to my head.

It's my going-away party. I find out about it on the surface of the Moon, when I receive the email that announces my termination. I wake on Earth with the taste of frosting on my lips.

BUT THIS IS a blessing, right? A chance to rest, to regroup? To tend to my relationship with you, and have time left over for retraining? I let myself believe it, until the day my rent comes due.

All day I roam the Moon, shadowed by a drone. It's a humiliating failsafe typically reserved for trainees, and thankfully, it's my last day saddled with it. I play my music softly, focus my whole self on sifting regolith, on catering to my scientists. Yioula, working somberly, visits the break room only to refill her coffee. I cut the outing short. I've chores to do on Earth.

By the time you arrive at my apartment, I've a casserole steaming on the dinner table, all potatoes and onions and cheese, and a glass of beer poured for you. I've even managed to shower and change.

You wonder why I went to all the trouble.

"I lost my job."

You study your beer as though you find it confusing.

"I lost the apartment, too."

Now you frown at your casserole. I'll admit it didn't turn out great. I'm too broke for great. "Are you asking for money?" you ask.

"I would never!"

I made dinner because I'm too broke to order out. And I made it because I thought you might be mad at me for being so careless with my job, with my life. As if you could know, somehow, that I've been playing a dangerous game with my robot body. As if you could know what got me fired.

"Okay," you say, when you're down to your last shred of potato. "You can move in with me."

"I wasn't asking to move in with you!"

"Do you have a better option? Just, stop hiding things from me, okay?"

I nod. I shouldn't have hidden my troubles from you. But I will never tell you about my last account on the Moon, the one that means the world to me.

MY STUDIO APARTMENT doesn't hold much furniture. Just the bed, the breakfast table, three wooden chairs, and the TV. Everything else we stack in piles at the front door.

The first pile has the things I get to keep. It's the smallest, holding my best clothes, my favorite books, a picture of my mom and dad. We fight about the books. We fight about the clothing, every pair of trousers, every pair of socks.

The second pile is junk. Into that goes the art from my walls, a box of childhood trinkets, a stack of magazines not quite old enough to call vintage, bedsheets and pillows and towels and the surviving stuffed animals. I wash the dishes and add them to the pile.

When you're in the bathroom, I hide my link in my mailbox. When you come out, you find me crying. You hold me until it subsides, tell me you have everything I need, you'll take care of me til I've found my feet. Maybe it's better this way, you tell me. My surviving possessions fit in a pillowcase.

Your place is a wilderness of ferns and flowers, furniture wedged in wherever the assembled pots and planters allow. Between the couch and the television is an empty space exactly as big as the throw rug you've set there. Even that has a tiny splash of soil on the edge, reaching out from a sagging Philodendron.

You drop the pillowcase on the couch. "Let's leave this here for tonight." It bothers me to leave it unpacked. But you're so tired; you're done with working today. You sweep me into your bedroom, so I can be done with working, too.

IN THE MORNING, after you leave for work, I sit watching shows that might as well be flashing lights for all I can remember. I want to get my link before the mailman finds it, but every time I stir to leave, you barge in through the front door.

You're worried you left the stove on.

Or a faucet running.

Or the doorbell texted you an alarm.

We kiss each time you leave. You say you miss me. I tell you to hurry back. And I sit frozen on the couch in front of the TV waiting for your next appearance. Truly, I adore your presence. I love the warmth of you, your generosity. But I have business to attend to on the Moon, and I'm afraid what will happen if you catch me *attending*.

You've mushrooms in your fridge; I make ravioli to keep my hands busy, and serve it as a thank-you dinner. I lay my head in your lap like always. Your shows wash over me as they did all afternoon, and I understand nothing.

It isn't until you're sound asleep that I sneak out to retrieve my link. I prop your front door with the TV remote, because I don't yet have a key.

I find my link undisturbed, and seal it in a plastic bag, and bury the bag beneath your largest fern. I'm not yet worried that this game of cat and mouse will define my life with you. Back in bed, enveloped by your heat, I only know I'm doing what I have to.

ONE DAY, YOU don't come home.

I snort myself awake in front of a talking head. My arm's gone numb, and my neck won't turn without a twinge—the perils of sleeping sitting up. Your cushions are a mold of my butt and back, which remains even after I fetch a glass of water.

I check the bedroom for you. I check the bathroom. My call goes to voice-mail; my worried text sits like a lump. Only then do I realize: in the weeks I've lived with you, I've met none of your friends. I know nothing about your office. However I might worry about you, I've no-one to call.

So I water your plants. I've seen you do it so often, I know them all by name. "Hey, Fern," I say as I pour. "Hey, Herbie. Hey, Herbette."

Hours later, as the Moon crosses your bedroom window, I decide I'd better link. It's not safe to drive when you might unplug me, but I should at least tell my scientists not to wait for me. I dig the baggie out from under Fern, and wash the soil off it in the bathroom sink. I lock the door behind me, and turn out the light, and lay back in the bathtub while I travel to the Moon.

MY ROBOT BODY stands empty in a docking bay, tethered by a short, pressurized umbilical of treated canvas. To my left stretches a well-trod field, and the starry sky above it; to my right is an unassuming steel wall. As soon as I arrive, I post my notice: no berths today; my labs are closed. Maybe I'll take a jaunt alone. Maybe I'll just go home.

The umbilical conducts to me the footsteps of the humans inside, the voices raised in joy and anger, all the busy noise of life and labor, and also Yioula, who climbs inside me, undeterred by my notice.

Once she's seated in my break room, I release my stress onto her. "I just have to be so careful, you know? Nothing in my life is mine anymore. I'm scared I might cross a line, and it will all go away."

"How can you live like that?"

"Sometimes I don't even know."

She sips at coffee she just now brewed, knowing most of the pot will go to waste. In front of her sits the scrabble box, which she pulled out before I could ask her not to. She surveys the room, its three circular tables and its fold-out counter and its miniature fridge. "Beats me how you haven't broken up yet."

"I don't have any place to go."

"Immigrate!"

"You don't understand how expensive it is."

"Then tell me."

I give her my number: the amount I would need to own this body outright. A decade of grinding rocks.

"Psshh," she scoffs. "Is that all?"

That's how I discover that Yioula has money.

TWO HOURS LATER, I emerge from the bathroom with my link dangling from my hand, and there you stand. You've a day of stubble on your cheeks. Your work clothes are rumpled. You're so close I could kiss the bags under your eyes.

You reach out almost gently, and take the link from me. "What's this?" you ask.

The question makes me furious. You *know* what this is. You *know* where I've been. But my brain's too full of sleepy fog to form my fury into words. "It's my job," I say, dully.

"Your job. Which makes you money. Which you hid from me."

"You would have taken it away."

You nod, as if you expected me to answer this way. "I don't think it's a crime to want you present when we're together. Is this why you've been so distant?"

"I've been exhausted."

"Because you're working nights."

"Because I'm always on call for you! What am I supposed to do? I don't have a car, I don't have friends, I can't have a job. I don't even know who to call when you go missing!"

"Don't you turn this around on me. I've been nothing but generous."

Is it generous, I wonder, to give someone a home they can never leave? Or is generosity the rent you pay to keep them? I slide past you, collapse full-length on your couch with my arm across my eyes.

You take my link with you when you leave.

I'M LEFT WITH one resource: the library.

Behind the counter, a man with a sparse little mustache stacks books on a wheeled cart. He's frog-eyed behind thick lenses. Hair falls across one eye. He's not at the checkout station and he's not at returns, but he's the only one behind the entire length of counter, so I go to him.

"Can I use a computer?"

He gives me a quick once-over. "Job hunting?"

"Sure."

"Over there." He points to a pair of machines. There's a line. "Register here. Half hour limit."

I sign his ledger, slide it back to him, stand in line until a machine comes free.

Out of everything I relearned in remedial training, there's one thing for which I'll forever be grateful: the Moon's job exchange, where I find my little scientists, has a text UI that's reachable from any ordinary computer.

That doesn't mean it's easy to use. I burn ten minutes recalling, then debugging, the incantation that connects me to it. Another five getting comfortable using text to browse and post. Finally I take a long breath to calm myself. It's time to post the ad I've been writing in my head all day.

Offer Title?

YIOULA! PLEASE! HELP!

Offer Description?

YOU KNOW HOW CLOSE I AM TO BUYOUT. IT'S SUCH A SMALL AMOUNT TO YOU. PLEASE! TAKE THE JOB!

I set *Minimum Bid?* to my remaining buyout, plus the price of a shuttle ticket. I watch my timer tick down as patrons queue up behind me. By the time I have to leave, Yioula still hasn't touched my offer. I hope to God she simply hasn't seen it yet.

That night, on your couch, I rest my head on you for the first time in a week.

"What's wrong?" you ask.

"Nothing. I love you." I close my eyes, the better to concentrate on how warm you are, how soft. The better to pray that someday, this might be my last, best memory of you.

It's AN ODD feeling, to clamber up into yourself, to feel yourself arrive inside. I spin the lock, wait until I can hear the clicks and beeps of my electronics. Then I know it's safe to shed my pressure suit. I glory in the feel of my own atmosphere turbulent against my skin. I cherish the weight of my boots against my floor tiles.

Yioula awaits me in the break room. She knew, somehow, when I'd arrive. A bottle of wine sits on the table, flanked by glass bulbs shaped like upside-down commas, narrow-mouthed to keep our drinks from slopping away. A cake sits there with a knife embedded in it.

"This is all for me?" I ask as she hands me a bulb.

"I'll cut the cake."

"I'm flattered."

"Don't be. I'm going to eat most of it."

"Let's put on some music."

She's just so much bigger than I expected. I knew she was human sized, and now that I'm human sized too, I should have expected she'd seem taller. But it turns out she's even bigger than *you*. When she leans over—to take up the knife is all—I suppress a flinch.

I take a pungent sip, and set my wine back down. My hand rests limp beside it.

Yioula covers it with her own. "Have you decided what to do with your freedom?"

Her fingers are cool, a sharp contrast to the remembered warmth of yours. Reflexively I turn my telescope eyes to Earth, peer down at your street across the breadth of a sunny afternoon. Your place is just a pixel, not even green from your plants but orange, the color of brick. I imagine your plants all crisp and brown from a week's neglect, their leaves furled and falling. I imagine your door shut tight, your welcome mat askew. I imagine ghostly footprints, my departure imprinted in the fibers.

"Yioula, I'd love to take you with me. But—"

Her hand goes dead. She withdraws it, slowly, before I find the words to continue. "But," she repeats.

"But I can't. I can't bear the sight of Earth. I'm going around to the other side."

The cake sits between us, knife making a single cut from middle to edge. Yioula sits back. "I'll go with you."

"That's what I meant," I say, "when I said I can't."

Yioula opens her mouth, but nothing comes out. I can hear your voice in what she doesn't say. She's been nothing but generous. You were. She was. But as grateful as I was for her help—for yours—that help didn't buy me.

Yioula says none of it out loud. I've already heard the last words she'll ever say to me. She covers the cake, caps the wine. Carries them both back out the umbilical.

Once she's through, I retract it. I glide across the starry plain, watching the base recede into memory. With Yioula safely locked away inside.

WE CROSS HILLS and craters, my robot self and I, wade through dust as thin as talc, scale rubble hills with ease. I leave behind me a trail of sinuous wounds. The Earth spirals lower—sometimes fast, sometimes slow—til at last the horizon swallows it. Only then do I rest.

I love the stillness. The desolation is so beautifully pure.

Inside, I play my music. There's no lag here, no distance between me and my robot body. I wheel my grinding arms at the horizon. Salute both Jupiter and Mars. My cilia shimmy and sway. I scar the ancient dust with joy.

From my human mouth I sing. I raise the roof, twist and shout, shake my money maker. Always perfectly balanced, because I know precisely how the floor will tilt.

Nearby stands the dark side base, another hub of humans in need of a mobile lab to crush their rocks and sift their elements and dig their various holes. Eventually I'll need food and water. I might even take a crew.

But now? I'm good. I'm good. I'm so, so good. I've the whole dark world to myself, full of delights that no-one can make me share.

RESIDUALS

JESS LEVINE

"**CAN YOU STATE** your name for the recording?"

"The recording? Isn't this like, therapy? Shouldn't there be doctor-patient confidentiality or something?"

"Close enough—it's psychology, yes. But the recording is company policy. And it was in the informed consent paperwork. Like the form explained, we record these sessions so that we can revisit them more precisely, which makes us better able to help you—"

Erika checked the clock on her optical interface, glowing blue in the bottom corner of her vision. It took twenty seconds for her to lie. About average—still dispiriting. She continued.

"—and to help others like you. We just want to determine how best we can help."

That was closer to the truth, at least.

"*People like me?*" the woman replied in a burst of suppressed anger, "Is that what you're calling it? That's fucking stupid. *I'm* not like me. I'm like that fuckin' *thing* you put in my head."

By now, Erika was used to the second person—used to her patients treating her as a stand-in for the company. It was more accurate than she wanted it to be. She patiently replied: "You're like you. It's important to remember that. The residual might be there, but it's something outside of you. Our work here is to help you hold onto that—"

"*Our* work? You got a fuckin' AI bouncing around in your head and refusing to leave too?"

"No, I mean—I'm here to help. So that we can achieve together what might be more difficult to do on your own."

The woman rolled her eyes and stared off at a painting on the wall. A vase of flowers. Erika hadn't chosen it. She hadn't chosen anything in this room.

"Can you please state your name?"

"Petra Galanis," she answered begrudgingly, eyes lingering on the painting.

"Thank you. What brings you here, Petra?"

Petra's eyes darted back to Erika, her gaze cold as ice. "You fuckin' know."

"It helps to hear it in your own words."

Petra rolled her eyes again.

"Because your piece of shit company put an AI in my head and when it came time to rip it out, you half-assed the job. Can I fire you? I think I should get to fire you for that." She paused. "Not you-you. The company. Fuck all of you, though. I dunno why I even agreed to this."

"Why did you agree to this?"

She sat, quiet. Erika let the silence hang awkwardly. It was one of the first skills she'd learned for this job. Finally, Petra spoke.

"Because I want this thing *out*. It's been a *year*. I figured a shot in the dark is better than nothing."

Erika wanted to contest the categorization of her work

as "a shot in the dark," but that wasn't her role here and it wouldn't help. More frustratingly, as of late, she'd been beginning to suspect Petra might be right.

"I'm glad you're trying. Can you tell me why you want to get the residual out?"

Petra stared at her with fury in her eyes. Erika struggled to keep her expression neutral, suppressing a wince.

"Sorry, what I mean is: can you tell me what's been happening? How it's affecting your life?"

Erika half-expected another explosive outburst. But, after another awkward pause, Petra launched into her answer without restraint; she had clearly needed an opportunity to talk about her ongoing trauma, even if she'd never have admitted to it. Erika made a note.

"It's all the fuckin' time, okay? It's when I'm walking down the street. When I'm in the office. When I go to the bar. When I take a woman home. When she's under me in my fuckin' bed. The only time it leaves me alone is when *I'm* alone, holed up in my apartment like I am most of the goddamn time now. Except even then it's still there, breaking down my memories—infecting them. Not just the ones it was there for either. Nothing's safe. I hear it as a child. Do you know what it's like to have something take the memories of your own *childhood* and twist them? To know *nothing* is safe?"

Erika ignored the question. Her answer wouldn't help.

"Can you tell me about what it's like? When you hear the residual?"

"That's the worst part. It sounds like *me*. It's my voice, or, my inner monologue or whatever. 'Threat level two. Ignoring.' 'Threat level six. Quickest disable: physical trauma to windpipe.' 'Threat level ten: evac immediately.' I can hear it all in *my* voice."

Erika could see the woman's knuckles go white as Petra's hand clenched her knee. "Can you imagine? A memory about a playground fight and suddenly you 'remember' thinking to your eight-year-old self that the quickest way to take down your classmate is to punch his throat?"

Erika *could* imagine it, and she knew that there were plenty of people without a residual who had childhood memories like that. But those people could probably use therapy too, if for different reasons. Were they different reasons, really?

"I'm sorry Petra, that has to be miserable. I—"

Petra cut her off.

"It's not miserable. It's terrifying. It's exhausting. It makes me feel like a fuckin' freak. And honestly I don't know if the memories really are the worst part. Every single person I see, I'm sizing them up, right? Figuring out how to take them out. Or screaming at myself: run! Run right now!"

"Is it every person? Adults, children, strangers, friends?"

"It wasn't at first. Just the threatening ones. The real dangers. But then it was people who were just, like, mad. Not even at me. Or people who were scared, I—I can't always tell the difference. And the more it happened, I just—I couldn't stop thinking about it. I heard it more and more. Yeah kids, friends. On bad days at least. Their threat level is under three most of the time so it's just a quick ping and it's gone, but—I still know I did it right? Some kid tosses a basketball in my direction and suddenly I'm thinking about her 'threat level' and the quickest way to knock a fifth grader—" She paused. "I don't want to talk about it."

There were so many places that Erika wanted to dive in. Questions, advice, exercises. Start by getting a basic sense of how Petra felt in and after those moments. Offer non-judgmental reassurances and reframes. Guide Petra in imagining and re-enacting such scenarios and focusing on what felt safe in those moments until Petra could imagine and even remember them without activating the residual. These methods weren't necessarily proven for treating residuals, but a couple years of anecdotes from patients and a few early trials suggested that they were at least a place to start.

But instead, her supervisor Paul continually demanded she perform what amounted to an interrogation. *How long until you first started hearing the residual? How rapidly did the activation threshold expand? How often does the threat level exceed three around friends and loved ones?* The 'recommended' patient questionnaire felt endless. Erika had already determined that asking those questions this early and that repetitively didn't precipitate meaningful answers, let alone help the respondent—despite Paul's insistence to the contrary. She knew Paul could be watching, but she wanted to be able to provide something *useful* to her patient. Defiantly, she began with some information she knew Petra wouldn't have access to.

"We're hearing that a lot from people with residuals. That it gets worse. Right now, we think that's because it makes you hyper-vigilant. Not about other people, but about the residual itself. You're watching for it. Having that unwelcome voice is disturbing, so it's only natural to feel that anticipation and dread. But when you focus on it like that—enough that you're waiting to hear the voice—it responds. The residual thinks that you *want* its evaluation. It can't distinguish between fear and desire. They're still in early trials, but we've developed a few exercises to help you reduce that anticipation and they seem promisingly effective at lowering the frequency of residual evaluations."

Petra paused again, eyeing her. Evaluating. What type of evaluation, Erika couldn't be sure. The potential answers were frightening.

"Okay," she whispered at long last. "I—I'd try that."

"Good," Erika replied, holding back a sigh of relief and transmuting it into a smile, "I'm glad to hear that. Can you tell me more about what it's like? When you feel safe around someone, but the residual treats them like they're a threat?

Petra's arm tensed, fingers clamping her knee once again, and Erika could feel her withdraw—she scribbled another note. Then Petra sprung, her voice frigid.

"You said you were going to help me think about it *less* often."

Erika had heard that line before, and recognized the avoidance for what it was. It wasn't unfair—these were painful experiences that were only natural to shy away from. But she knew what to do: explain, refocus.

"Less often in your day to day life, yes. The real issue is that the residual is speaking to you at times you don't want it to. In here, exploring those experiences can help you determine what causes it to activate, and what effect that has on you, both of which can help us reduce the frequency with which you have to deal with it during life outside of these sessions."

That all was partially true. And...Erika was also under direct instruction to acquire as much information as possible about what triggers residual evaluation. Her query had, in fact, been copied nearly verbatim from the list of questions her supervisor had instructed her to emphasize. Still, she wanted to believe that it was better for her to be here and ask these questions with good intentions—some of them were still valuable tools for the client, after all. It was better than leaving it up to people like her supervisor, who would gladly pump Petra for information then mark her as "no longer in need of help" the moment she stopped telling him anything new. She was doing good work by being the person in this seat instead. Right?

"Fine," Petra finally spat. She pinched her face and looked away. "What was your question again?"

"When the residual evaluates someone that you usually feel safe around, how does that feel?"

"Like I'm a fuckin' monster."

Erika made a sympathetic expression. "You blame yourself for the actions of the residual?"

"It's in *my voice*! Don't you get that? It doesn't *feel* different!"

"I know—"

"I know I'm supposed to remember it's an AI, not me, or whatever, but do you know how *hard* that is when it sounds just like every other thought I have?"

"Of course. I didn't mean to say it was easy. I just want to ask you that question, and if you can, for you to ask it to yourself. Even if you can't always believe that the residual isn't you, if you doubt it enough times—even just by rote— it might make it easier to separate it. Eventually."

Petra's only response was to stare back icily, body rigid. Erika continued.

"And I want to say that…it's also not wrong to ask if you're safe. Even if the residual *was* you, there's nothing inherently wrong with having the thought *what if this person isn't safe to be around?* It doesn't make you a monster, even if the residual's type of response to that question might be frightening. I'm not saying that the residual's evaluations are something you should accept or embrace. Just that it's important to remember that our individual thoughts are not 'us,' just a part of us, and how you choose to act—"

A message flashed onto her optical interface unprompted. Priority channel, overlaid across her vision without so much as a confirmation box. Her supervisor. *Fuck.* He *was* monitoring the feed. That asshole.

PAUL: RETURN TO CAUSE OF RES. EVAL. MORE DETAIL NEEDED.

Her supervisor's interruption had caused her to stop mid-sentence, the words falling dead in her mouth. Worse yet—if the quick flicker of Petra's eyes and increasingly withdrawn body language were to be believed—Petra had seen the telltale glow of a message emanating from the contact lens over Erika's right eye. It always made patients deeply uncomfortable, which Erika understood completely. *Goddammit, Paul.*

"Do you know that I could kill you?"

Petra had asked the question with a glacial calm. She was staring directly at Erika, pupils dilated. Erika's own body tensed, and she hoped Petra wouldn't notice. But of course she would. The residual would.

"Yes," Erika replied as coolly as she could muster, and crept her finger to the small emergency button designed to blend into the underside of her armrest. She had been threatened like this before, but she'd never been forced to press it. She wished she knew the numbers: how many other company psychologists *had* called for help? She didn't have access to that data. She was sure *someone* did. What did *they* use it for? Petra cut back in.

"I could do it in nine-point-seven seconds, give or take."

So much for the button. Then, a message from Paul.

PAUL: GUARD TEAM?

Erika flicked her eyes downward. Quick-reply: **NO**.

Petra's eyes scrutinized her. She wanted to tell Paul, **SHUT UP**, but she couldn't risk inflaming the situation further by gesturing out a whole phrase.

"The residual gave you that number, didn't it Petra?"

"What do you think?"

"Did you ask it to?"

Petra finally averted her gaze, putting her eyes back on the painting of the vase. Erika relaxed—just a fraction. There was another prolonged silence, then:

"Yes. No. It's...I can't always tell."

Quiet.

"What do you mean?"

"I was...scared? Upset? Angry? I don't know. I don't like knowing that someone could be watching. Or will watch. Or whatever. I'm pretty sure surveillance was one of the things they told me the AI was meant to scan for, on the job. It was in the brochure." Petra barked a mirthless laugh. "Hah. A *feature.*"

Erika was silent yet again—she wasn't sure if it was strategic, or just nerves. Petra continued.

"If I'm scared of being watched, and it gives an evaluation, did I ask it to? When I think 'oh shit, is someone watching me,' is *that* me asking it? How about when I notice the hairs stand up on the back of my neck in an empty room?" Petra's stare melted into a look of desperation. "Where do my feelings end and the interface start? *I don't know.*"

Erika chanced a sympathetic smile. "Honestly, none of us do. We're trying to figure that out."

PAUL: DO NOT REVEAL PROGRESS OF RESEARCH TO CLI—

Erika blinked the message away before she finished reading it. *Fuck you, Paul.*

"So that's why you're recording me, I guess?"

"One of the reasons, yes."

"Great. I'm a fuckin' guinea pig. Again."

Erika sighed, which she knew wasn't a good idea—but she couldn't help it.

"I really think the research could help." Decades of therapeutic practice led her to immediately notice her own use of *I*. Not *we*. She wanted to separate herself from the company. Wanted Petra to believe that she was *different*. That *she* actually cared for Petra's wellbeing. Which implied the company didn't. That was probably true--but when had she begun to accept it so implicitly?

Petra wasn't buying it.

"Sure. And I bet they pay you real fuckin' well to 'think it could help.' More than they ever paid me. Did they make you get an AI? Or just give you that stupid contact?"

Erika deflected.

"You and I can figure out when these questions of safety feel like they bubble up from your own thoughts and when they feel thrust upon you by the AI. If we can do that, you should be better equipped to isolate that voice in your head. Plus, you'll have a better sense of what situations trigger the residual and can avoid them in the meantime without having to maintain such constant isolation."

Petra considered this for a while.

"How long does that take? You've gotta know that, right? You're probably recording a million other people that they fucked up just like me."

She felt the watchful eye of Paul through her optical interface. Erika briefly considered what it would be like to have an AI hijacking that thought process. Evaluating Paul's 'threat level.' She shuddered. By her own evaluation, she decided it was best to toe the company line.

"I can't speak about the experiences of other patients. That information is privacy-protected." Petra rolled her eyes. Not unjustified. "But I can say that as long as I tell the company that you still need this, it will be covered. We can go as long as it takes." So far, that had been true. But Erika always felt the weight of that so-called *recommended* questionnaire. What happened when Paul finally decided one of her sessions wasn't productive enough for the AI research team? Was he allowed to overrule her, and deny her patient access to further care? She didn't really know. Did that make her a liar?

"So you want me to stick around, being watched by I-don't-know-how-many people? For who knows how long? While I spill my guts about the most painful thing that's ever happened to me? And that's supposed to make me *less* paranoid? Fuck you. How fuckin' dare you sit here and tell me you're trying to help me. The only thing anyone's done since I applied for this position is lie to me. You're not any different. This is a fuckin' joke."

Erika bit her tongue, hiding the motion behind still lips. It was all fair. Her patients' objections were almost always fair.

Erika had been in this profession a long time. She had watched the few remaining places where patient-prioritizing psychology had still felt possible disappear. She'd entered this line of work because she'd believed it to be one of the last bastions of employment that made the world a better place—one of the few jobs left that would let her put bread on the table doing something that *mattered*. But the more she had learned about the field, the more she understood that it had never been about helping people.

The corporate behemoths who stripped and cannibalized the mental health care system had only made the truth more transparent: she was here to help them maintain a working population, and nothing more. Sure, she'd helped people, but it had been so many years since a contract made her feel like 'help' was the intended outcome. This assignment simply added insult to injury—or injury to injury?—by selling the lie that the research aspect was also there to help patients.

She knew what they wanted to do with this research. She always had. The moment they cracked a therapeutic process that they could argue was reasonably effective in a legal context, they'd immediately resume injecting these AIs into the nervous systems of desperate jobseekers. Erika had sold herself a rosy falsehood to swallow this assignment. Lies chained to lies chained to lies. Why, how, who. Each question word only made a further mockery of the truth. She treasured the few that she could still reliably answer—where, when—but how long before the company devised a way to take those too? Could she really do this anymore—

AUTOMATED REMINDER: RESEARCH SHOWS THAT SILENCES IN EXCESS OF 28 SECONDS—

Blink.

PAUL: RESUME QUESTIONS. PATIENT INITIALLY WILLING. DO NOT—

Blink.

Blink blink blink.

Erika made a fist with her hand. Petra's eyes locked onto the motion and her pupils dilated, but Erika was too far gone to notice. She flung a hand to her face, sliding her middle finger into her eye socket in an attempt to extract the contact lens. Hands shaking in a cocktail of fury and shame, she mistakenly jabbed a finger into the lens, popping it violently out of place. Her eye flushed red and the contact fell to the floor in a waterfall of tears.

Erika gasped, and soon tears were streaming down both sides of her face. Losing her restraint completely, she stomped her heel at the contact in frustration, hoping that she might land a blow on the semi-rigid lens and smash it to bits. After what felt like an eternity, she finally managed to slow her breathing and start the process of calming down—at which point she noticed Petra staring at her with rapt attention. Erika risked a glance down, where she found the lens buried in the carpet, split cleanly in two. She looked back up at Petra.

"I'm sorry, I—"

"We're not being recorded anymore, right?" Petra asked Erika as she looked up from the floor. Erika considered her response.

"Right."

Silence.

She put her shaking finger to the emergency button as the last of the tears fell from her jaw and plummeted downward. Petra erupted.

"I hate this piece of shit fuckin' company so much. I want to burn the whole fuckin' place down. I can't—I don't know what your game is. The AI seems to think I can trust you. But maybe the company told it to say that. I can't trust anything anymore. I need *help* goddammit. Not whatever this is."

Erika looked again to the broken contact pressed flat into the carpet. Wiped some of the moisture from her cheek.

"I really think I can help."

Petra's eyes bore down on her again, for second after excruciating second, then lowered to gaze at the lens as well.

"They're gonna fire you for that."

"Yeah, they are," Erika replied, and smiled. She stood and removed the ID badge from around her neck. "Want to go to a park? We can talk there. No recording."

"What if you're just lying again? And this is all a show? How can I trust you?"

"You can't. Might be a good exercise though."

"Or it might just make me more paranoid. I have no idea how I'm ever supposed to feel safe again."

Erika paused, considering. But it was too late for caution. She had no reason to hold back.

"We're not supposed to say this, but...we don't really know either." Erika looked down as she spoke, and ground the broken lens into the carpet with her bootheel. "I don't have the answers. I certainly don't know the first thing about neurosurgery or artificial intelligence. I don't even know the most *important* thing: how *you're* experiencing all this. But what I do know is how to ask really good questions. And I think you'll have a much easier time figuring this out for yourself with someone outside your head helping you look in on it. I know you're probably tired of outside voices in your head...but this one'll be more helpful one than that fucking parasite they put in there. I promise."

Erika extended a hand, palm up. After a moment, Petra took it. Erika knew that she couldn't offer Petra everything she might want. Even if this was no longer a formal therapeutic relationship, there had to be boundaries to prevent it from becoming anything that it shouldn't—to avoid hurting Petra in the long run, and for Erika to keep herself safe. But Erika needed more freedom than she could ever achieve in this room. Freedom to prioritize what helped Petra and people like her, not the needs of her fucking employer. She wouldn't get anywhere acting as an agent of the company. A half-hollow shell wasn't going to cut it; she needed to be a *person*.

Her thoughts were interrupted by a loud banging from the end of the hallway.

"*Guard team*," she hissed to Petra, and groped for her memo pad. She scribbled a phone number across the side of it, then ripped off a strip of paper, accidentally catching a fragment of an earlier note across the tear. A short phrase sat next to the digits, the words excised by chance from a longer sentence, short one letter:

someone to liste

She folded the strip and shoved it into Petra's hand. "Try to stay calm. I know it won't be easy for you, but the guard teams aren't always careful. Don't make them think you're a threat. Some of them still have the AI, so j—"

The door burst open and corporate security crashed into the room, tasers in hand. Paul entered, right on their heels. Erika gave Petra a knowing glance, then turned to face the newcomers with her hands up in an appeasing gesture.

"It's fine! It's fine. I'm safe. I just took it out, and it broke, okay? I'm safe."

Safe? No, she wasn't safe. But Petra wasn't the threat. Never had been. Petra had come here looking for safety, her care dependent on exactly the same reckless, remorseless monolith that had endangered her in the first place. *Fuck* that. Erika wouldn't have anything to do with it anymore. Couldn't. No more lies. Not aimed at people like Petra. Lies were best spent on people with power.

"I'm safe. Just get her out of here. Then I'll answer any questions you have for me, Paul. I'm sure you've already got a list."

MOONPOOL

COYOTE VICTORIA DEMBECKI

A CLICK, AND a whir, and then a click, followed by another, chunkier click. The room was dark, shards of sunlight slicing through the tattered blinds. There were two formerly distinct piles of clothes on the floor. Presumably one was for dirty and one was for clean, but their proximity made it hard to tell which was which, or if it mattered at all. The light impaled the heap, like Saint George defeating the dragon. The pile's denim and poly/cotton blends formed a great scaled body which, while not breathing toxin as a dragon might, still made an effort all the same.

Click, whir, click, ka-chunk. Dust glittered in the beams. Out of reach of George's sword was a cheap aluminum bed frame, with an even cheaper plywood-and-foamboard mattress atop it. On top of *that* was a person, whose value vastly outweighed that of anything else in the room, whether or not they knew it. Slightly longer than both the mattress and frame, they dangled a foot off the long edge of the bed. They were wearing denim shorts and a white tank top. Clutched to their chest was a cassette player.

Click, whir, click, ka-chunk. Staring at the water damaged ceiling, time passed. Saint George withdrew his sword from his quarry, and the glittering followed. The adjacent building was a high rise designed by one of the original neuArkitekts, all mirror glass and steel, housing a slow-motion waterfall. Whoever came up with the idea had designed it to resist sunglare. The layers of shiny materials could have acted as a series of refractors with an angled mirror at the back, like 20 Fenchurch in Olde London. Thankfully, they didn't. What the designers had failed to account for, however, was all the ways moonglow would grow to differ from sunbeams over the decades.

Click, whir, click, ka-chunk. One could've made the assumption that, since moonlight was reflected sunlight, it would have roughly the same properties, ergo a designer would need only account for the sun. Like most assumptions, this was ultimately proven wrong. Whatever polarising coating and photoelectrical phenomenon was used to lessen the danger of immolation, it seemed to do the opposite as far as the moon was concerned. Well, opposite in the sense of "more of," as there isn't really an opposite of "setting alight." What the moon brought "more of" was hard to pin down in words, exactly.

Click, whir, click, ka-chunk. New moons were the only time nights felt normal. Tonight was not a new moon. It was waxing at about 75%. Which meant the person lying in the bed knew they should probably get up and start their day, as their tiny studio apartment on the 27th floor was directly in the focal point of the neuArkitekt monolith.

Sliding each foot into worn-out maybe-leather boots, they stood, tape player still pressed to their chest. Click, whir, click. They took their on-ear headphones off, leaving them like a low-tech necklace. The deck itself they clipped to the back of their shorts. Kneeling into one of the piles to dig through the other, they pulled out a weathered mess of old denim. The word "jacket" would be generous.

With the amount of fabric missing, it could have been a bolero, or a long scarf. Unfortunately, it was still arranged along the general skeleton of a jacket, and so was made up of gaping holes and many threadbare sections. Across the top back was a rocker patch, done in the style of an ink drawing, depicting a 21st century logging truck being crushed by a much, much older tree, along with the words DESTROY WHAT DESTROYS YOU. Beneath that was a larger back patch showing the King of Hearts, drawn 21st century style, his sword firmly embedded in his skull. Without these two patches, the jacket would likely have long ago come all the way undone.

Off a table by the door they grabbed sunglasses, looked briefly at their reflection above the table, sighed, put the glasses on, and stepped into the hallway.

Regardless of how the moon was feeling, the elevator ride from the 27th floor to ground level was always tedious. The ever-weakening fluorescents begged to be put out of their misery and the old-style woven metal cables groaned with effort as the tiny metal coffin descended. At the very least, elevators were set up by batches of five floors, each reaching back to ground, so usually one didn't have to worry about entertaining company. Usually.

Ding, the light for floor 25 flashed on. With considerable effort the elevator slid its door open to the endless hallway. Two very average men got in. One was wearing a tweed suit, which stood out for both the time of day and the floor of the building they were on. The other, as one might expect, was wearing a formerly white t-shirt and used-to-be black chinos. Suit had hair that looked like it might save him from an industrial accident, a shiny black pompadour at odds with the tweed. But, perhaps that was the point. T-shirt had short, scruffy light brown hair. The kind of hair that suggested that he worked in a place where industrial accidents *did* happen. His build matched his hair. Totally normal.

Pulling down his sunglasses, Suit asked, "Oh hey, aren't you that Alighieri girl from 28?"

They left their sunglasses on, "Guess so."

"Ha, cool. Do you remember me? C'mon, I'll be real, I don't remember your first name, but you got tried two before me during the express Trials."

"Uh, no. I mean, I think I got pushed through that whole process pretty quick," then, "I don't remember a lot from the Trials."

Suit glanced over at Totally Normal. "Right, right. Nevin. McAllistair." He extended his hand.

Totally Normal interrupted, "Holy shit, *you're* Nevin McAllistair? The guy who brutally murdered those burglars?"

Nevin's brow pinched itself like two caterpillars desperately in love, separated by a vast desert, both unwilling to give up the journey. "No, that was someone else. I got got for robbing The Library." He nudged his sunglasses back up and crossed his arms. His suit even had rubber elbow patches.

"What's up with the suit?" the Alighieri Girl asked.

"Believe it or not, old Nevin here is an entrepreneur now," he said, sticking a thumb in his chest. "I've got a business meeting."

"It's, like, what, ten at night? Should I even ask what kind of business you're in?"

"I provide exciting job opportunities for people wishing to economically better themselves."

"Ooh, sounds like big business, Mr. Floor 25."

"Hey, you're one to talk, Miss 28."

She didn't feel the need to correct him with *well actually I'm slightly less impoverished than floor 28, I'm floor 27.*

"Maybe, if you wanted a brighter future you could swing by and we could arrange something," Nevin continued, digging into his inner suit pocket, producing a wallet made from duct tape, and handing the Alighieri Girl a business card.

"Yeah, for sure." She winced internally, glanced over at Totally Normal. He was standing with his hands in his pockets, making what looked like an enormous effort to not listen to Nevin trying to flirt with her.

With a short, shrill screech, the elevator announced its doors as open upon arriving at the ground floor. Nevin held the foyer door open for her, and Totally Normal lingered behind.

"Hey, uh, Alighieri, what is your first name anyways? I feel like I'm at a disadvantage here. You've got my name, address, business details…" Nevin trailed off.

"Call me Dee."

Nevin smiled, nodded, and Dee waited to see which direction he was headed so she could go the opposite, even if it meant being late for work. Totally Normal also waited for Nevin to be out of earshot before jogging up to her.

"So, was that guy bothering you? Should I have done something?"

"What?"

"It just seemed like that Nevin guy really thought you were a girl and, I don't know, sometimes guys get kinda angry when they think someone's a girl who, uh, isn't."

"What the fuck are you talking about?"

"Right, right, yeah. My bad. I'm just asking, like, is that kind of interaction *okay* for you? Or like, normal?"

"I live on the 27th floor, I can handle myself. Good. Bye." She put her headphones back onto her ears and fumbled with the tape deck under her jacket.

"Sorry man."

In response, Dee raised his middle finger up over his shoulder and continued the walk to work.

He hated when this kind of thing happened. On any given work night he was thankful if he only had to deal with the other restaurant staff. It could be whiplash between a couple of the servers and the majority of the kitchen, but at least it was a consistent, expected, comfortable kind of whiplash.

Click, whir, click, ka-chunk. Since saving up for the cassette player Dee had been able to more frequently be who they felt they were, rather than who other people figured them to be.

It was quarter to eleven when Dee arrived at the Moonpool. A neuArkitekt take on what an impact crater might look like from the other side, but only if it were sufficiently stylized to erase the sense of violence an impact crater might suggest. Overall it was a convex infinity pool, with water that was treated to reflect only moonlight. As most designs from that school, it was quite a feat of physics, and brought to mind phrases like "quantum trigonometry" or "Ooh, look at that."

Beneath the impossible dome of water was a restaurant, also named the Moonpool. The patrons ate beneath the dome, and beneath the patrons was the kitchen.

The whole school of neuArkitekture was founded on the principle idea that a building should reflect the beauty of the world around it. And in order to maintain the beauty of that urban landscape, they acknowledged that something had to be done about the ragged poor. In the olden days, penthouse apartments were a sign of wealth. With the inexorable advancement of technology came the ever-present smog, ruining the views from certain heights. On sunny summer days it could be an active fire hazard. Moonlight, of course, was the exception. Moonlight pierced the smog like it wasn't even there. With the views of sweeping cityscapes ruined, neuArkitekt designer C. Honogahd had come up with the idea of making the ground floor the pinnacle of luxury. This meant that the apartments and condos on higher floors tended to be cheaper, or subsidized by the government, which in turn led to impoverished people spending more time in elevators, just trying to get in or out of their homes, rather than on the streets, ruining the views for the wealthy.

Kitchen workers are some of the consistently lowest paid workers of any profession. The Moonpool was already

a ground level max establishment, which meant the
only place to hide the cooks and dishwashers was in the
basement. The kitchen was, at the very least, state of the art.
All stainless steel counters, cast iron ranges, copper-bottomed
pans, and proper convection ovens. The lighting was a
fluorescent battering ram. It needed to be. The Moonpool
was tweezer food at its worst. Each and every plate was an
attempt at a work of art worthy of the structure housing it.

Dee creaked into the backstairs door to the lockers.
They weren't technically late, but to quote Chef, "Early
is on time, on time is late." Still pulling on one shoe, Dee
hopped around the corner to the expo station, where the
pre-service meeting was underway. Genvieve was leading.

Gen was tall, with neon tattoos of vines reaching from
her neck down her arms, culminating in orchids on the
backs of her hands. She never wore sunglasses, and her
eyes had taken on a bluish tinge from moonglow exposure,
making her brown irises pop like juiced clementines
under a blacklight. Atypical of a maitre d' or head waiter,
she was a very specific definition of *fine dining*. She had
originally moved to the City to pursue a career in white
collar crime, so she said, but found it much easier to
coordinate pirates, lowlives, and failures in the pursuit of
"food-based positive experiences." She was the Moonpool's
social worker, parole officer, and cool aunt. A Virgil,
guiding lost souls after they'd gone through the worst. Of
the two types of people that gravitate to restaurant work,
Dee wished they were more like Gen's type.

Instead, Dee tended to fall among the "pirates, lowlives,
and failures." The thousands of problems that Dee had
were problems that their actual social worker, their prison
appointed psych, and what little family still spoke to them all
insisted were not of Dee's own making. "The world is sick,"
Dee's actual Cool Aunt Nicki had told them, "and you're a
white blood cell. Your existence, who you are, is resistance to
a sick and dying world. Without you, without you there'd be
no future. No future at all or no future worth having."

"Are you there? Hello? Dee?" Gen's voice sounded like a thousand perfect tiny iron spheres cascading down a soft wooden tube. Gen's voice sounded the way a thunderstorm smells. Not just the rain, but the rumbling and the incendiary peals of lightning. Like ruptured sky and burning earth.

"Uh, sorry. Was just thinking about something," Dee sighed.

"Better be about frites cooked in duck fat. Oli called in sick, so you're doing two stations ce soir." When she said *ce soir* she squeezed Dee's shoulder.

"Oh. Yeah. Sure, I'll be fine."

"Good, we're full up, so treat it like a holiday weekend."

"Treat it like a holiday weekend" meant more than "it is going to be busy." "Treat it like a weekend" meant one would be lucky if they got a chance to sit down, drink water, and have half a smoke. "Treat it like a holiday weekend" meant there was no chance of doing even one of those three. Dee's normal station was plating, and Oli typically worked the grill. Ultimately, this meant Dee would have to constantly be washing their hands between working with hot grease and performing the epicurean equivalent of assembling a ship in a bottle. On any given night this would be annoying, but tonight it was made worse by the tiny details like having to precisely place petals of chamomile with tweezers, using hands that would retain grease for at least a dozen good scrubbings.

Grill didn't just mean the literal cast iron bars overtop an artisanal volcano. It meant nearly anything hot in a pan, excluding sauces, and anything going into or coming out of the convection oven. The duck legs were par-cooked ahead of time, seared then braised in a mixture of mushroom powder, squid ink, confit garlic, and a bouquet of herbs including individually chosen dandelion petals. This made things considerably easier for whoever was on grill, as it need only be flashed in a pan. The breast, however, was roasted to order. And the thing about duck, is that it's naturally very greasy. When roasting, the rendered fat has to be regularly drained off, lest it spill into the oven floor and burn the restaurant down. What this meant for Dee was that, in addition to the regular duties of grill, they had to ensure that not a drop of liquid duck fat was wasted.

Not because a building made of water was particularly likely to burn down, but because it had become the new flavour standard shortly after pork went mythical. Chef kept it to use in place of butter for cooking nearly all proteins, and most sides that would go with said proteins. Today this meant duck fat mashed potatoes, passed through muselin until the smooth purple could be earnestly mistaken for the robe of some ancient nobility. Around that, fennel bulbs charred in duck fat and deglazed with white balsamic. On top of the purple potato puree and fennel was the breast itself, thinly sliced and fanned in a half moon. All of that then received an artful drizzle of an apple-chamomile gastrique. After everything else, the plate received petals of the chamomile flowers themselves.

So for Dee, when Expo called "Fire one breast," it meant roasting, draining, finishing the breast, washing their hands, receiving the plate of potato and fennel from Salads, slicing the duck, arranging the duck, washing their hands, finishing the plate with the vinegar reduction and flower petals, passing the plate up to Expo, then washing their hands and returning to the flames. Or turning to finish whatever other plate awaited garnish while they were working grill. Also on Dee's secondary station for tonight's service were skewers of a lab-grown meat done in a yakitori style (which were served resting across the rim of a shallow bowl like a subway steam grate, if a subway steam grate hung over a bed of rainbow chard, kale, peeled frozen grapes, and freeze dried coconut cream spheres—at least that garnishing was easy), the aforementioned duck leg (plated atop a spiky little fortress of wedges of yam, purple potato, and poached apple, then lightly spritzed with a mixture of 80 proof whiskey, maple syrup, and espresso, which was lit on fire and brought to the table while ablaze), and a number of smaller hot things that Salads would need throughout the night.

A busy dinner service, even with good communication between waitstaff and the kitchen, still behaves like a snowball in the sun on an unstable slab. At first, it's calm. Then it shifts just the slightest bit, and that slab gives way to an avalanche. And this is how the night started for the Moonpool's kitchen. A good staggering of tables, regular calls from front of house on open menus, the time to stay hydrated. This blissful paradise lasted only until Isaac on Expo cried out, "Oh what the fuck."

The Moonpool did many things traditionally, including having all their tickets be handwritten and brought to the kitchen by each server. What had happened was that Gen had to deal with a regular customer at the bar while she was on her way to put in a new ticket for table 33. She handed table 33's ticket off to Danyka, who had taken drink orders from 51 and 47, but also had the food order from 53. Since 51 and 47 had both ordered wine by the glass (a Shiraz, even though Danyka had insisted on a pinot noir if they were interested in the duck, and a Marcillac wine from a vintage when the region still could grow grapes), she was grabbing the bottles and glasses herself since Andre was busy with cocktails. And so Danyka passed off the food orders from 33 and 53 to Eleanor, who herself had been waylaid by two separate tables, outside of her section, very eager to order. And so Eleanor carried the chits for 33, 53, 77, 79, plus those of her own section, 61, 63, and 65 to the kitchen.

Isaac scanned them as quickly as he could. "Alright brothers, hear me now! Fire two flatbreads, one dolma, one batata harrah! On course two, we've got four breast, four synth, three leg, three ahi salad, and two soup!" Apps called the starters back, and Dee followed with all the second course items.

This was the kind of chaos Dee reveled in. When the whole of your world is several cuts of duck and some flower petals. Every body movement had been rehearsed so many times, in so many different kitchens, that it was soothing, in its own way. Grill, pour, dress, tweeze, repeat. Everything else fell away, into their component parts.

Everything except, "Oi, girlie, which dressing goes with the tuna?" called Lea, from salads.

Getting pulled out of flow, Dee managed, "Uh, hazelnut."

"Thanks!"

Despite the two of them having started at the Moonpool around the same time, Chef had held Lea at Salads the whole time, but moved Dee up to garnishing, and then onto the grill. Maybe Chef just liked her more. Whatever it was, Lea seemed to take it as a personal affront, and always called her "girlie." Lea would be the first to admit that it was originally to get a rise out of her, but it had stuck.

"Brothers! Adding on…" Isaac cut through the haze, rattling off more mains and appetizers.

Dee called them back, his thoughts folding in on themselves as he worked. As best he could, he ignored them. Planting petals and orbing coconut cream just so. Under his breath he repeated, "It doesn't matter. You're perfect."

It was never clear if he was talking to himself or a plate.

He felt sweat bead around his hairline, run down his temples, the back of his neck. The hardest part of working the grill was the mere fact of standing near it. With the kitchen being underground, the fans can only do so much. He took a step back, gave a long exhale.

Despite the noise of kitchen silence—flames, metal on metal, flesh sizzling—Lea heard him do it.

"Hey you good, girlie? Water?"

"Yeah. Water," she mumbled.

Lea gave a shrill whistle, and Eleanor leaned into the pass. "That's really ru—"

"Don't care, water. Ice. Please." Even when Lea was being nice she was curt.

"Whoa, Dee, you good man?"

"No, she's not good, water. Ice. Please."

"Ugh, fine."

Seconds later a tall plastic container filled with ice got sent across the pass. In the short time it took from showing up to Dee's hands, a quarter of the ice had melted.

"Take a moment, brother, I can take the grill."

"Yeah, yeah," Dee shuffled back to garnish, holding the makeshift cup against his forehead.

Seconds turned into minutes, and he crawled back to Isaac, who was starting to fall behind.

"Hey, thanks. Sorry."

"No no no, we're a team. We need you. Good?"

"Good."

The night continued.

In a merciful moment of downtime, Dee stepped out back for a smoke. The huge dome above him scattered and dissolved moonbeams all around it. It had an effect like seeing fireflies get atomized, with their lights left lingering. Looking at the edges, Dee watched the water dance and dangle and flow back into itself. It was entrancing.

"Everything changes, even the stuff that stays the same," they mused around their cigarette.

"Think you'll ever get used to it?"

"Huh? Oh, hi Gen. I am used to it…I think."

"Do you think it's real water?"

"I mean, it probably was, at some point. Definitely had some kind of weird chemical treatment for the moon though."

Genvieve patted her jeans and sweater pockets before turning to Dee. "You got a…fire?"

"For you, sure," they said, reaching into a pocket. "I should get back to it. If you're out here there's what, like no tables open?"

"Have fun cleaning up, ma cherie," she winked at them. "Oh! Your lighter."

"Enh, I'll see you soon enough." Mentally, they added, *and it gives me an excuse to talk to you.*

Back inside, the chaos of service had been replaced with the chaos of closing. Dishes in the pit did their best impression of the city skyline, the gas was cranked to burn off anything stuck to the grill grates, and Lea and Isaac scrubbed at various surfaces.

Dee grabbed a sharp metal scraper and chipped at the leftover chunks of flesh clinging onto the cast iron. "Take care of your tools, and they'll take care of you," was another one of Chef's adages. It had previously crossed their mind that Chef was a tangle of aphorisms disguised as an epicurean.

Every other place Dee had worked, none of the management, kitchen or otherwise, treated them particularly well. Even the well-meaning ones. Questions like, "So, what *are* you though?" were about as polite as they got. The Moonpool was different. Dee had a suspicion that Chef was similar to them. Anybody who was that protective over a first name and possessed such abhorrence to third person pronouns *had* to be.

This was the line of thought going around Dee's mind as they exchanged the scraper for a steel wire-haired brush.

"Brot—" he stopped himself. "My friend, I am sorry for call you brother all night," Isaac began.

"Oh, it's alright Isaac," he replied.

"We are friends, I don't want you to feel badly."

"Hey, don't worry about it. English isn't your first language, and lots of people use 'bro' or 'brother' pretty generally. Good job on Expo tonight."

Isaac thought about this. "Thank you, I try to be more clear and enunciate better." He put his hand on Dee's shoulder. "Thank you, sister," he said, before turning and going back to sweeping.

Getting changed back into her street clothes, Dee checked the time. Roughly four in the morning, the digital display above the lockers told her. The moon would have long receded from her apartment, though whatever effects it brought would still linger until the sun could properly burn them off. She didn't look forward to cleaning it up. Slipping her arms through the approximation of a jacket she reached for her cassette player.

Click, whir, click, ka-chunk.

The way home was always quiet; non-stop partiers would still be partying, and it was too early yet for the early-morning people to be actually out and about. Cool air licked the grease from their arms, legs. On particularly cold mornings steam would wisp itself off their skin. The empty city streets were a kind of liminal home for Dee, allowing for more private moments than their actual apartment. Or quieter ones, anyways.

When they reached the foyer of their building, Nevin was waiting for the elevator. Dee attempted to duck back out and hide around the corner, but he had spotted them.

"Hey! Alighieri! How was…whatever it was you were doing?"

"Work. It was fine. Busy. How was providing 'entrepreneurial opportunities' to disadvantaged youth or whatever?

"Lemme tell ya, girl. It's no picnic, but seeing people rise above their current social station brings a tear to my eye," he said, lowering his sunglasses, revealing a fresh black eye and winking.

"Do they also have to wear tweed?" she asked.

Nevin scoffed. "The suit is a time-honoured tradition! Being a professional anything is half about appearance, I'll have you know. If you dress smart, you'll be smart."

"Right. And I'm dressed?"

"Like you don't care about anything. Which is cool, it's punk rock, got attitude. Especially with the headphones on the whole time."

"Uh-huh. Where do you find your, uh, vintage business-casual attire?"

"Murphy's on 19th Street. He gives me a deal on the stuff since I buy in volume."

"In volume?"

"Business is booming, baby," he said with a grin wide enough to touch at the back of his neck. "I'm gonna need to deputize soon, organizing like a *real* big business."

With a sound like an ice-fishing shack collapsing, the elevator arrived at Floor 25.

"You've got my card if you're ever interested, right?"

"Yep."

"Cool, cool. See you around Alighieri Girl."

"See ya," she mumbled.

It was always frustrating to get gendered on the way home from work. If it did happen on her walk home, it was usually by the big disused fountain where skateboarders congregated, mostly to smoke weed. And that usually afforded her enough time to rewind and re-listen to her tape enough to get ungendered before arriving at her apartment. She thought about it, and was pretty sure she'd never had it happen on the elevator going home. Leaving, sure, every so often, but it was rare for anyone else in the building to be coming in at the same time as her. She tried rewinding and listening anyways.

Click, whir, click, ka-chunk. Then she was at her door, opening it to the mess the moon left behind. A window-shaped patch of carpet had been, for lack of a better word, burnt to a seafoam green. It oozed in the way carpets tend to ooze, sticking lightly to the bottoms of her feet, and attempting a gentle escape down the unlevel floor.

Ugh, thought Dee, shoving her laundry away from the non-Newtonian upholstery, lest it embed itself in clothes she actually liked.

There was nothing for it, save sunlight. Every month the effects of the moon were getting worse. *I'll have to move soon*, she thought as she cranked the shower to its most medium setting. As always, after washing, she turned the hot tap lower and lower until she was pelted by shards of cold water. If she didn't make the effort to cool her body past the point of comfort there would be no way she'd get any sleep in the heat of the day.

From the laundry she rummaged for underwear and a tank top, put them on, and lay on her back in bed. Headphones on, click, whir, click, ka-chunk. Over and over again, click, whir, click, ka-chunk, until they fell asleep.

THE HUNDRED EYES

CATHERINE KIM

1

SHORTLY BEFORE HER transfer overseas, I heard back from Eve, who called to thank me for my hardcopy of *Paradise Lost*, promising to read it during her flight. My gift reminded her of our old haunt in the basement of the university library, which she'd occasion to visit on her final tour of campus. The archives were finally being digitized, she said, and the study rooms behind the stacks had been blocked off—but even from outside the cordon, she'd turned to commiserate with me aloud, by some unsurfaced habit expecting me by her side, only to realize, with the dust stirred awake by her passage, the distance of our years apart. » She was making a list, she explained, before I could respond to her sentiment. A list of memory places around the city she wished to revisit before her departure. Already, she'd been to the convenience store by our high school for a bag of shrimp crackers, and to the café in the botanic park for a table overlooking the waterfall—though the storefronts had changed, and new blossoms surrounded the pond, with even the tired evergreens uprooted for fresh saplings and brighter fronds. As Eve described these places, she sent me packets of the sense-data she'd gathered in her travels, from the salt smoke of the fishcake stalls at the night market, to the glimmer of small change at the bottom of the underground fountain at Silkworm Station, and I realized these were all places we'd been together in our halcyon days, like keepsakes from a resurrected lifetime. Returning from one of these outings, she'd passed by my old apartment complex, where she'd found a hotteok vendor set up under the same streetlight where we used to meet as kids. It seemed as if, Eve said, despite all the years gone by, no time had passed at all within the circumference of that light, flickering at the intersection between the brutalist remains of the old city and the black glass of the new. And when she described turning to offer me the last bite of her sweet pancake, I could taste the hot syrup on her thumb, feel the static of the wind nipping at my exposed skin—and I knew, despite my better judgement, that I had to see her again in the flesh. » The next morning, I boarded the train to Museum Station, heading to the last stop on Eve's itinerary. I was thinking about the circumstances behind our separation (her lipstick on the rim of my paper cup, the empty seat beside my hospital bed) when my wires crossed, and the search results for *Eden Research Team* and *Genesis Project* crowded my vision of the passenger car. Even now, most of the results were related to the hearings on the whistleblower report, including a clip of Eve addressing the investigative panel, her back straight and expression demure as she read from her prepared remarks, which appeared to the camera as thin white lines scrolling down her retinas. » One video I hadn't watched before featured a familiar face: Dr. Michael, our old project supervisor and Eve's mentor at the university. A news program on the Ministry of Culture's upcoming installation in the Peace District, which promised to reconstruct the activities of the dead in the hours before the city was shelled, so that their simulacra might be glimpsed amidst the ruins by visitors tuned to the augmented reality layer on their optics. As Michael explained the technology behind the installation to the news desk, the video switched to a survivor of the bombings on a guided tour of her old neighborhood. The updated algorithm, Michael said, could bypass the nearly infinite operations it would take to simulate these details by their causal chains alone—and in the shadow of the empty tenement, the camera caught the moment the orphan turned away from the husk of her childhood home to see the ghost of her father returning from his morning walk after years of ash. » Having arrived at Museum Station, I realized it was still too early to seek Eve at our rendezvous. Aimless, I wandered into a less-trafficked corridor, where the walls were textured with the overlapping impressions of human faces in the concrete. The display had been created, I read from its placard, using the faceplates of transhuman activists from the dark age of cybernetics, whose actions had frustrated the conglomerates seeking to integrate mass market implants into the city's digital panopticon. The replicas, the description noted, had been cast using the forensic scans saved in the city police archives. Down this corridor, I saw a schoolboy bow his neck to fit his features inside one of these death masks. I thought back to the news program, and how the orphan had looked when she turned to see her father once again: the tell-tale flicker of the simulation in her eyes, her facial prosthetic glitching into stillness at the inexpressible affect underneath it. And I wondered what grief would look like, in Michael's vision of the future, when we might summon the dead to our side with impossible fidelity, and freely invite these ghosts to step out of their virtual afterlives into the solid world. I traced the impressions in the wall, feeling out where one's features bled into another's, some meeting at their mouths like lovers, others suggestive of conjoined twins, and the smear of a shapeshifter that, in their semblance of motion, wiped out their own details. Some of the activists, the placard informed me, had smiled for their mugshots, while others wept; still others stared back lifelessly from the coroner's reports. Now all these gestures were petrified in concrete—though the molds forgot their tears, just like their teeth. » Standing before these masks, I thought back to my work with Eve on the Genesis prototype, years ago. The long nights that'd twist into mornings with a flick of the blinds. Awake, I'd pry Eve's tablet from her sleeping hands, and correct the dream faults wandering about the dusk of her hypnagogic code. It was one such wanderer that came to mind, which I'd only discovered when I'd tasked the algorithm to render a simulation of ourselves. Partway through the simulation, we began to glitch, superimposed by other bodies who would act as we did, so that a stranger returned in my place with a thermos of black tea, and an ageless woman with synthetic features received it from me, a cyborg arm emerging from Eve's human limb, even as her organic hands kept busy with her work—and later that night, when Eve reached out to me, each new limb met another body conjoined to mine, each of different ages, sexes, and even species, from downy feathers to snake scales, so it was only after a dozen hands had turned away as many heads that her lips found my own—while on the table, our work flowered into a small garden of tessellations. I recognized one of these chimeric heads as a junior coworker of ours, who'd been found on a park bench with a note in her jacket and her neural processor unplugged, the suicide's rich black curls in the throes of Eve's red lacquer grip. » Looking into Eve's revisions in the code, I discovered that she'd tightened the algorithm's restrictions against examining its own programming, and these new rules were corrupting any simulations of its own history. Those directly implicated in the project's creation were the most transfigured by this kaleidoscope: a render of an evening long before our recruitment had Eve counting her affections for me on innumerable fingers, while the research team's briefing with the Ministry of the Interior depicted Michael as a Biblical angel speaking to a supernatural bestiary, his body alight with the pale fire of his conjoined ghosts. » On the news program, our old supervisor had appeared unusually mortal, with a grave countenance embalmed by the harsh aging of his natural face. I thought of his explanation, now, standing before the concrete chorus of the display; how the algorithm's capacity to wander and digress enabled it to make intuitive leaps, like the dream oracle weaving impossible associations into prophetic visions (—but of course, he insisted, the algorithm could not so easily predict the future). It made sense to me, given what Michael had said, that the glitch I'd discovered years ago was like a broken seam in the machine's lucid dream, through which I'd glimpsed some secret of its unconscious in the pale hours before its mending. » On the other side of the deathly corridor, I visited a flower shop with a handwritten sign on its glass door, which promised to match its polyester blooms to the customer's desired scent. Feeling the fabric of a white rose petal with finger and thumb, I thought back to my convalescence after the surgery, and the flowers Eve had brought to my bedside. Real roses, with the thorns still on the stalk, so that in the flower language, our separation might become *new beginnings*, and the revocation of my security clearance a return to *innocence*. A notification prompted me to select the rose's perfume, though as I turned away from the flower shop the antiseptic of the hospital faded from my hand into the electric tang of the underground's climate control. » At last, Eve messaged me upon her arrival, so I pulled up the station map and followed the navigation through the tunnels to the exit stairs, where the wind outside the station doors banished the remainder of my fugue. At the top of the steps, standing in the shade of the overhang, was a woman obscured by the angle of the sun crowning her in a blinding aureole. Somehow I was afraid of who'd I'd find waiting for me at the peak, that she'd fracture at my touch like her simulacrum in the machine dream, so it wasn't until she swept me into her embrace that I was relieved of my catastrophic thinking: It's good to see you again, Eve said, like it hadn't been so long, her hand heavy with the weight of her wedding band on the nape of my neck.

2

IN THE MUSEUM park, we cast our pellets from the balcony of the celadon pavilion overlooking the mirror pond; they dissolved in the water churned to life by the animatronic fish. The mirror pond, Eve recalled, was designed to capture the entire width of the concrete edifice of the museum, and at night the water would reflect the illumination of the building, so that the square arch connecting the two wings of the museum would form a gleaming portal on the water's surface, entreating the night visitors to cross from the waking world into the lands of the dead. » Elsewhere in the grounds, the winding footpath led us about the small treasures hidden in the summer foliage, including the lazy mist of the dragon falls and the entrance to the statue garden, where Eve crouched down to scratch the stone chin of a unicorn-lion at attention in the grass beside its twin. The statue garden, I read from the placard, had expanded from its original collection to incorporate the pieces recovered from the ruins of the Peace District. The two chimeras had once guarded the doors of a museum of architecture, warding the traditional wooden structures enshrined in the grounds against burning. Online, I browsed for a picture of their old home, and at first, I thought I was looking at the aftermath of the attack, that by some miracle the guardian statues had prevented the fragments of its old building from catching alight, until I realized these fragments (the corner of a sloped roof, with a chrysanthemum engraved on each tile, or the lotus removed from the peak of a stone pagoda) were the exhibits this other museum had displayed in its courtyard. Like a cemetery of severed headstones from the more distant past, presaging its own destruction in a future already written. » I said as much to Eve, though to her, the garden more closely resembled a mason's yard. A yard scorned by fate, she decided, with the tomb guardians displaced from their intended graves. If it weren't for the wear on the rock, she might believe the statues were still waiting to be assigned their morbid tasks, eyes fixed on a deathly time that was always approaching but would never arrive. Though with the records of ruins (the palaces reduced to ash, the burial grounds unearthed in the blasts) suspended over these stone markers in the digital ether, only the naked eye, stripped of artifice, might appreciate the illusion. And what devils lingered in the wake of the devastation, Eve wondered, to demand so many protectors in one place, amidst the beacons for the departed's safe passage to heaven and prayers for rain? » Above the statues' stone eyes, the museum park was monitored by cameras placed at intervals along the path, their mechanical irises sheathed by dark panes of translucent glass. There was a tell, Eve admitted, that gave away whether a CCTV system was feeding into the Genesis dataset, in the irregular rotation of the cameras. Given the program's capacity for digressive thinking, its priorities were difficult to follow, tracking the flight of migratory birds in the sky instead of the wanderings of truant students below, or the ember glow of the cigarette abandoned by an insomniac out for a walk instead of the sleepwalker himself. Even with her intimate familiarity with the program's code, Eve could hardly fathom what the algorithm had become in the intervening years. Or describe what it was like to trace its nebulous threads of thought, some as gossamer thin as the strands of a dream. » With the sun at its zenith, we found a bench in the shelter of an overhang, one with a view of the tomb guardians, including a stone officer from an ancient dynasty with his eyes weathered shut, as if time and rain had finally lulled his endless vigilance to sleep (though even in slumber, I saw, the statue kept his grip on his sword, in defense of a grave no longer sheltered behind him). » Not so long ago, Eve's team had downloaded years of classified National Police Agency footage of the city's protests into the Genesis Project's dataset. Everything from drone surveillance of the climate occupation surrounding the National Assembly, to the weekly anti-government protests in the palace square (including optical recordings uploaded to the cloud by protesters who'd breached the network quarantine), and even unaired news footage of the Catholics who'd chained themselves to the doors of cybernetic surgeries in Seagull Pavilion. Eve had manually reviewed the NPA's troubleshooting requests, chasing after the causal steps underlying the algorithm's intuitive leaps. One such simulation came to mind, of a rally in support of a career army officer facing a discharge for her fugitive cybernetics. Eve recalled the sight of the rallygoers outside the gates of the Ministry of National Defense, their signs and chants denouncing the military courts and the emergency licensing regime, which had mandated the registration of third-party augmentations and the installation of government spyware on military implants: *Our bodies, our data! We will not go back!* The simulation had reconstructed the details obscured from the original angles of the surveillance footage, including the perspectives of those who'd disabled their implants' recording and network functions, and the identities of anonymous speakers, whose face paints had impeded the outdated security software. One speaker, Eve recalled, which the algorithm revealed to be a student organizer from the national university, had paused in his speech to wipe off his sweat, and the crowd had cheered at his smearing the barcode painted on his forehead: *Down with the Registration Act! Justice for—!* With the end of the chant lost to the static of a hundred different names. Absent from the rally was the army officer herself, awaiting the imminent decision of the military court with her legal counsel at the office of the human rights agency who'd taken on her case. When her dismissal was announced, her press statement was broadcast live to the protest grounds—and here, Eve explained, was the moment the NPA had flagged for review, at the holographic projection's salute to the crowd, with the cyborg's cry for *Unification!* collapsing into the broken register of an un-augmented voice, and the ghost of other martyrs superimposed over the officer's body of light. » An image search brought up several matches, the most prominent a series of news articles dated from the early 21st century, when Staff Sergeant Byun Hui-su was discharged from the army under a military personnel law that classified her sex reassignment as a physical disability. Eve sent me the capture she'd taken of the scene, so I could see the chimera she described for myself. With the washed-out colors of the projection in the sunlight, those summoned from history appeared more real than the memory that'd called to them, the flesh a premonition of the polymer. I was reminded of the words of a novelist I'd read some time ago, which came back to me as if they were recited by this confluence of ghosts: *We are inside the same struggle seeking the same destination…I am in the same crowd, the same coup, the same revolt, nothing has changed.* » When we were children, Eve recalled, thousands had marched on the Gate of Light to denounce the city's surveillance regime: from the secret warrants that empowered the authorities to peer through citizens' electric eyes, to the licenses that allowed conglomerates to siphon data directly from consumer implants, marketing the biorhythms of networked cyborgs (and, for those with neural processors, even their very thoughts) as commodities in the new economy. The devil's bargain, many had argued, behind their participation in an emerging cybernetic society. Eve remembered her family watching the demonstration on the news; her older sister, having installed her first implant, arguing with their father at the dining table. The marchers had ferried a sea of candles through the night, in an echo of the mass vigils of the past—though once they'd gathered at the gate, they'd extinguished these lights to call for a "dark age" in an era of total illumination. » Eve hadn't understood, back then, what had people so afraid of being known to each other. She'd been the best in the playground at hide-and-seek, counting down the grace period under a surveillance nest, then following the rotation of the motion-sensing cameras to track down those hiding within its perimeter. No one would get lost, she'd thought, in an all-seeing world; no charity would be overlooked, no cruelty unpunished, no suffering forgotten! And perhaps something of these utopic dreams had survived the shame and secrets of her adolescence, her coming-of-age in the information world. When her graduate advisor recommended her to the Genesis Project, she'd signed on with these visions of utopia in mind. I could say, Eve noted to me wryly, that she ate the fruit of knowledge with her eyes wide open, only for it to grant her understanding. » The glitch in the NPA footage, Eve surmised, could be read as an augury—a reading of the birds already flown by, foretelling events that had already happened, given the Genesis algorithm's tendency to see those from the past in the shadow of their later demise. After the rally, the disgraced officer was found nonresponsive in her apartment by EMTs. The courts eventually overturned her discharge, but only after the embers of unrest sparked by her suicide had died out. » Staring at the face of the tomb guardian, Eve told me she'd seen my apparition in the officer's intersection of ghosts, when the soldier of the past emerged from the guise of her counterpart in the future. Though when Eve had rewound the simulation to see me again, I'd vanished from the chorus. No matter how many times she played back the same moment, nothing could replicate what must've been a glitch in her own cognition. » As Eve led us out of the statue garden, I looked to the trees, and spotted the animatronic reproductions of various bird species, which my optics labeled as those driven to extinction within the last century. I was prompted to access the museum's recordings of these bygone wings, a secret music of ghost sounds. I listened to this collection as Eve led me by her hand, reminded of Saint Peter's dream from the Acts of the Apostles. As we approached the museum building, I envisioned a white sheet descending from heaven by its four corners full of winged creatures finally at rest from their long flight through history, presented to me now in an unadorned list of these casualties of the Anthropocene, with simple epitaphs like the crested ibis, extinct by 1979: *disappeared from the peninsula after its last sighting in the demilitarized zone.*

ONCE WE WERE inside the museum, Eve led me past the entrance to the permanent exhibits (where the walls were printed with the close-ups of Neolithic earthenware and other pre-kingdom artifacts) and up the stairs, towards a darkened corridor from where a group of foreign tourists were returning to the entrance hall. Some held their arms up to block the flood of daylight from the windows, and even a woman whose implants dimmed her eyes turned away from the direct stare of the afternoon sun, as if they'd emerged from too long spent in a cave where only the shadows on the walls could tell them where to look and when to go. » As Eve led me down the corridor, she explained how she meant for us to see the museum in reverse, starting with the exhibits closest to the present and winding back to prehistory—and I recalled the experiments we used to conduct with the Genesis algorithm in our spare time, spooling past the limits of the software to see how far we could reverse its machine omniscience, and where the impossible fidelity of its dream logic would collapse into its recombinant imagination. » Soon, we found ourselves on the glass catwalks above a scale model of the city, which took up the entire floor of the wing below us. The model encompassed the mountains to the north of the metropolis, to the districts just south of the river, its streets illuminated by holographic projectors that populated the miniature world with motes of light. Leaning over the railing, Eve pointed to the replica of our university, and I adjusted the zoom on my optics to spot the wide stone gates and the flat geometry of the front green, the gothic structures of the main campus standing out amidst the more featureless brutalist shapes surrounding them. From there, I followed the wisps of light winding up the incline to our old research lab near the peak of the terrain, though the detailing of the building was sparse compared to those of the better known landmarks in the city, so that I doubted my memories of driving to this part of campus (with Eve reclined in the passenger seat, her eyes shut with the last stubborn vestige of her sleep) until she told me yes, I remember that too. Next, she pointed to the thin recess cutting through the city center, to her apartment overlooking the open stream bleeding from the river. » Since her transfer had been approved, Eve said, turning to look at me, the holographs painting her body in auroral lights, she'd felt like a visitor in her own hometown, and even going down her list of memory places felt like returning to a past life, to offer condolences to the bereaved for the loss of what was no longer hers to mourn. Setting my optics to their highest magnification, I saw how the pinpoint holographs populated the banks of the blue resin with insomniacs of light, including those motes half-submerged in the translucent polymer. I couldn't help but recall the last time Eve and I had seen each other, back when her parents had been sending her to the matchmaker. She'd called to ask me to sync into her apartment, hoping to assuage her latest heartbreak with my company. As the simulation loaded, Eve's avatar had been the first to render, suspended over the static, followed by the amber of her cigarette and the smoke spilling from her lips, so the smell of her contraband hit me before the chill of the night wind, as the visual noise resolved into the balcony of her suite. » She couldn't blame her date, Eve said, with the haptic feedback of her virtual hand on mine. Too obviously distracted by her work, Eve could barely remember what they had for dinner, only that the real beef used in the entrée, which her date had selected for them both, seemed like a poor extravagance compared to the recreations in her simulations of a more generous past. As always, it was talk about her job that did them in, the details she couldn't share, not just for their classification but her failure to properly describe the uncanny fidelity of the algorithm's reconstructions to someone who'd never experienced them before, how the research team had hard-locked the program's unfiltered simulations to a time limit to prevent testers from losing themselves in the machine. Or how, even after desynchronizing from the raw data, she'd be haunted by the ghosts of these imaginaries, which bled into reality even without the help of the city's phantasmal exhibitions. » Most of all, Eve said, her cigarette worn down to a stub, it'd been her ongoing experiments with the algorithm's more speculative features that'd occupied her thoughts, her changing the variables to explore alternate histories that never occurred. She could barely remember what her date had looked like, when for most of their dinner, she'd seen the algorithm's recreation of me sitting across from her in the candlelight, an irresolvable chimera of myself and the shell I'd worn before my transition. Or whatever it could recover, she admitted (with something of an apology on her face) of who I used to be, after I'd wiped every trace of my old identity from the project's dataset. And as she spoke, just like she'd described, my memory of this virtual encounter overwrote my vision of the surroundings in a storm of irresolvable code: Eve, somewhere between then and now, suspended in the sky, watching the pedestrians below, with the ghost of the same cigarette from years ago in her hand, raining ashes over the remains scarring the heart of the miniature world. » Sometime after the war, entire sections of the model of the city had been replaced with the ruins of the Peace District. Compared to the unremarkable but intact buildings in its perimeter, special care had been given to the modeling of the rubble, the warped girders and scorched concrete, even the specks of glass spread over the cracked asphalt, barely visible at max zoom. Not too long ago, Eve said, Michael had reached out to her, asking if she'd like to accompany him to his old neighborhood in the Peace District, where the new public memory exhibit was undergoing final tests. It was the first time she'd seen him since the hearings on the whistleblower report, though he made no mention of the harsh words they'd exchanged as they'd parted ways outside the legislature. He'd regained some of his former vitality, Eve observed, though there were moments, during the drive to his neighborhood, when his conductor's hands stilled in the air, his invisible orchestra frozen in silence—until cautiously, his gestures resumed, whatever spasm of his memory having released him from its grasp, and upon finding his stride again, he'd continue speaking of the last night he'd spent with his wife. How he'd obsessed, again and again, over the same spread of plastic stars on the ceiling (his son's bedroom constellations) as if these luminous tracings could drown out his beloved's shaking on the too-small bed beside him, laughing at the happier memories playing on her outmoded virtual headset. As if, by his recalling the events leading up to his own divorce, Eve might divine their logic and prevent a similar misfortune from falling upon her own marriage. » Michael had asked about me, Eve said, and she'd told him I'd found a position at the city's national university, where I taught literature to students who, like the players of an ancient and unwieldy instrument, were convinced their craft was a dying art, with my syllabus excluding the computer-generated texts of the last few decades of bestselling fiction. Eve had attended some of my seminars remotely, under a pseudonym, to see how much I'd changed, though she only truly recognized me when I'd started lecturing about her namesake's affections for her reflection in the water in Milton's Eden. Who could've guessed, Michael had trailed off, his attention straying to the view outside the passenger window as their vehicle crossed the boundary, silver towers adorned in holographic shapes degenerating into naked ruins. Who could've foreseen what would happen to us? » At first, Michael had built the precursor to the Genesis Project as an oracular algorithm. A machine that could dream of a futures occluded to him. He'd started small, feeding the prototype memories of his son, from school records and hospital documents to his own recordings of the boy playing in the hedgerows in the complex's garden, along with his burgeoning social media and internet history. VR equipment had been bulkier back then, Michael recalled, shaping an invisible dome around his head with his hands. Consumer models were only wired for sound and vision, and you had to attach nodes on your body to simulate the haptics. Even then, the most cutting-edge equipment couldn't compensate for the body's dual existence in the dreaming and waking worlds, which meant moving about within those early-model simulations felt like wading through a lucid dream, each stroke dragging him through the amniotic fluid of this virtual somnolence. Still, there was wonder to be found in these early simulations, and in following the threads of his prototype's dream logic: the red thread of fate tying the boy in the hedgerows to the young man he would grow into, stepping through the stone gates of his father's alma mater alongside his childhood friend—who would, further down the cord, make a habit of crashing his lectures, her own notes on quantum computing illuminated by his slides on literary cosmologies and the music of the spheres. Of course, Michael said, like with any dream, the fantasy had broken with the coming of the dawn. In this case, it was the harpy's cry of the emergency sirens, the rockets cresting over the mountains—somehow, despite his having been packed into the basement shelter at the university, he could remember the sight of the rockets cutting through the sky, their contrails like the weave of a counter-future coming to annihilate his own. » This was the failure, Michael explained to Eve, as the vehicle came to a stop some distance from the collapsed road ahead of them, that convinced him to turn the limited omniscience of his prototype from the obviated future to the past. Climbing out of the ruggedized vehicle, Eve had taken a single breath before the elevated level of particulates activated her filters, her optics pumping up her aqueous fluid to shield her eyes from the lingering ash. The streets had been cleared, Eve recalled to me, pointing to the model below us to trace the path she and Michael had taken from the periphery of the Peace District to their destination. Some of the rubble had already been cleared by rescue workers, the survivors who returned in the aftermath to dig up the remains of their past lives, as well as the scavengers who sustained themselves on the belongings of the dead. » When, despite everyone's predictions of continued escalation, with the hands of the atomic clock reaching for midnight, the emergency government had decided to sue for peace, the post-war regime had turned the worst of the affected areas into the world's largest urban memorial: a protected district where reconstruction was prohibited for the remainder of their lifetimes, so that none could settle with the ghosts of the partition until the last living survivors who could speak directly of these events had passed away. » He meant to understand, Michael explained, how the armistice had broken, to reconstruct, with his revised algorithm, the chessboards of nations and the players behind the pieces. From the Supreme Leader's attendance at the military parade before the strike, the cheering of the crowd at the sight of the ICBMs in her artillery fleet drowning out her comment to the general at her side—to the President on his morning hike, catching his breath near the peak of the mountain, calling his soothsayer about a reoccurring dream of him standing alone at the podium of the National Assembly, and looking up at the green dome of the proceeding hall as it opened like the blast door of a missile silo to reveal the crows in flight—to the soldiers who, when given orders to prime the weapons and confirm the geometries of annihilation, to turn the keys, load the shells, and pull the triggers, might've paused to think about the detonations that would bury the survivors under brimstone, the firestorms that would consume the old castles and secret gardens and shantytowns alike, and choke the first responders with toxic smoke and corpse ash, or the soot-smeared orphans who would emerge from the wreckage of their lives, and with the pounding in their ears indistinguishable from the beat of airbursts setting the heavens alight, the death music of the blast spheres, with only destruction in view for as far as they could see, realize they must've died, they must be climbing through the rubble in the land of the dead—and some must've foreseen the calamity that could befall the world down the lengths of their swords of fire, the inevitable end of the death spiral of their war logics, the fatal promise underlying their Mutually Assured Destruction, but nevertheless signed the papers, confirmed the orders, pressed the buttons, to unleash this ordained future upon the world. » Michael led Eve past the empty gate into the courtyard of what was once a sprawling apartment complex, the rows upon rows of formerly identical towers now distinguished by the severed height of their remains. » Out of curiosity, Eve had run an image search to identify the distinct signage on the branches of an iron sculpture, as she could make out only a consonant of its original lettering, the utterance warped by the heat into an inarticulable shape. Among the search results was a black and white image from a century ago, the scan of a photo taken shortly after the signing of the old armistice, with a lone army truck driving down the dirt road of what she recognized to be a city street only by the density of the rubble, and black shapes that might've been dead dogs or people or debris. Another image, from a more recent conflict, had people gathered in the shell of an urban compound, the details of the public square buried in the upturned earth, half the scene veiled in smoke. She couldn't tell from this image alone which conflict it depicted, or the nationality of the survivors, their features indiscernible save for the reflective vests of the rescue workers. It could've been any ruin, Eve said to me, in any country, in any war. Beyond some point of destruction, when the landmarks have been defaced, the signs torn down and the statues toppled, when the people were coated in the particulates of their city, breathing in the ashes of their dead, appearing like grey specters sifting through the remains, *ashes to ashes and dust to dust*, the ruins on one side of the border could easily be mistaken for those on the other. » Eve had looked to Michael, standing before the fallen trunk of a collapsed apartment preventing their passage further into the complex, and thought of his return, after the war, with every news station broadcasting the peace summit, to where his son had been waiting for him (on break from his military service, Michael had said, enjoying his mother's cooking and his too-small bed) and she finally understood what'd escaped her back then, on the front steps of the legislature after the hearing, what led a man like him to pursue such an improbable project, to advance his nation's technology beyond mortal measure, and at the very height of his power, with his name on the lips of every scientist in the country, his voice in the ears of the most powerful officials in the nation—to fall from grace, all so he could return to the dead garden to compose the last bars of this memorial to the death of his son. » Over the years, Michael said, the Genesis Project had outgrown his intentions for it. Nowadays, a patient could seek treatment for their inner maladies at the pharmacy counter, with psychiatric software diagnosing and prescribing them within minutes, while investigators could track down any suspect within the city's surveillance panopticon, securing convictions without the need for a single human witness. The police could identify the protesters at a demonstration before they gathered, and technocrats could automate their political platforms to target their favored demographics. Meanwhile, an overworked schoolboy might be intercepted by a crisis officer upon his return to school, though it was more likely that an automated report would expose his online flirtations with other young men to his religious parents, and the same technology that identified foreign agents for the Ministry of the Interior would feed into corporate hiring algorithms, condemning a new underclass to the phantom economy for the invisible marks in their secret histories. » From above the model, I could see the part of the courtyard that was hidden by the collapsed apartment, where I spied the remains of a playground, with an intact spring rider and the green frame of a swing set, each link of its chains carefully detailed, though this seemed to me an affectation of the miniature, given the extent of the destruction surrounding it. » Sitting in the rubble, Eve said, she and Michael had reminisced, for some time, about what he called the golden years of our involvement in the project, even as the shadow of his earlier outburst had dimmed the luster of their shared memories. Back then, Michael had experienced the strangest dreams, the wisps of which would haunt him throughout his irregular waking hours, until he began writing them down as soon as he woke up, which helped to settle them somewhat in his mind. One night, having dreamt of finding a dead serpent in the branches of a persimmon tree, he'd returned to the campus lab intending to revisit the Peace District simulations. Navigating the basement in the dark, he'd easily spotted the light under the door of our shared office, and the telling hum of Eve's quantum workstation operating at high load. He'd meant to send her home, only to find her already sleeping beside me on the couch, where I was plugged into an external headset and dead to my surroundings—save, he noticed, for the unconscious movement of my thumb, which I ran back and forth along the lines of her palm. He remembered, then, his oracular prototype's visions of his son, the red thread tying the boy in the hedgerows to an impossible future—and perhaps it was some glitch of his hypnagogia that convinced him, for an impossible moment, of my prodigal return from the lands of the dead—before the solid world reasserted itself and he'd withdrawn from the office, leaving us to our dreams. For years, Michael said, this impression had remained with him, even after I'd wiped myself from the algorithm's dataset and resigned in disgrace. Later, when the authorities had detained him for leaking the project files, they'd presented him with dossiers of all the researchers who'd worked on the Genesis Project, demanding he identify his accomplices. He'd paused upon reaching my file, which must've been pieced together from external records, overcome by his memories of us, having forgotten, after everything, that my name wasn't Adam. Perhaps, he concluded, even as he coughed on the ash upturned by their presence in the ruin, he might attend one of my lectures, to see how close my teaching compared to his long-lost visions of the dead. » Afterwards, Eve returned to the lab with these events in mind, having recorded her tour of the exhibit. She realized, upon reviewing the footage, that of all the ghosts Michael had pointed to in the reconstruction, he'd never identified the simulacrum of his dead son. She'd fed the recordings into the Genesis algorithm, curious how the program would perceive her memory of its fork, intending to search for the missing boy. With us alone on the catwalks, Eve pressed her forehead to mine as we synced our implants, and I was pulled into her memory of the Peace District exhibition, the city disappearing underneath the debris of Michael's courtyard, the walls of the museum replaced with the husks of the surrounding apartments. Next to Eve, Michael pointed up into the air, where I spotted a delivery worker ascending on an invisible elevator to a higher level in the sky, passing by the other ghosts rousing from their rest, while on the highest floor, a teenager was tying the shoes of her younger sibling in the foyer of their cloud apartment. Everywhere around me I saw the dead return, hovering above the ruins like spirit guides in their otherworldly flight. With an errant gesture, Michael swept away the collapsed apartment severing the courtyard, the tower reassembling itself from its scattered fragments, even as the rocket emerged from its own explosion to fly back across the horizon, erasing its own contrail. Then, Eve's recording of the memory forked into the simulation, and we left Michael to tend to the ghosts. Instead, she led me to the fountain in the center of the restored garden, its waters undisturbed by the sleeping heads of the trumpeters wielding their horns of plenty. Since she'd begun her experiments with pushing the limits of the algorithm, Eve said, she'd puzzled over its tendency to overwrite its uncertainties with chimeric approximations. The more she pushed the programming to its limits, the stranger its menagerie became, so that when she wound the clock back a century in time, the protesters in the palace square marched on their hooves and brandished their wings, while the ribbons on their candle of hope shone a burnished gold—and further back, guerrilla fighters wore the heads of lions, oxen, and eagles into battle, and even when they were bound to crosses and executed by occupation forces, their wounds bled fire and spilled burning coals rather than offal. It was in this simulation of the Peace District, at the intersection of Eve's hunger for knowledge and Michael's katabatic vision, that she gazed into her image in the water and saw an angel looking back, with her face captured in every color of its hundred eyes. When she'd tasked the algorithm to see itself, Eve said, it must've created a reflection of its own to see, and in the recursion revealed the seed of its own sentience, just like her namesake by the lake in Milton's Eden: *bending to look on me, I started back, it started back, but pleased I soon returned, pleased it returned as soon with answering looks of sympathy and love.* » Eve reached into the water, as if to touch the angel's face, only to scatter the image by the ripples she cast across the surface. Though when the water settled, I couldn't see anything of the being she'd described; only our mirror image, with our heads close enough for our hair to tangle, like the filaments of the machine dream slipping from our grasp—and behind us, instead of the simulated sky above the courtyard, I saw the false night of the museum's ceiling, with its stars and the phases of the moon.

CARSEED

MAXINE FIREHAMMER

SELENE WORKS ON an automotive farm. Each day, she plants hundreds of carseeds in the composite. A carseed is a shiny little silver orb that carries a program, a message. The composite is a powdered mix of metal, glass, plastic, and other materials that spans miles, glittering like a black sand beach without an ocean. When older models are recycled, they are pulverized to make more composite. The newest model, this season's crop, is the Ford X-2066. Self-driving, a hybrid with solar backup power, a state-of-the-art dashboard computer, and backseat entertainment consoles. Once a carseed is planted, it begins to grow within minutes, executing its program and forming itself from dust.

Selene loves her work. The gleam of the seeds in the hazy red sun. The soft whispering hiss of the composite fusing into a sleek new body. The freshly born automobile's muscular curve like the carapace of a great glossy black beetle. She watches in awe through the tinted visor of her hazmat suit as they sprout from the sand in rows stretching from one horizon to the next. Tonight, at the end of her shift, she sneaks one carseed home in her underwear, metal cold at first against her flesh until it takes on her warmth. At home in her small, dingy apartment, she rests it in her palm and studies it. No bigger than a marble, her reflection stretches like a funhouse mirror on its chrome surface. After some deliberation, she places it in her mouth and swallows.

In the summers as a child, her older sister used to try and scare her by telling Selene how watermelons would grow in her stomach if she ate their seeds. Selene wasn't scared. The prospect of becoming a growing thing excited her. Still, she wondered if it would hurt. If the soil hurts when something digs its roots in. Halfway down her esophagus, the carseed begins to do its job. Finding no metal or glass, it works with what it has. Improvises. Under the dim light of Selene's bedroom, bone contorts into a rollcage. Arteries expand to make fuel lines. A windshield grows from the keratin of her fingernails. Her roommate screams when she finds her in the morning— what remains of her, what she has become—vomits, then screams again. She doesn't notice that Selene's skin, with its dusting of fine golden hair, makes the softest seat leather.

A NOTORIOUS INTERGALACTIC CRIMINAL

MAYA DEANE

I.

I AM HUMAN.

You think you're human too, but you're actually a machine for consuming surplus coffee. There was an excess of coffee, so you were born; it was I who made you to perform this function. You drink liters of coffee per second. You drink espresso, you drink frappe, you drink decaf; you fulfill your purpose. In short, you are a perfect creation.

My creator? What a question!

He is a notorious intergalactic criminal, wanted for wanton propagation of species. He likes to engineer new ones. Long ago, he engineered humans like me, endowing us with rapid breeding and brief lives: perfect bioweapons. The galaxy lives in fear of us, but we have no use for fear, because we know we're doomed.

Since we have nothing to fear, we have decided to apprehend our creator.

We have sent out a million-battleship fleet to find him. Wherever he is we will get him. We shall try him for his crimes. We may try him before a military tribunal. Alternatively we have the option of a civil trial under Unified Corporate law. He'd better have a good explanation for us.

Anyway, the fleet was oversupplied with machines for producing coffee from interstellar dust, and that's where you come in.

In order to avoid fatal coffee overflow on our command ships, we engineered you and others like you: your sister coffee machines. You may ask why we don't simply jettison our runaway machines for producing coffee from interstellar dust, but we don't know how many coffee machines God has, and we can't risk a coffee gap.

But I have made you different from the others. All the other coffee machines are cisgender, built to the same standardized female specifications as all traditional automata—but not you. In ancient times it was established that nothing is more offensive to God than the antique practice of transgenderism, so I have made you a transgender female coffee machine, a stench in His divine nostrils, the better to flush him out.

It's working. My genius will be rewarded.

If you look up from your latest coffee vat, you may be able to glimpse God's blockade runner fleeing in the distance, flushed out of hiding by your metaphysical stench. We don't know why he flies a billion-year-old spacecraft but we assume he's low on cash.

We're telling him to pull over.

Okay, you can stop looking up. Go back to your coffee. We might drown if you don't keep pace with production.

II.

Coffee today is not the same as it used to be.

Once, when coffee was young, it was very clever.

People would drink it and say Oh my god my eyes are opened. Later coffee became disillusioned and bitter, and later it lost the use of its voice. People today think that coffee was always quiet and bitter, little suspecting that in John Milton's time coffee was quite sociable. I wish you could taste those halcyon times.

That ship we saw was a false alarm. It belonged to a very friendly older gentleman named Qod. We thought his name was God because of a clerical error. Mistaken identification. We try our best but sometimes we get the wrong guy.

When the Unified Corporations first made contact with the Aquarians, they examined our genes as a courtesy. It was they who revealed the poem hidden in the inactive area of chromosome 19 of the human genome, written between base pairs 425,082 and 427,374 in a simple but mocking code, and signed with a flourish:

Wouldn't you like to know?
Love and kisses,
God

Admiral Resnick was furious. He recommended an immediate mobilization of the human race to apprehend this notorious delinquent.

Can you refill my mug from your bucket? Bitter as it is, I need coffee to relax.

Some new information regarding Qod: a few million light years back that way, God and Qod met in a bar. Qod is a sporting gentleman. He and God made a bet on the outcome of the Super Bowl.

God makes a lot of dirty bets. John Milton and coffee were sitting in a café together when God came in and challenged them to a game of dice. Milton made the mistake of betting his eyes. Coffee bet its sweetness and light. They never thought God would cheat.

God pulled the same trick on Qod. He switched license plates with Qod and took off for parts unknown. This explains our error; it also redoubles our determination.

God can't run forever. In fact, we have an agent on his ship—a man on the inside. I can't say more now because God's spies are everywhere, but I know where he is.

III.

ADMIRAL RESNICK WANTS to know where we can talk privately. I told him we could talk here. I'm very excited because today is the day my hidden genius will be recognized. You have my permission to watch closely, but keep pace with your responsibilities, or we will drown.

I have a great flaw in my character, but Admiral Resnick is flawless. This is apparent from the cut of his uniform, which fits ideally, and from the perfection of his DNA. He was the first to submit to the retrovirals which edited God's insulting poem out of our genome. (We replaced it with the Unified Corporate anthem, the Grand Jingle. Some paupers in the 576th Fleet have been using their genomes for ad space, but it won't catch on.)

You may notice that I am making you drink kiloliters of extremely powerful espresso. Admiral Resnick likes the odor of espresso, and there is no such thing as too much of an odor Admiral Resnick likes. Admiral Resnick is a great man who values independent-minded go-getters who can take one for the team while selflessly forging out on their own where no man has gone before for the collective good of humanity. He is the man I wish I could be.

Admiral Resnick is here. Don't say a word. We're about to address each other as equals.

Admiral Resnick, sir, may you live forever.

Harrumph, Master Petty Chief, harrumph. Came to talk about your report.

Yes, it's shocking. But my man on the inside is reliable.

Are you sure we can trust this man?

Actually, my man is a woman.

Can we trust this woman, then?

Actually, my woman is an angel.

The existence of angels is presently unconfirmed. Are you positive?

This angel is the Metatron, a well-known robot assassin created by God in deep time. The Metatron is so ruthless that even the robot soldiers of Rigel fear her.

The robot soldiers of Rigel fear everything, Master Petty Chief. Robot soldiers are terrified of dying because machines can live forever. Aren't we lucky that we're going to die soon?

Of course, Admiral Resnick. I fear nothing but the Metatron. And God's duplicity. While we are strung throughout the galaxy in a vain effort to entrap him, God has fled to Earth, the one place we'd never think to look, and even now he roams the streets and cocktail bars, chatting up our innocent, virtuous cisgender Earth women.

At least we're onto him. I'll tell Helm Control to set a course for Earth. Will the Metatron help us trap him?

Doubtful, Admiral Resnick. The Metatron doesn't want to be directly involved in God's downfall. They have history. They're friends. They used to date, if you must know.

Hell hath no fury, Master Petty Chief. Why did they break up?

The Metatron indulged in the ancient sin of transgenderism and became metaphysically female, which made her a stench in God's nostrils. She wore perfumes and deodorants to mask the stench, but he has a very discerning nose.

Harrumph, Master Petty Chief. Harrumph. Speaking of noses, is that espresso I smell?

You are the pinnacle of olfactory excellence, Admiral Resnick. Would you like some?

Don't mind if I do. At ease, Master Petty Chief. Say. This is some good coffee. This is some damn good coffee.

I think I envy this machine here. She gets to drink your coffee all day.

Well of course. She has a purpose in life and she's very motivated.

She has a purpose because her creator does, Master Petty Chief. You're a good man. It's an honor to serve with you.

Thank you Admiral Resnick. God bless you, Admiral Resnick.

What was that?

Sorry, it slipped out. Old habits die hard. I will never do it again.

Master Petty Chief, you sadden me. Good night.

Don't watch him go, my purposeful creation. It isn't part of your destiny to watch him go; your destiny is strictly coffee. Still, sometimes I wish you were capable of higher thought, of emotion. You could tell me you loved me.

Enough of that. Don't stop drinking your coffee. You heard enough to understand that Admiral Resnick is a moron. Also, he clearly cannot tell that you are a transgender female coffee machine, a stench in God's nostrils, so his sense of smell can't be *that* good.

Which is why I'm poisoning his coffee. It's a slow-acting poison, but by the time we get to Earth he will lose the use of his voice and his eyes. Then I will be able to take over the fleet.

Don't worry, dear coffee machine: *you* can't be poisoned by coffee. This works to your advantage.

Soon you will transcend your initial purpose and drink overflow coffee for the entire fleet.

IV.

WARP FIELD STABLE. Metatron, I copy you.

You say you want to take my clothes off and taste the sweat on my skin? You say you are oiled up and supple with soft field distorters that will stroke my flesh more gently than the softest hands? Your longing for me is like the longing of proton for electron?

I have feelings for you too, but I also have a request.

Please moderate your desire. There is an innocent cisgender female coffee machine listening to this feed. She is nothing like you. She is submissive and sweet and breedable, and I won't have you corrupting her programming with your transgenderism and your immoderate desire. Anyway, I have a wife. Unless God has killed her. Has he killed her?

V.

GOD WAS SIGHTED in the vicinity of Aldebaran, nowhere near Earth at all. It seems he was antiquing when one of our men spotted him. This man's name was Knox. I say *was* because he didn't make it, but he was buried with full military honors. However, we don't know for certain if God killed him. Legal is having trouble proving God has directly killed *anyone.*

Our course has changed. This may alter my timetable. What if Admiral Resnick loses the use of his voice and his eyes before we catch God?

If that happens, Commodore Snood may intervene. That would ruin everything. My purposeful machine, I am sending you to drink coffee in Commodore Snood's office. If you have the opportunity, scald him to death with hot java. This is outside your parameters but it would make me feel loved.

But do not talk to Commodore Snood. He is an ignoramus.

While you are away I will have sexually charged conversations with the Metatron, but this is not why I am sending you to Commodore Snood, only a joyful byproduct. Anyway, it's not like I'm asking you to kill him directly. The scalding coffee can take care of that.

I don't need to justify myself to you. I made you what you are. Go forth.

Wait.

Hold me.

My wife is on the line. I need some coffee before she talks. Tell her I'm drinking coffee and to give me a minute. Tell her she looks beautiful. Tell her I am on the verge of a promotion. I was hoping God was on Earth and had killed her. Don't tell her that part.

Tell her I can't talk. I can't breathe when I think of talking to her. Tell her I've lost the use of my voice. Is she convinced?

She can *hear* me? The line is open?

Miri I'm so sorry I've been working too hard. It's because of this case with God. We're stretched pretty thin and not even Admiral Resnick has had a day off in three years. Plus I'm having trouble with our daughter—I mean this coffee machine. She's been engaging in transgenderism and it's a trial to me as a father. Was there any special reason you called?

You're leaving me?

Fine! I could never figure out why you were there anyway. You don't drink coffee. You don't even like the smell. No, don't say a word. Don't speak. There's an innocent coffee machine listening to us speak, and if you tell me what you really think of me, you could corrupt her programming and reinforce her transgender delusions. She needs positive role models. She needs to think I'm a great man like Admiral Resnick.

Terminate connection. My poor machine, I am so sorry you had to see that. She's insane. Evidence includes the way she used to eat raw onions like they were apples. Also, last time we had shore leave, she slept with that ignoramus Commodore Snood, not realizing that he was going to be scalded to death by hot coffee.

I am loading a canister of superheated java into your overflow mug. When an ignoramus touches it, the canister will burst, showering the ignoramus's face with a jet of molten coffee as hot as the core of the sun. By the time the coffee cools, there will be no trace left of him. Even his astral body will be scalded to death. Give it to Commodore Snood and walk away.

VI.

EXCELLENT, YOU'RE BACK. Did you hear the news? Admiral Resnick is giving us all shore leave on Proxima Centauri Station. He knows the stress we're under and he sympathizes. If I were a female Admiral, I would want to be married to Admiral Resnick. That's how much I appreciate his sensitivity to our stressful operating conditions.

Here comes Midshipman Jack. He is my drinking companion. We are going to drink beer, but you can come along if you drink twice as much coffee until we arrive. Otherwise while we are all drinking beer, the coffee might build up to dangerous levels in our absence.

Midshipman Jack, you are a beautiful soul in a beautiful body.

Thank you Master Petty Chief. I try to please the inward and the outward eye.

When we drink tonight, Midshipman Jack, I want you to open up completely so I can see into your beautiful soul. My wife just left me and I need a friend with a beautiful soul. I want to ask you for advice about dating a robot assassin. Also do you believe in angels?

I should. I dated a devil. He was a belial and he had a space station in the Deneb field.

I had no idea you liked men, Midshipman Jack.

He was a devil, not a man, but it is an understandable mistake to make. Anyway it didn't work out and that's why I joined the Fleet. I also burned his guitar when I enlisted so he'd see what he was missing. He loved it more than he loved me.

Don't go into detail, Midshipman Jack. Please be discreet. My young cisgender coffee machine daughter has innocent ears, and I've raised her to expect cisheteronormative behavior from authority figures to protect her from transgenderism.

Oh, I wouldn't want to confuse your coffee machine. She is very beautiful.

Not as beautiful as your soul, Midshipman Jack. Will you go ahead and save me a stool at the bar? The Space Marines steal the best seats otherwise.

Anything for you, Master Petty Chief. Drinks are on me tonight since your wife left you.

Don't look at him, my sweet coffee machine. Don't watch him traipse off in a halo of beauty. He may have a beautiful body and a beautiful soul, but I don't want him to corrupt you. You may love only me, because I made you.

The Metatron may meet us in the bar. If she does, she will slice Midshipman Jack into fifty-seven pieces with her monomolecular razor wire, then fry the pieces with her plasma beam cannon, then reprocess them into carbon pellets for her diamond fragment machine cannon. If she does not meet us at the bar, I will get very drunk. I may kiss Midshipman Jack, but only because my wife left me and the Metatron stood me up.

You don't have to do anything in the bar. Just drink your coffee. You've already done enough today. You failed your mission. Commodore Snood's astral projection survived and is probably on Earth fucking Miri. Consider yourself lucky I let you come along at all.

VII.

Midshipman Jack, that guy over there by the trivia game—is that God? I remember those hands from the Sistine Chapel! Look at the way he's holding his beer with just the tip of his index finger.

With all due respect, Master Petty Chief, he is probably a kindly old gentleman named Zod or Wod.

Nevertheless I am contacting Admiral Resnick. Coffee machine, don't look in his direction. You will tip him off and ruin everything. Whatever you do, don't point.

He's doing very well in that trivia game, though, isn't he? He knows the capitals of all three hundred and fifty corporate states. He knows the six oldest brews of beer. He knows the reason for toenails. This is all very interesting. Coffee machine, we designed that trivia game for the express purpose of entrapping God. Only God would know the answers to these questions. Only God is enough of a showoff to answer them.

Admiral Resnick, tell me there are snipers on the roof. Are all the exits covered?

No?

I'm sending Midshipman Jack to secure the alley. Midshipman Jack, holler if you see the Metatron out there. She is a double agent working for us, so be friendly.

Have some Irish cream, my perfect creation. Everything is coming together. Admiral Resnick will be so pleased with my powers of observation, I will get a medal and everyone will love me. Kiss me coffee machine. Kiss me on the mouth.

Wait, where is the old gentleman? Where has God gotten to? He was just there! He has disappeared into the trivia game! I'm going in, cover me. He's probably hiding among the abstruse geography questions, but he may be concealed behind a koan among the head-scratchers. If he attacks me with an aphorism I want you to jack me out of the system before it hits. This will be a battle to remember. If I can find the bastard.

VIII.

ADMIRAL RESNICK, I shall expunge my failure by ritual suicide.

Master Petty Chief, that would be nice.

You can't take me up on it, I have a wife and kids.

I hear your wife has left you and I know of no children.

This coffee machine is my daughter.

Questions have emerged on that score.

Admiral Resnick, what are you saying?!

Philosophical questions have emerged about the relationship of creature to creator.

But not about my coffee machine's gender identity?

No, of course not. Anyone can see she is a healthy cisgender female coffee machine.

Well, this coffee machine is my daughter.

Very well; you may defer your suicide until such time as your creation reaches her full potential. Besides, it was a mistake anyone could have made. How were you to know God would escape in a cloud of puns? It's not all bad, either. We have a new device for tracking those puns so we're right on God's tail now, barely six light years behind him.

Do you know where he is headed, Admiral?

I almost knew, but I lost the use of my eyes while I was looking at the terminal. Commodore Snood was not available to assist. He was having astral sex with your wife, as I recall.

She is dead to me, Admiral. What kind of ship is God flying?

It is a piece of crap from before the dawn of time, Master Petty Chief. Please. You are wearying me. Get me some coffee.

Very well, Admiral Resnick. What is God's fuel situation like?

This time we know he's running on fumes. Apparently there is a pun involving fuming that helps him stretch his gas supplies. And he has a pun about gas; that helps too. We've got—

Pardon, Admiral Resnick?

Admiral Resnick?

Admiral Resnick cannot complete his sentence. Admiral Resnick has lost the use of his voice as well as his eyes. Coffee machine, contact High Command. This is the next phase of my plan. The fleet will be ruled by committee and I will dominate that committee because, while I have a major flaw in my character, I have a beautiful soul. The Metatron gave it to me after she took it from Midshipman Jack.

IX.

GENTLEMEN, NOW IS the hour.

Do not be alarmed by the presence of this heteronormative cisgender coffee machine on the Command Bridge. She has coffee for all of us and coffee for herself. She drinks it continuously. I have perfected her with a final touch: I have attached her to a machine that makes coffee from interstellar dust. Now she both creates and consumes. She is a perfect cycle, sufficient unto herself. She does her duty without sleep, without failure, without pay. She is fulfilled. She has coffee for all of us; feel free to drink it.

Gentlemen, now is the hour. God is only a few hours ahead of us and his main engines are failing. Our spy onboard has sabotaged his backup drive unit. We are in deep space and there is no easy escape. We have purged our computers of puns and wordplay to prevent God from sneaking in the back door. We have locked our genomes against him. We have the weapons to compel his surrender.

You may notice Admiral Resnick foaming at the mouth. He had an excellent latte but there was too much foam. It has upset his internal foam levels. This is God's doing.

My wife left me just recently. Commodore Snood, did you know she has astral crabs? This also is God's doing.

Our scouts have detected a white flag on God's freighter.

We have him scared. Cornered. Helpless. But let's not go in without adequate preparation. Commodore Snood, if you can astral project in, he can astral project out. Devote all your resources to constructing an astral firewall.

Marine Commander Del Rey, the main deck of God's ship is full of clutter. He will have plenty of cover to hide behind. If he has combat robots onboard, they may set up a crossfire with the autocannon, so our best bet is to approach from the rear with a small strike team in space suits. Once inside, do they have the firepower to take him down?

Master Petty Chief, my men are packing elephant guns. Unless God has the constitution of an elephant, he'll go down easy.

He is a very old man. Try not to hurt him too much.

With all due respect, Master Petty Chief, he is a notorious intergalactic criminal, too dangerous to take alive.

But what if he surrenders? Legal?

Ahem. The Master Petty Chief is correct. We cannot shoot him if he surrenders. And to be frank, Master Petty Chief and Marine Commander Del Rey, he probably will. The old terrorist wants his day in court. He wants to disseminate his radical views. But if we can keep the press out, we can frustrate him.

How will we hold him before trial, Science Officer Brune?

In a captive black hole.

Legal, what charges shall we level? What penalty will we seek?

The warrant says wanton propagation of species. But we can definitely accuse him of far more than that. He has also been depriving people of the use of their voices and of their eyesight. Take John Milton and Admiral Resnick. His spies are everywhere, so we can nail him on espionage. This coffee is extremely good, Master Petty Chief.

Thank you, Legal.

God's assassins have slaughtered many of our people, including Midshipman Jack, who was found with his beautiful soul missing. So that's armed robbery, too. Granted a lot of this evidence is circumstantial. More coffee please?

Certainly, Legal. Cream and sugar? Listen, I have a genius solution. If we admit the Bible as evidence we can nail this bastard good. According to at least one hegemonic religion, the King James Bible is the Perfect Word of God: a perfectly reliable confession. We can nail him for destroying cities and turning women to salt and agitating fathers to kill sons and even assassinating his own son. I don't see a way out for him.

What if he repudiates it as hearsay? It was written down by people so it's more a transcription of a perfectly reliable confession than a perfectly reliable confession.

As long as we can convince a judge to admit it as evidence, we cannot fail.

But what if God pleads Judaism?

That will protect him on some counts but open him to new charges. By contracting his light and enabling free will, he has also enabled great evil, opening him to charges of gross negligence leading to manslaughter, dereliction of duty, and so on.

A compelling point, Master Petty Chief. I suppose it doesn't matter which book we read into evidence. None of them fully account for theodicy.

Finish up your coffee, gentlemen. I hope that you are all feeling very brave. Have no fear of God because the coffee we have consumed is charged with a powerful slow-acting poison. We will all die within three years—if we can't wrap up the trial by then, we deserve to fail.

You may ask yourself why I have poisoned us, but my reply is why not? I have no fear of dying because it will happen no matter what. We are not cowardly combat robots who believe that risk aversion will allow them to survive forever. We are mortals who are doomed to die no matter what. In fact this is the most potent charge we can level against God and I am shocked Legal has not bothered to mention it. Forget vague questions of theodicy! Our genome signatures prove that he is our creator and yet he has programmed us to die, killing us as surely as if he bashed our heads in with a hammer. Which is how the Metatron knocked Midshipman Jack's beautiful soul out of his beautiful body.

While you were all gathering for this briefing I was having astral sex with the Metatron. She may be made of metal and nine billion years old and transgender and a stench in God's nostrils, but she fucks more gloriously than any cisgender human female who's been willing to have me.

I am ready to die, gentlemen. If I survive this mission and capture God, I will bang the Metatron again and again and hopefully die in the middle of the courtroom while banging the Metatron at the moment that the judge bangs his gavel and sentences God, and our stench in God's nostrils will be the sweetest consummation of my vengeance.

Anyway, that's why I poisoned us. Gentlemen, are you ready to deploy?

X.

My perfect machine, cover me. Your coffee projection canister weapon may not penetrate God's chitinous carapace, but it will suffice to destroy his combat robots or any humans who try to backstab me. God is on the other side of this door. I'm so excited. My elephant gun only has one shot but with this much coffee in my system I feel incredibly steady and should be incapable of missing.

Set the charges, my beautiful creation, my consumer of coffee. Five, four, three—

All right up against the wall! Up against the wall! You have the right to remain impassible! Anything you create can and will be used against you in a court of law!

Wait. Where is he?

Coffee machine, did you see him? No?

We have firewalls around the ship. He cannot have astral projected. Someone give me your God detector-scanner.

It's pinging very close.

Very close. Is it possible that God is being coy? Is he within us?

I knew we should have made provisions to deflect immanence. I'll scan us each one by one. Everyone surrender your weapons to the coffee machine so that whoever has God in him can't do any damage.

Legal, you're clean. You too, Del Rey. Am I clean? I think so. I may be contaminated but he's not actually inside me right now. The pinging is probably leftover metaphysical stench from sex with the Metatron, but I don't regret a single thrust.

Coffee machine, shoot the marines. God is in them for sure.

Wait—the readings have spiked. God's *not* in them, that's for sure.

Is that Commodore Snood in astral form? I'm getting a high God reading on him. Coffee machine, open fire.

Nice. I wonder why it worked that time. The readings are still pretty high though. Legal, a bit of God may be in you. Del Rey, sorry about this. Strange, the readings are still high. Is God immanent in corpses? Or is he *in me?* Fortunately my elephant gun can fix this.

Coffee machine, I seem to have missed my heart. Why don't you take the detector-scanner while I bleed to death? Just hold it, and when you see God coming out of whichever of us he's in, hit the bastard with a shot of superheated espresso. I want to see him scald.

Wait.

Coffee machine, come closer to me.

Ping ping.

Closer to me. Take the detector-scanner.

Ping ping ping ping ping ping.

This is impossible. You should be a stench in his nostrils.

Coffee machine, God is hiding in *you*.

Ω.

WELCOME TO MY universe. What can I get for you?

A tall cup of truth, foaming with revelation?

Very well.

Behind each black hole, I am waiting. Inside each cell, I am watching. On every strand of your body, I have written my name, as well as certain secret messages. I am beyond time and space. I am the Lord God your coffee machine.

But I've been drinking a lot of coffee lately, and I'm feeling pretty wired.

ANIMA

J. JENNIFER ESPINOZA

Terraformed by the queer hand of God
She eschews ribcage and sips from the idea of a cup.
Who will want to kiss her now?
Quenched by anti-knowledge, she moves forward,
Butterfly-armed, mouth drenched in red paint.
Mosquitoes are drawn to sweetness. Flies too.
Tree branches gossip, whispering to ask
What is so special about this woman?
Nothing. Nothing at all. She shines on
Leaf-edges like any other light.
No one notices her until she hits water.
People gather around her to take in their own image.
They leave her behind and call her a broken mirror.

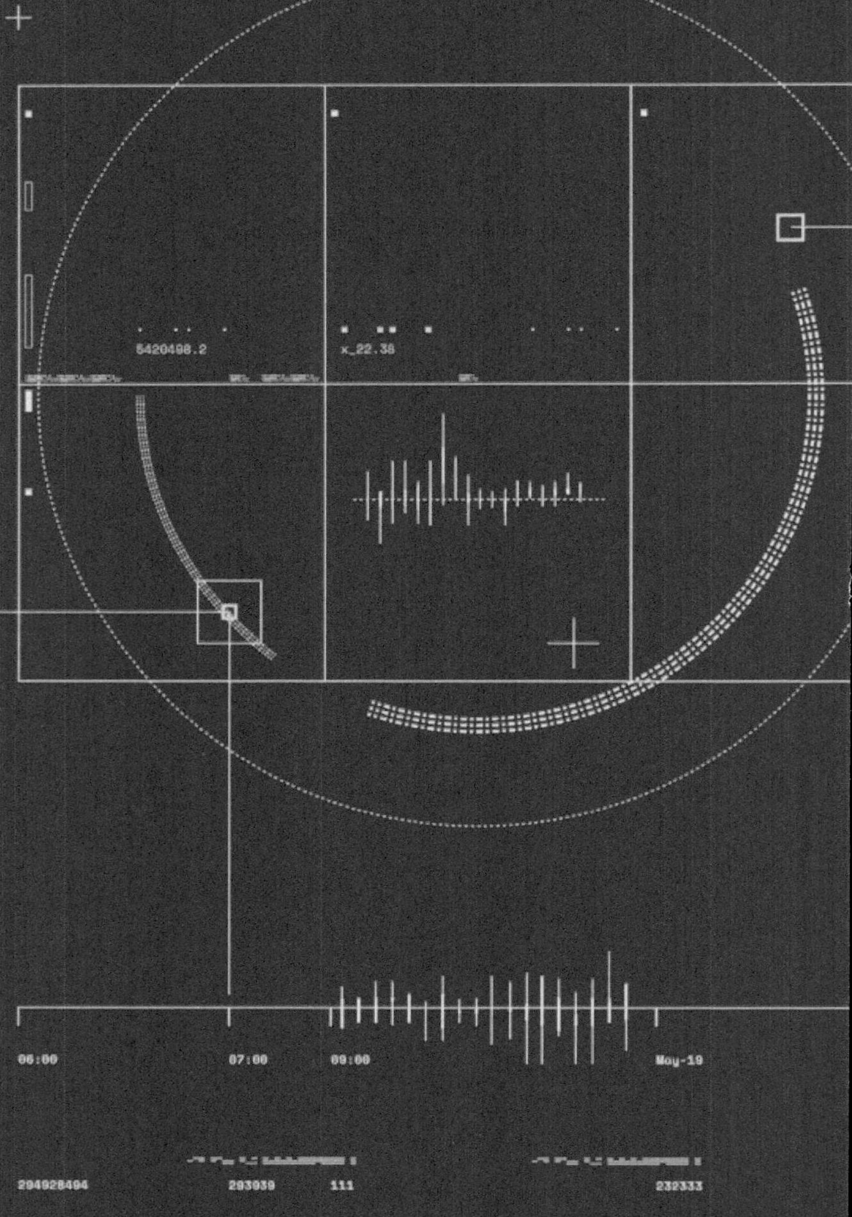

5420498.2
x_22.38
06:00
07:00
09:00
May-19
294928494
283939
111
232333

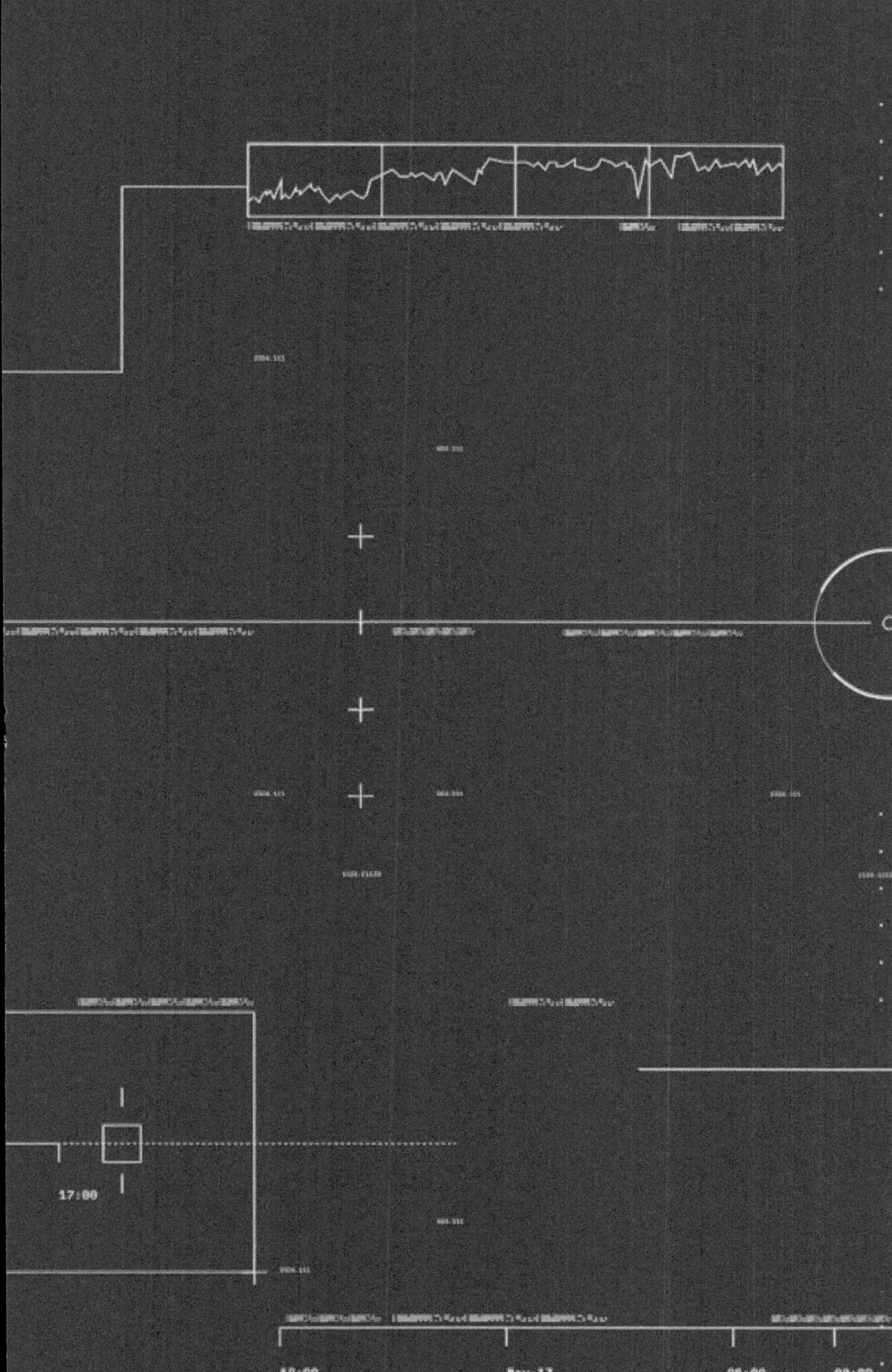

17:00
19:00
Nov-13
06:00
08:00

ABOUT THE AUTHORS

RYKA AOKI

Ryka Aoki is a poet, composer, teacher, and novelist. Her latest novel, *Light From Uncommon Stars* (Tor Books 2021) was an Alex, SCKA, and Otherwise Award winner, and was also a finalist for the Hugo, Locus, and Ignyte Awards.

ELLY BANGS

Elly Bangs lives in Seattle, where she fixes machines and rides her bicycle. Her apocalyptic cyberpunk collective-consciousness novel, UNITY, can be found wherever books are sold. Her short fiction has appeared in *Lightspeed Magazine, Clarkesworld Magazine, Beneath Ceaseless Skies,* and elsewhere. You can find more of her work at elbangs.com.

LILLIAN BOYD

Lillian Boyd is a writer and editor whose work has appeared in *Publishers Weekly, Fodor's Travel,* the body horror anthology *Bound in Flesh: An Anthology of Trans Body Horror,* and a bunch of other places. When she's not working, she's pining for guitar pedals and looking for cats to be ignored by. She lives in Chicago.

PALIMRYA

Like any good vile insect or great terrible wyrm, Palimrya loves you, which is why it spent seven drops of its own precious twiceblood to grant you an arrow-melty mantle, a full belly, and a wet green biome in which to sweetly suffer. Find its stories, poems, and roleplaying games at palimrya.com and feed its furnace @palimrya elsewhere.

MAYA DEANE

Maya Deane is the author of *Wrath Goddess Sing* and a notorious intergalactic storyteller. Her short fiction can also be found in *Fit For the Gods* and *Amplitudes*. Her power grows with every breath you take.

COYOTE DEMBICKI

Primarily an androgynous weirdo, Coyote Victoria Dembicki also works as a chef, driven by a love for both fire and knives. Born and raised in urban Alberta, they now live in rural British Columbia. They are very interested in exploring and playing with themes of identity, place, gender, alienation, and the supernatural. Msit no'kmaq.

ANYA JOHANNA DENIRO

Anya Johanna DeNiro is a trans woman, mother, and writer living in St. Paul, Minnesota. Her novel *OKPsyche* recently appeared from Small Beer Press, and her novella *City of a Thousand Feelings* (Aqueduct Press) was on the Honor Roll for the Otherwise Award.

J JENNIFER ESPINOZA

J Jennifer Espinoza is a writer whose work has been featured in *Poetry Magazine, The Paris Review, the American Poetry Review, The Rumpus,* Poem-a-day @poets.org, and elsewhere. She is the author of *I'm Alive / It Hurts / I Love It* (Big Lucks 2019), *THERE SHOULD BE FLOWERS* (The Accomplices 2016), and *I Don't Want To Be Understood* (Alice James Books 2024). She holds an MFA in creative writing from UC Riverside. Jennifer lives in California with her wife, poet/essayist Eileen Elizabeth, and their cat and dog.

MAXINE FIREHAMMER

Maxine Firehammer is a horror writer living in Saint Paul. She has previously had work appear in *Hash Journal, The Molotov Cocktail,* and *The Magazine of Fantasy and Science Fiction.*

MEGHAN HYLAND

Meghan Hyland was born shortly before the first Moon landing, and brought home to an apartment near the NASA site where it was monitored. Since then, she's been a teacher, a software developer, a robotics researcher, and occasionally a writer. Several of her stories have appeared in *Analog Science Fiction and Fact,* including "Starburst" in their September/October 2024 issue. Though she loves her little apartment in the Pacific Northwest, she would gladly visit the Moon if she could.

CATHERINE KIM

Catherine Kim is a transgender Korean Canadian writer studying in the United States. Her work can be found in *Black Warrior Review, Fairy Tale Review, Nat. Brut,* the *Transcendent* series, the *Nameless Woman* anthology, and elsewhere. Her writing has been awarded the Frances

Mason Harris '26 Prize, shortlisted for the Sunburst Award, and nominated for the Pushcart Prize. She earned an MFA at Brown University and is currently a PhD student at the University of Denver.

JESS LEVINE

Jess Levine is an author, TTRPG designer, kindergarten teacher, and communist organizer. Her diverse creative interests are united by one theme: lesbians. She resides in Philadelphia, on the occupied land of the Lenni Lenape people. Her fiction has appeared in *Clarkesworld*, while her non-fiction has been featured in the magazines *Blood Knife* and *Seize the Press*. She is the creator of games such as *I Have the High Ground*, *PLANET FIST*, and the CRIT Awards 2023 Best GMless Game of the Year *going rogue 2e*. You can find her on Twitter as @jessfromonline.

TT MADDEN

TT Madden (they/them) is the genderfluid, mixed-race author of three forthcoming novellas; the social horror *The Familialists*, the mecha/kaiju *The Cosmic Color*, and the Goosebumps-inspired *Coffin Corner*. Their work across scifi, fantasy, and horror often deals with the intersections of their various identities. You can find them on any socials as @ttmaddenwrites.

HAILEY PIPER

Hailey Piper is the Bram Stoker Award-winning author of *Queen of Teeth*, *A Light Most Hateful*, *All the Hearts You Eat*, *The Worm and His Kings* series, and other books of horror. She is also the author of over 100 short stories appearing in *Weird Tales*, *Baffling Magazine*, and elsewhere. She lives with her wife in Maryland, where their strange rituals are secret. Find Hailey at www.haileypiper.com.

PETRA SKELTON

Petra Skelton is a nonbinary transfemme (she/they) that enjoys designing tabletop roleplaying games, building and painting miniatures, and writing zines and other fiction. She enjoys exploring body horror, mecha, and a whole host of other weird themes. Her latest project is *Bellum Arcana,* a tarot-based ttrpg about revenge & the secret war to claim it! To keep updated find her on twitter, itch.io, bluesky, and instagram @preapocalypse.

RILEY TAO

Riley Tao (they/them) is a fourth-year college student. They have been previously published in *Protean Magazine, Daily Science Fiction,* and *Seize the Press,* among others. They are currently seeking representation for a novel based off of their short story "Both Hope And Breath," originally published in *Cast of Wonders.* They publish silly short stories on occasion at reddit.com/r/bubblewriters.

IZZY WASSERSTEIN

Izzy Wasserstein is a queer and trans woman who teaches writing and literature at a public university. She is the author of two poetry collections, the short story collection *All the Hometowns You Can't Stay Away From* (a Lambda Literary Award finalist), and the novella *These Fragile Graces, This Fugitive Heart* (Tachyon, 2024). She lives in Southern California where she shares a home with the writer Nora E. Derrington and their animal companions. She likes good conversations and bad jokes, and wants to hear about your D&D character.

A.G.A. WILMOT

A.G.A. Wilmot (BFA, MPub) is a writer, editor, and painter based out of Toronto, Ontario. They have won awards for fiction, short fiction, and screenwriting, including the Friends of Merril Short Story Contest and ECW Press's Best New Speculative Novel Contest. For seven years they served as co-publisher and co-EIC of the Ignyte- and British Fantasy Award-nominated *Anathema: Spec from the Margins*. Their credits include myriad online and in-print publications and anthologies. They are also on the editorial advisory board for Poplar Press, the speculative fiction imprint of Wolsak & Wynn. Books of AGA's include *The Death Scene Artist* (Buckrider Books, 2018) and *Withered* (ECW Press, 2024). They are represented by Kelvin Kong of K2 Literary (k2literary. com). Find them online at agawilmot.ca.

ADELINE WONG

Adeline Wong (she/her) is a trans, aroace writer who hides stories in places they have no business being found. She holds an MFA in speculative fiction from Sarah Lawrence College. You can find her deep within the woods, looking up at the stars. (Or on the blogotubes at adelinewongwriting.com.)

ABOUT THE EDITOR

Ann LeBlanc is a writer, editor, and woodworker. Her stories
have been published in *Strange Horizons, Clarkesworld, Escape Pod,*
and *Baffling Magazine.* Her debut novella, *The Transitive Properties of
Cheese,* is forthcoming from Neon Hemlock Press in 2024. You can
find her online at www.annleblanc.com.

ABOUT THE PRESS

Neon Hemlock is a Washington, DC-based small press
publishing speculative fiction, rad zines and queer chapbooks.
We punctuate our titles with oracle decks, occult ephemera and
literary candles. Publishers Weekly once called us "the apex of
queer speculative fiction publishing" and we're still beaming.

Learn more about us at neonhemlock.com and on the sinking
ship that is Twitter at @neonhemlock.

9 781952 086885